PRAISE FOR THE AUTHOR

"Ryan is that rare breed of thriller writer,
a craftsman and an artist!"
—Acclaimed American writer Lee Jackson,
author of *Redemption*

The Ottoman. Conspiracy

ALSO BY THOMAS RYAN

In the same series:

The Field of Blackbirds
The Mark of Halam

Short Stories

THOMAS RYAN

The Ottoman. Conspiracy

THOMAS & MERCER

Published by Thomas & Mercer, Seattle

www.apub.com

Amazon, the Amazon logo, and Thomas & Mercer are trademarks of Amazon.com, Inc., or its affiliates.

ISBN-13: 9781503942196
ISBN-10: 1503942198

Cover design by @blacksheep-uk.com

Printed in the United States of America

For Meg,
to whom I owe everything

CHAPTER ONE

A gear change and a turn caused the Starliner bus to lurch to the right. The sudden movement stirred Barry Briggs from his catnap. He opened an eye. The early afternoon sun caused his eyelids to flicker as they adjusted to the light. His head bounced off the window pane. Neck muscles stiffened, holding his head steady until it settled back against the glass. Bethany, his fiancée, her head on his arm, remained undisturbed by his fidgeting. For two hours the bland music filtering through the bus speakers had caused him to drift in and out of sleep. He had wriggled about each time he woke. He envied Bethany's ability to sleep in such uncomfortable conditions: to sleep well, he needed a comfy bed and a flat pillow.

The vehicle pulled to the side of the road. Barry checked his watch. It wasn't a scheduled stop. Outside, through the misted windows, he could make out shadowy, uniformed figures, but not how many. He would be pissed off to hell if the driver had stopped to take on passengers. The trip to the ANZAC commemorations on Turkey's Gallipoli peninsula had been in part to celebrate his thirty-third birthday and in part a pre-wedding gift from Bethany. In a few days, they would leave for Rome, and in Rome they would be married. A trip to the battlefields of Gallipoli was not the most romantic lead-up to the most important day of their lives. But he was Australian and Bethany was a New Zealander, and ANZAC Day at Gallipoli was a pilgrimage for the citizens of both countries. They were in the region and Bethany had readily agreed when he suggested the visit, so why not?

He had joined an organised tour group. The group had chartered the bus to take them from Istanbul to Gallipoli and back to Istanbul, and they had paid good money to have it to themselves. Even if he was in a generous mood, and he wasn't, where would the extra passengers sit? Okay, there were spare seats in the rear and a couple in the front, but that wasn't the point. What if one of the group wanted to stretch out? Turkish bus drivers might look to make extra cash on the side by taking on extra passengers and not declaring it, and good for them, but not on this bus.

A hiss of compressed air and the door opened.

The driver climbed out of his seat. Barry put him at fifty years old, could be younger. He was overweight, with a round face that had not been shaved for a week. The driver glanced down the aisle: twenty-five rows of light-grey, soft-leather upholstered seats to the back, with two seats either side. Barry thought there was something shifty about the driver's actions, like a shoplifter in a department store checking if anyone was watching. Satisfied there was little interest in his movements, the driver pulled on his mustard jacket with its sheepskin collar and stepped off the bus. Barry lifted himself up in his seat and quickly checked the passengers. Some were sleeping, some reading a book or leaning heads on hands, but no one seemed interested in the bus driver. Barry turned back to the window.

He blew hot air on to the window and used his sleeve to rub a space in the moisture. Now he could see clearly. As the driver spoke with the men, he repeatedly looked over his shoulder. The men, agitated, waved their arms. One poked his finger at the driver's chest. An argument, but over what, Barry couldn't hear. The driver must have lost. He kicked at the ground then stomped to the luggage compartment and loaded two bags. The bus was an expensive, luxurious experience, fitted with the latest gadgets, and Barry was not happy to share with freeloaders. He would need to complain.

When the driver climbed back aboard, four men dressed in Turkish police uniforms followed. A fifth man, scruffily dressed in unironed civilian clothes, jumped on to the first step and the door closed behind him. The civilian had piercing slate-grey eyes, set in a face chiselled from granite. At first, Barry thought he might be a prisoner. But the man looked too relaxed. And the manner in which the police spoke to him was respectful, not authoritative. The police looked scruffy, the uniforms unkempt. Not the smart look of the cops in Istanbul.

The man in civilian clothes sat.

The police remained standing, speaking in whispers with the driver. The driver was shaking his head. It looked as if the police were demanding the driver take them somewhere and, wherever that might be, it didn't appear the driver was keen. Barry dismissed any ideas he had of enforcing his authority as self-selected tour manager. Even in Australia, if the police wanted a free ride, there was no argument. If these guys wanted to go all the way to Istanbul, what could he do?

Two of the cops walked to the rear of the bus, casting their eyes over the forty passengers. The tour group was mostly couples from New Zealand and Australia. Barry and Bethany were the youngest couple, Reg and Mildred the oldest – in their eighties, Barry thought. Two American women, not much older than twenty, were travelling with the group. Barry had no idea why they had tagged along. They had kept to themselves, and other than a friendly smile whenever he caught their eye he'd had no communication with them. Another passenger had passed on that the request for them to join the trip had come via the American Consulate. All he could think was that, despite their youth, they were a token response from the US government to add an American presence to the Gallipoli proceedings.

As the cops passed each seat, heads followed their movements, but no one asked what it was they were looking for. They were cops. No one questioned cops. Barry's first reaction was it might be a passport check or a search for drugs. When they reached the seats he and Bethany occupied, sly eyes slid in his direction. Cold and calculating was Barry's reading of the police officers. Most cops he had met on his world travels had a surly manner. Why would Turkish cops be any different? He considered asking one of them, 'Why the hold-up? Start the bus and let's get moving.' He didn't. When the two cops returned to the front of the bus, he relaxed. Maybe now they would be on their way. He leaned his head back against the window and let his eyelids close again.

The sound of metal tapping against metal roused him.

One police officer was tapping the barrel of his side arm against the handrail next to the driver's seat. Barry swivelled and looked behind him. Heads rose above backs of seats. Graeme Beattie, in the seat across the aisle, a can of beer in his hand, looked Barry's way. His eyebrows arched. 'What the hell is going on?' was the unspoken question. Barry shrugged a response. How the hell did he know? Graeme's wife looked at the beer can and then directed a frown towards Barry. 'This is your fault,' she seemed to be accusing him. Barry wanted to yell back at her, 'Your husband's an alcoholic, lady.'

Bethany stirred beside him. "Who's making the noise?" she mumbled.

"I think we're about to find out."

Confused, she saw something amiss in Barry's face and sat upright.

The police officer said, "I have your attention? Good." He stepped back.

The man in civilian clothes stood. He squeezed past the men in uniform and moved up the aisle a few paces.

"I am known as The Sheriff," he started, his English not fluent but clear enough to be understood. "My men and I have taken control of this bus. Before boarding, I placed explosives in the luggage compartments." Forty pairs of eyes glanced at the floor. "Enough, I assure you, that if the bombs explode not even your teeth will survive the blast. A black mark on the ground is all that would be left. Identifying your bodies will not be possible." The Sheriff held up an object the size of a cigarette packet. "This is the trigger mechanism. If I push this button it will send a signal to the detonators. And boom, in the blink of an eye you will be dead."

Barry stretched his neck as he looked out the window and down the side of the bus to the baggage compartment. He didn't know what he expected to see, and he saw nothing. Bethany, now fully awake, looked to Barry for an explanation. He stroked her arm.

"I do not wish to blow the bus," The Sheriff said. "This is a last resort, but be assured: if I need to, I will. As long as you behave and do nothing silly, when we have reached our destination you can walk away."

Graeme Beattie jammed his can of beer between his thighs. He grasped the back of the seat in front and pulled himself to his feet. The can fell to the floor and brown liquid splashed over his wife's leg. She slapped him on his thigh and glared.

"Who the hell do you think you are, mate?" Beattie yelled, his words belligerent, slurred. "You can't tell us what to do. Now take your fucking bombs and get the fuck off this bus."

A sneering grin broke across Beattie's face. He looked round for support. But, instead of an encouraging en masse thumbs-up, the passengers' shocked and pale faces turned away, careful to avoid his gaze. Over the last few hours, his companions had slept off the booze. Beattie had kept supping.

Barry ducked down in his seat and waved to attract Beattie's attention. He wanted to warn him to shut his mouth and sit down. The gesture went unnoticed. Beattie's wife pulled at her husband's jacket to try and make him sit. Beattie pushed her hand away. His brain was sodden with alcohol, and now he had become the centre of attention, he was too caught up in his bravado-induced theatrics to spot the perilous course he had embarked upon.

The Sheriff's eyes narrowed. His lips thinned.

Barry likened The Sheriff's sudden transformation to the mannerisms of a trapped animal in the wild. He had seen it in men in the mountain villages of Kosovo and Albania. They were hard men who survived in uninhabitable regions, eking out an existence for themselves and their families. And like wild animals, when threatened, a welcoming smile became a snarl in an instant and their reaction was swift and savage. Barry would bet every cent he had in his wallet that almost from the day The Sheriff could walk, any fight he participated in had been a fight to the death. Queensberry Rules did not exist with such men. He would have a primal instinct for survival and, in Barry's opinion, had been in survival mode for many years.

The Sheriff's slate-grey eyes twitched and then fixed on Beattie.

"Your name is what?" The Sheriff's icy voice cut across the silence.

"Graeme Beattie, mate, and I'm not taking any shit from you or your buddies. Now you guys get off this fucking bus before I take matters in hand. Do you dumb shits get what I'm saying here?"

The Sheriff's eyes narrowed even further. He seemed to pause and consider things, and then a tiny hint of amusement flickered across his lips.

"As with all Westerners, you have a mouth that is very big. When it drops open there is much noise, but always the noise is bluster. You should have learned to keep your mouth shut, Graeme. Because of you, I have to do this."

The Sheriff stepped back a few paces. With each step, he held Graeme Beattie's eye. He pulled a handgun from his belt and held it in the air for Beattie to see. The action brought gasps. Barry couldn't stop an involuntary inhalation of air. Was Beattie about to be shot? Then The Sheriff swung his arm away and brought his weapon down until the barrel was inches from the side of the bus driver's head. Just above his ear. The driver had been sitting face forward, scanning the road ahead and waiting for the order to drive on.

The Sheriff pulled the trigger.

A loud crack exploded through the bus. Blood and brains splattered across the steering wheel and on to the windscreen and side window. The Sheriff stepped aside for the passengers to see the driver slump from his seat.

"Fuck!" Barry blurted out. "Are you fucking kidding me?"

From his seat, Barry had had a clear view of the killing. Those seated behind the driver would not have seen; a partition wall separated the cab area. But everyone had heard the pistol shot.

"What happened, Barry?" Bethany asked.

"He shot the driver."

Bethany's eyes widened in disbelief. She looked at Barry for confirmation. He nodded and Bethany paled and began to shake. Her fingers stroked the cross round her neck. Elsewhere, there were stifled screams and sobbing.

Barry fixed his eyes on the four Turkish cops and the killer in civilian clothes and then across to Graeme Beattie. What an idiot. Bethany gripped Barry's arm. Her nails dug into his flesh. Without looking he pulled on her fingers until her grip eased. In Kosovo, they had lived through civil unrest, been shot at on occasion and hidden in doorways as rioters roamed the streets. Barry had fought with terrorists while Bethany stood at his side. She was a strong woman. The shock would pass. His main concern right now was whether Beattie would survive the day.

"Look what you made me do, Graeme," The Sheriff said. His voice was raised, angry. He pointed at the dead bus driver. "This man has a family. Now they have no one to care for them. No more income into the home. His wife, what can she do?" He shrugged. "Beg on the streets, become a whore, and why? All because of you, Graeme. You and your big mouth. Now tell me, do you have more to say? I have no more bus drivers. I will have to kill your friends. I will start with the woman next to you. Is she your wife?"

Beattie swallowed. His shoulders sagged. Pale and open-mouthed, he shook his head and fell back into his seat. His eyes picked a spot on the floor and his head did not move.

His wife made to touch his arm, but pulled her hand away.

"Good, Graeme. Good decision. Anyone else want to speak?" A broader smile now showed a row of worn, yellowing teeth. "Good."

The Sheriff returned to his seat.

Two of the police officers dragged the driver's body to the back of the bus. Frightened eyes followed the trail of blood, and then followed the policemen as they made their way back to the front. One of them climbed into the vacant driver's seat.

The police officer who had tapped the railing said, "Now the unpleasantness is over, I have one more task. We need to collect your mobile phones. Please do not play games with me. It is the modern age and you people come from first-world countries. I know every single one of you will have a phone. I will shoot anyone who does not pass a mobile to my man."

He nodded to one of his men.

The man, gun in his right hand, held out a plastic supermarket shopping bag in his left and moved along the aisle. Trembling hands dropped mobile phones into it. Barry focussed his attention on the gun barrel when his turn came. He pulled his phone from his jacket pocket. Bethany had taken her pink phone from her purse. He dropped them both into the bag. The man moved on until he had collected the last of the phones. He returned to the front of the bus and deposited the bag into an overhead luggage compartment.

"Good. Well done. It is good we have reached an understanding," the policeman said.

He nodded to his companion in the driver's seat. The engine gunned into life, and the bus moved forward.

CHAPTER TWO

Ex-Special Forces soldier Jeff Bradley looked for a table that would give him the best view of the gates into the Port of Bari. Not that there was much choice. There were only two roadside cafés opposite the entrance to the docks. They were fifty metres apart. Between them, a stone stairway wound its way up a slope, but as far as Jeff could see it led to nowhere. He chose the café to the right.

From where he sat, he could see through the gates to the wharves and berthed ships. He had come to the port at 8:30 a.m., the listed arrival time for the ferry from Albania. By 9:30 a.m. his second coffee was almost cold. He was about to search for a shipping office and check if the delay might be permanent when he saw the blue-hulled Adria ferry cruise into view and manoeuvre into its docking position. A few minutes later his phone vibrated to an incoming text. Sulla was aboard.

Jeff had travelled to Italy to attend a wedding in Rome. His two friends, Barry Briggs and Bethany Bridge, were to be married. He had met them both in Kosovo.

"The engagement has gone on too long," Barry had said when he phoned Jeff. "It's time to marry the woman and I want you to stand with me at the altar as my best man."

Jeff had cringed at Barry calling Bethany – 'the woman' – and imagined Bethany punching his friend on the shoulder if she ever heard him use the term. But the thought of meeting with them again warmed his heart. He missed his friends and hadn't hesitated to accept Barry's offer. The invitation had said bring a guest. Jeff wasn't in a relationship so came alone and a week early. The wedding ceremony was to be held in Rome, but today, he was in Bari, on the eastern side of Italy. And this was not a holiday. He was here on business, hunting prey: the international terrorist Avni Leka.

Jeff had first encountered Leka in Kosovo when he travelled to the former Yugoslav province in search of his friend, and the manager of his Auckland vineyard, Arben Shala. Arben had been kidnapped and held for ransom and as Jeff drew closer to uncovering that the abductor was the master criminal Avni Leka, Leka ordered the murder of Arben to end the trail, perhaps thinking that with Arben dead there would be no reason for Jeff to stay on. But Jeff had not returned to New Zealand as Leka had hoped he would, and instead Jeff continued the hunt for Arben's killer. When he finally discovered Leka was the murderer, further investigation revealed that Leka was not just an opportunist kidnapper but an international terrorist. He had a team of contract bombers operating in Europe. Leka's men would explode bombs for maximum casualties, and terror groups such as ISIS, who had paid Leka huge sums of money, would claim responsibility.

Jeff set a trap, but Leka escaped capture.

Months later, Leka sent men to New Zealand to bomb an American nuclear submarine, the USS *Ulysses*. A small squad of the terrorists was reassigned to find Jeff and kill him. Jeff survived, but many innocents died in the city of Auckland. Jeff made a promise to the dead to find Leka and put an end to him. Jeff blamed himself for the loss of lives. If he had killed Leka when he had had the chance, it would have prevented the many deaths. He knew eliminating the man responsible fell short of atonement, but at least the dead would be avenged.

And he had a lead.

A member of an Apulian crime family had made contact.

The Italian told Jeff criminals from Albania were making inroads into their activities and were costing them much money. The Albanians were greedy and not willing to share; they wanted it all and had made life difficult for their Italian counterparts. They were well organised and had networks across the Balkans and far into Europe. This control over such a large territory had brought them great wealth and, with the wealth, they bought influence in Bari regional government departments. Once local government was the sole domain of the Italian criminals, but now, weakened government protection was undermining their operations. Raids were taking place on business enterprises that had previously been protected. The Italians wanted rid of the Albanians. Information had been given to them that a Kosovan, Avni Leka, was the money man and planner. Remove him and the Albanians would crumble.

The contact told Jeff they had received information he was looking to kill Avni Leka and they would help him. He added they could take care of Leka and the Albanians themselves, but to do so carried risks. If the Albanians found out a member of a local Italian gang killed their boss they would seek revenge. If an outsider took care of Leka, it would avoid an unnecessary war. The contact told Jeff that whatever he needed from them to help get rid of Leka they would supply. If he failed in his task, so be it. They would go to war.

"We will ship their Albanian carcases back across the Adriatic," the contact stated. "But we do not wish to do this if it can be avoided. It would not be good for business. The police and the military would intervene."

The comment on getting rid of the Albanians had amused Jeff. If it was that easy, why had they not done so already? When Jeff weighed the comments, the only conclusion that made sense to him was the Albanians were strong and the Italians fearful of them. At any rate, he didn't care for the problems of the Italians, and he had no intention of letting them turn him into their pawn; he was not going to become embroiled in a gang war. He wanted Avni Leka, and that was all. The Italians offered Jeff money if, when tracking Leka, he fed them any information he uncovered of the Albanian plans for future expansion, but Jeff had said no. When the killer Leka was dead, he'd move on with his life.

From the moment the Italians made contact with him in New Zealand, Jeff was suspicious. Why him, when all the international intelligence organisations, especially the Americans, wanted Leka? All they needed to do was contact Interpol and give them Leka's location. So there were alarm bells, but his personal need to exact vengeance on Leka had made him ignore them. The only stipulation from the Italians was that Jeff had to come to Bari if he wanted the information. The Italians said they wanted Leka taken care of on the spot and quickly, and if they handed over the details while he was still in New Zealand he might change his mind.

Jeff hadn't believed it then, and he didn't believe it now.

But he was in Bari, and he considered himself a well-hooked fish. At the end of today, he'd either be dead or knocking on Leka's door, gun in hand.

Another thirty minutes and another coffee, and finally the first passengers from the ferry walked through the gates. Jeff's arse had numbed from sitting too long on the uncomfortable plastic chair. The morning sun had chased away the chill. He had eaten breakfast. Not the bacon and eggs he craved, but a plate of sliced salami and cheeses, washed down with orange juice. Now, legs stretched out in front of him, he scrutinised the disembarking passengers, searching beyond the row of motor scooters parked outside the café for the tall figure of Sulla Bogdani.

Sulla managed a vineyard in Kosovo for Arben Shala's family. They had come to New Zealand as refugees from the Serbian/Kosovo war, and now lived and worked on Jeff's vineyard in Auckland. When Arben was murdered, Jeff stood at his friend's graveside and promised he would look out for his family. He and Sulla had recovered the family's Kosovan property stolen by Avni Leka. It included a vineyard and house, but Arben's widow, Kimi, did not wish to bring their children, Drita and Marko, to the country that killed their father. Jeff had appointed Sulla Bogdani as manager. Sulla proved to be a good businessman and an equally reliable ally.

Two men walking towards the café caught his attention.

They wore dark suits without ties, and were slim and clean-shaven, with tidy haircuts. Jeff kept an eye on the pair as they approached, and received a token glance, which he initially dismissed without consideration. Strangers looked at strangers. It was normal human behaviour. But his instincts began to scream a warning. Be wary. Out of the corner of his eye he kept them under observation. They walked on to the next café. He caught them looking his way. Not the casual look of a diner scanning his environment, more the furtive, sly look of a fox eyeing a rabbit.

Fifteen minutes elapsed.

The two men had finished their coffees, as he had, and remained seated, as he did, but their waiter made no attempt to move them along. Jeff's waiter wiped the table many times, glaring as he did so, with loud sighs for effect. The tables in both cafés were full, but only Jeff's waiter wanted him gone. Jeff's assessment was the two men were local Italian hoods, and he was under surveillance.

It was no secret he was in the country. The Italian crime family knew he was coming. And if the Italians knew he had arrived, so might Leka. He didn't care if Leka knew, as long as it drew him out. If these two were Leka's men, finding Leka had become easier. If they were here to kill him, Jeff figured he had time. They wouldn't attack him in daylight. Not with so many witnesses, and not with port security everywhere. But it *was* Italy, and it *was* Bari, and maybe they could kill him and take off and no one would care. Or, the more likely scenario was his paranoia was out of control and the men were only two friends enjoying a morning stroll. But, for the moment, he would let paranoia rule and stay vigilant.

The line of disembarked passengers making their way through the dock gates grew. He shaded his eyes and at last saw the head of longish black hair bobbing above those around him. Dressed in familiar black, the tall figure of Sulla Bogdani emerged from the crowd. Jeff stood and waved. Sulla, his mobile phone to his ear, raised an arm in acknowledgement. Jeff sat back down.

The waiter, who had rushed to the table as Jeff got up, stood, legs planted wide and hands on hips, when he saw Jeff had no intention of leaving.

He leaned forward. "You must order something. If you want to sit at this table, you must make an order. It is for customers."

Sulla stepped between them. The big Kosovan reached across and shook Jeff's hand before slumping into the seat. He turned to the waiter.

"An espresso, a bottle of water and a juice for my friend," Sulla ordered.

The waiter flung his cleaning cloth over his shoulder and went inside the café. Jeff glanced across to the next café. No sign of the two men. He scratched at his stubble.

"There were two men earlier," Jeff said. "Sitting in the next café. I'm certain they were keeping an eye on me."

Sulla nodded. "Bari is a bad city. Lots of criminals. Just like in Prishtina. The criminals know you are coming and will know when you arrive. Of course they will follow you." Sulla shrugged. "On the other half of the coin, they might be petty criminals looking to steal your wallet. As I remember it, your wallet is always full."

"The saying is 'the other side of the coin', Sulla," Jeff corrected.

"Yes, this is what I have said. The other half. Do you have the address where we are to meet these informants?"

Jeff slid a piece of paper across the table. "I'm to ask for Marius."

The waiter returned holding a tray with a bottle of water, an espresso and a small bottle of orange juice. When he left, Sulla wound the top off the water and took a swig.

Then he sipped his coffee and read the note.

He tut-tutted. He glanced at Jeff, a wrinkle across his brow. "I know this place. It is in the older part of the city. Narrow lanes. In the American films I have seen, the leader of the posse would say we are riding into a blind gully. Good place for an ambush. It is not far. We can walk there."

Jeff climbed to his feet. "Right then. Let's go get ambushed."

CHAPTER THREE

Sulla, where the hell is this place?"

"Maybe one, maybe two more streets, no more; of this I am certain."

"You've never been there, have you?" Jeff asked.

Sulla shrugged, and a sheepish look followed. "No, but remember I was a guide before I took charge of the vineyard."

Jeff shook his head. "In Kosovo you were a guide. Have you ever been a guide in Bari?"

"Does this matter? I have never been to Paris, but I could find the Eiffel Tower."

Sulla stopped at the top of the next entry. An apartment building had been constructed over the street, creating a ten-metre tunnel through to a narrow alley of tightly packed medieval houses on the other side. The lane, paved with squares of stone polished shiny by centuries of Italian feet, was wide enough to take a small car, but little else. Motor scooters and motorbikes stood against the cream-rendered apartment building walls. Balconies protruded from the second floor. On display were an array of non-flowering pot plants and the day's washing, drying in the limited amount of sunlight that eked past the high-rise buildings and tiled roofs. Jeff surveyed his surroundings. Sulla had been right: this was a great place for an ambush.

There were no pedestrians.

Jeff walked behind as Sulla counted off the door numbers. He stopped in front of a green door. A large white enamel box encasing an air-conditioning fan hung on brackets to the left of the doorway. Sulla read the Italian on the brass plate and checked it against the paper in his hand. "This is it." He thrust the paper into his jacket pocket.

Sulla stepped aside for Jeff. "Are you armed?" Sulla asked.

"No, of course not."

Sulla grinned. "Then you should go in on your own."

"I've missed your very bad sense of humour, Sulla."

"I try to be a funny man."

They had fought side by side against Avni Leka's criminal gang in Kosovo and it had almost cost them their lives. Jeff remembered how Sulla's cynical sense of humour blossomed in dangerous situations. It reminded him of the humour shared with fellow soldiers during his days with the Special Forces.

Jeff rapped on the door. From the inside, he heard footsteps approach. The door opened.

Two overweight men filled the doorway. Beady eyes studied their visitors.

"My name is Jeff Bradley," Jeff said.

A few words of Italian passed between the two men, followed by a nod of heads. They stood aside for Sulla and Jeff to enter. Jeff made to move forward. Sulla grabbed his arm. He spoke to the men in Albanian.

"I have told them you are here to meet with Marius. They said Marius is inside waiting for you. At the top of the stairs."

One of the men spoke with Sulla and waved for him to enter. Sulla took a pace back, drawing Jeff with him. He spoke to both men, this time in Italian. He held up his wrist and pointed at his watch.

To Jeff he said, "I have told them to tell their boss we will meet him at the fish markets in one hour. If they are not there on the hour, we will go."

The two men looked confused.

Sulla turned and took Jeff by the arm, pushing him back towards the archway. Jeff allowed himself to be manhandled. He trusted Sulla's decision-making; he knew his friend was looking out for him, and now was not the time to argue. Halfway through the arch, Jeff looked back. One of the two men stood on the step. He assumed the other had gone to tell Marius what had taken place.

Jeff turned his attention to Sulla.

"Okay, Sulla, what just happened?"

"You said you were meeting Italian criminals. At least one of those men was Albanian. Now, it might be he works for the Italians. After all, half the criminals in Italy are Albanian and don't care who the boss is as long as they get paid. But they could be Avni Leka's men, and that would mean we were walking into a trap. For me, this is a problem." Sulla grinned. "I am not wishing to die in Bari."

Jeff shook his head.

"Okay, but what if they do not show at the fish markets? They were my lead to Leka."

Sulla said, "Relax, my friend. If they are Leka's men, they will show because they will still want to kill you. If they are Italian criminals and do not come, we know it is not a trap and we can come back and knock on the door." Sulla tapped the top of his head with his forefinger. "I think this is smart."

Jeff laughed.

"On the surface, your logic is sound, Sulla. Let's hope you're right. Where are these fish markets?"

"On the same road as the ferry terminal, but I am not certain where exactly. But where the fishing boats are is where the sea is. If I am right, our noses will smell the fish before we get close. If not, we can ask someone."

"Okay, if it is by the water it will only take fifteen minutes. Why did you say they should meet us in an hour?"

Sulla rounded the corner. A man standing next to a taxi waved.

"I phoned my cousin, Gani, when I got off the boat. He has been following. From here on, no more walking, we drive. But I think we need help. I need the hour to contact Blerim, my brother-in-law. He has men in Bari."

Jeff nodded. "Help would be good."

CHAPTER FOUR

Gani weaved his Fiat through the labyrinth of narrow streets before exiting through a tunnel in the shadow of Basilica di San Nicola. One more turn and they were driving along the seafront promenade of Lungomare Imperatore Augusto. A waist-high railing secured between metre-cubed blocks ran along the shoreline. Atop the blocks, spaced every twenty to thirty metres, sat lamps shaped like four-pronged candelabra. Pretty, Jeff mused. Pedestrians strolled along the wide boardwalk, enjoying the sea and the sun.

Sulla's cousin pointed at a construction in the distance. Concrete columns, holding up a flat roof, ran a couple of hundred metres back into the port. There were no walls, only the overhead cover; beneath was completely exposed to the elements.

"The fish markets."

Jeff opened his window.

Sulla had been right. Jeff could easily pick up the definitive smells of seafood mixed with salty air. On the seaward side of the markets was an inlet. Red mooring buoys bobbing up and down had small boats roped to holding chains that had been secured to the seabed. And directly behind the markets, a concrete slab ran the length of the one-hundred-metre-long structure. It sloped into the sea. Fishermen, having secured their small wooden boats, were dragging nets filled with the day's catch up the concrete launch ramps. They then set about disentangling the fish and dumping them into plastic trays.

Sulla's cousin turned off the promenade and into a side road that ran along the front of the markets, then continued on another half-kilometre to a yacht club and marina. He slewed into the parking area and stopped between two diagonal lines. The sign said thirty minutes. Jeff saw no parking wardens. Did anyone police the time limits? Jeff could see a man on one of the boat ramps smashing an octopus body on to the concrete. Tenderising the meat, he guessed, not killing it. The bloody thing would have been dead after the first whack.

He and Sulla climbed out.

"Gani will stay with the car," Sulla said. "We might need to scoot in a hurry."

From a distance, Jeff had thought the overhead cover was for the traders, but as he and Sulla walked closer, it appeared not. The sellers were not undercover but out in the open on the pavement. Wood planks lay across the top of upturned Peroni beer cartons and plastic buckets. Sitting on the planks were plastic trays of whole fish, shellfish, and a wide variety of species he couldn't readily recognise. Behind, on small plastic tables, were sets of scales.

Sulla said, "The Bari council built those cement counters in the rear for the fish sellers to display the day's catch. But as you can see, no one uses them. They want to be where the customers are, so they stand on the footpath, in the rain, and not under the shelter."

Jeff noted the especially built counters were not entirely unused; they held empty Peroni beer bottles.

In summer, there would be flies. Lots of them.

Jeff walked with Sulla as they mingled with morning shoppers. All the time, his eyes scanned the surroundings. It was more exposed than he would have liked. On either side of the market road was ocean, and the only way out was back on to the promenade. Opposite the market stalls, a small park served only to split the road coming from the marina, giving drivers the option of turning left rather than having to drive past the fishy smells. The park was no more than fifty metres across. It did have decorative trees and some artistic rock formations, and was perhaps somewhere for Sulla to hide while he waited, but if the meeting went wrong and they had to flee, then anyone running into the park and trying to hide would be easily seen by their pursuers.

"This is a good spot, Sulla, if you think many witnesses will put off a gunman shooting in the open, but if the gunman doesn't care, we have no escape. There is only open ground for a couple of hundred metres, whichever way you look. And running into the ocean is not an option."

"I agree." Sulla grinned. "I have learned a valuable lesson. A good guide should visit locations."

Jeff ignored Sulla's wisecrack.

He said, "I think how we handle this is, you wait in the park. There are a few trees that will give you some cover and you'll have a good view. If it is Leka's men and they mean to take me out, maybe you can come up with something that might distract them. If we stand here together, it makes it too easy. We'd be sitting ducks."

"Yes, I agree. I do not want to be a duck. But I should stay close. You do not speak Italian. If you need help, and panic, everyone will think you are a madman or a lost tourist because you will be waving your arms about and, to them, speaking gibberish. They will not understand you."

Jeff frowned and shook his head. "I will not panic."

"Smart men smell fear, Jeff."

With a shrug of his shoulders, Sulla left to get in position in the park. Jeff loitered near the middle of the markets. He stood back, allowing pedestrians and shoppers to walk about without tripping over him. The traders, unshaven men in denims, knitwear and leather jackets or windbreakers, accosted each passer-by with well-practised sales pitches.

The shoppers ignored the harassing banter, and instead studied the wares before shaking their heads and moving on. Now, closer, Jeff studied the species of fish on offer. Used to fishing New Zealand waters, he thought the seafood on display looked undersized. But, undersized or not, he was thankful the goods had brought people out of their apartments. The fishmongers and the growing number of shoppers might increase his chances of survival.

Sulla had been right not to enter Marius's apartment. Another reminder, as if he needed it, that when working unfamiliar territory a few alliances with the locals might save his life. Sulla was not strictly a local, but he knew the terrain and the language and had contacts ready to support him. He was putting his faith in Sulla. In the past, Sulla had never let him down, and he trusted him enough to know he wouldn't today.

Standing about and showing little interest in buying seafood brought an occasional glance from a few of the fishmongers. One held up a flounder not much bigger than a human hand and waved it towards him. Jeff shook his head, but the attention made him uneasy. The seller turned back to the housewives, but Jeff noticed that an eye was cast his way every so often.

When they arrived, Marius and his men were easy enough to spot.

The black SUV drove into the street, ominous in its disregard for pedestrians and other vehicles. It stopped, two wheels on the park-side pavement. It blocked Sulla from Jeff's view. Sulla was smart; he'd find another spot. The Italians climbed out. Jeff recognised two of the men from the apartment. The man walking between them had an authoritative swagger. That had to be Marius. The driver followed behind.

Jeff rolled his head, enough to loosen his neck. It was stiff from sitting too long at the docks. He let his arms hang limp and flexed his fingers. A technique he used to relax his body. Four armed men against one unarmed. Jeff weighed his options. He couldn't think of any. But four against one gave him a chance. He'd fought more. A number of the fish vendors waved to Marius. They smiled the smiles of servants to master. A touch of acid rose from Jeff's gut into his gullet. No wonder Marius looked as casual as he did. These were his people. A whole bloody army; even some of the old people out shopping nodded deferentially to him.

Jeff had not needed a sign round his neck with his name scrawled across it to be recognised by Marius. Like a rooster about to have sex with a brainless hen, the Italian strutted towards him. Jeff allowed himself a quick look behind. The shifty eyes of the vendors flickered between him and Marius, but none had moved closer. For the moment, his back was secure.

The theatrics of the arrival of Marius and his men had stamped an air of darkness over the market. The fish sellers were talking among themselves, shoppers eavesdropping. As word spread, the sellers seemed to stop selling and the buyers suddenly found a reason to slink away home or at least move to a safe distance. The stepping back of the crowd had created an amphitheatre.

Marius had a babyish face and looked too young to be a gang leader. Dressed in casual clothes – leather jacket, denim jeans, ankle boots – he might have been coming home from high school. Marius fixed his eyes on Jeff. Lifeless was Jeff's first thought; they had none of the hopeful sparkle of young people. Aged beyond their years and lacking in humanity. A quintessential, dispassionate killer was Jeff's assessment of the young Italian. Not a man who would show mercy or be reasoned with.

"Mr Bradley, we had arranged to meet at my apartment," Marius said. "It upset me when you refused my hospitality. Not polite for a man who comes from a country that prides itself on manners."

Jeff resisted the urge to seek out Sulla. He knew the Kosovan was not far away, but a flicker of his eyes in any direction would tip off Marius where Sulla was hiding. They knew he had not come alone. As if on cue, one of the men from the apartment scanned the crowd. As long as Sulla stayed hidden, Jeff had an edge of sorts.

"I'm a cautious man, Marius. My first instinct is to not trust a man until I get to know him."

Marius glared then laughed.

"Perhaps you are right to be this way."

Jeff said, "You have information on the whereabouts of Avni Leka. Tell me what it is and I'll be on my way."

"You are an impatient man, Mr Bradley. In Italy, we discuss such matters over a coffee or a cognac. There is a café a short drive from here. Let us take this conversation there. We can use my car."

With a slight movement of his head Marius gestured towards his vehicle. Jeff remained passive.

Marius's driver was sidling to Jeff's right and one of the other men to his left. When they were in position, both backed away. Far enough that the distance between them meant Jeff could not get to either before they pulled their weapons. Professionals. The fish vendors further along the line watched on, uncertain. Jeff's head was spinning as escape scenarios flashed through his mind. But in all his SAS training, this situation had not been practised. The special ops manual spelled it out: whenever possible, avoid direct contact with the enemy.

He said, "Avni Leka has killed many innocent people, including friends of mine."

"This is not my problem," Marius said. "I do not know this Avni Leka. My boss has said you are messing with his business, and he has ordered me to bring this interfering to an end."

And there it was. Confirmation he had walked into a trap. Marius straightened. His shoulders drew back and there was an almost indiscernible shift of weight on to the balls of his feet. Jeff trained as a boxer. He never fought as a boxer, but he recognised the signs of a man readying himself to fight. His own reaction was to let his arms fall limp. Relax. If it did come to a fight he could flick a jab to the jaw as quickly as any pugilist. But Marius had a noticeable bulge under his left armpit. Jeff didn't need to have x-ray vision to know the bulge held six to twelve rounds, depending on the weapon model. He doubted Marius had any intention of indulging in fisticuffs. He would be pulling his handgun.

Jeff glanced over his shoulder. The fish vendors on Marius's payroll had stepped forward. Others, uncertainty across their faces, stepped back. The number of assailants wanting to rip him to pieces had jumped to twelve. Jeff shook his head. He'd misjudged his foe; a serious error that might now cost him his life. His SAS commander would have kicked his butt for being such a dumb-ass. His only hope now were the men Sulla's brother-in-law had sent to Bari to oversee the smuggling of goods into Albania. They were tough men. Ex-Kosovan Liberation Army fighters. Sulla had said they could be with them in an hour, but had they arrived yet? There was no obvious sign of them, but the crowd of onlookers had increased. Were they hiding in plain sight?

Sulla himself was nowhere to be seen.

Jeff turned his attention back to Marius. Marius raised his eyebrows and gave a slight tilt of his head.

"It's not looking good for you, Mr Bradley."

Jeff said, "If your choice is to protect Avni Leka, you are my enemy."

Marius's lips tightened into a thin line. "As I said, I do not know any Avni Leka. I only know what my orders are."

Again, Jeff searched for Sulla.

To his horror, more men were drifting across the street. Marius was making sure he didn't escape. Murmurs from his men distracted Marius and he turned in the direction of the approaching newcomers. Something was wrong. Instead of increased confidence, he looked confused.

Then Jeff saw Sulla.

He nodded to his friend and allowed himself a hint of a smile.

Sulla waved his arms and his men moved in behind Marius's gang. Marius's eyes narrowed as each of his men reaching for their weapons received a nudge in the back. Weapons remained inside their jackets.

Marius tightened his lips and turned on Jeff.

"Shall we call this a draw, Marius?" Jeff said.

Marius lifted his right hand towards the bulge in his jacket.

"Don't go there," Jeff warned.

Marius dropped his hand away in a gesture of defeat, but Jeff did not relax.

"Smart man, Marius. Now where can I find Avni Leka?"

Suddenly, there was the deafening sound of sirens.

Jeff recognised the blue-and-red cars of the Carabinieri, Italian military police. Tyres screeched as cars slid to a stop around them. Police officers leaped from their vehicles, side arms in hand. Marius glanced sideways at Jeff and gave him a quizzical look. Jeff shrugged. Two officers ran to Jeff and, taking an arm each, guided him to a car already turned and facing the boulevard. Bemused, Jeff had little choice but to allow himself to be led away. He looked out for Sulla. The big Kosovan scratched the top of his head, then looked about him seeking an answer. A frown appeared on his forehead. The message to Jeff was that it seemed neither Sulla nor Marius knew any more about who had called the police and what was happening than he did.

The police bundled Jeff into the back of the waiting vehicle. Sirens blared, and the motorcade sped away. Looking back through the rear window, Jeff saw Sulla's brother-in-law's men gather round Sulla. Marius and his men shuffled back and forth. An angry Marius was gesticulating as he conversed with his driver. He pushed him in the chest. The driver held up his hands and turned to his companions for support. The shoppers, pedestrians, fishmongers, and Marius and his men could only puzzle at what had just happened. Jeff was doing the same.

CHAPTER FIVE

The Starliner bus continued en route to Istanbul. There had been no further incidents. Barry and Bethany, like the other passengers, were in shock. The murder of the bus driver had dulled their senses. They were unused to such naked violence. The blast of a gun and the sight of a man's brains splattered across a bus windscreen had left everyone traumatised. No one dared speak or make any sort of contact with the other passengers, fearful they might be singled out and suffer a similar fate. Barry and Bethany had swapped theories on why they had been hijacked and what the kidnappers' end goal might be. Nothing they had come up with made sense of their predicament.

Barry watched cars pass. How he would have loved to have held a sign to the window: 'Help! Hijackers have taken control of our bus.' A sedan coasted alongside for a few hundred metres. A young boy harnessed into a safety seat caught Barry's attention. The boy waved at him. Barry did not return the wave. He looked away. Any misinterpretation of the gesture might lead to a bullet in the head. When he looked again, the sedan had gone.

The sound of gun metal tapping on the railing beside the driver's seat brought an instant reaction. Forty heads looked to the front of the bus. This time, The Sheriff was already standing. He waited until he was certain he had everyone's attention.

When he spoke, there was a harshness to his voice.

"I think we have an understanding. You have been well behaved, and this is very good. I am certain you must be asking yourselves, why have we done this to you? What are my friends and I doing here? Why have we stolen this bus, and you along with it? The time has come where I can tell you a little of what is happening. Not everything, of course. Some aspects must remain a mystery.

"We are to take a journey together, to the Syrian border. It will take thirty hours, maybe longer. For you, time does not matter. You will be my guests until the journey is ended. It won't be too boring, and for those of you who have an interest, we will pass through Cappadocia, one of Turkey's most famous tourist spots." The Sheriff changed his tone to conciliatory. "Think of me as a guide. Our first stop will be Istanbul. Not far away. There you will leave the bus. Bathroom facilities and food will be provided. I repeat: as long as you behave yourselves, no harm will come to you. And you will be treated with civility. Talk among yourselves. Do it quietly. Even walk about if you wish, but I remind you, do not do anything silly. You know the consequences."

The Sheriff turned his back and spoke to the police officers. He lowered his voice. When two of the policemen spoke to each other it was loud enough to be heard by Bethany.

"Those policemen are speaking Albanian," Bethany whispered to Barry.

"Are you certain?"

Bethany nodded. "I'm positive."

Like Bethany, Barry worked for the UN in Kosovo. She worked in research. Barry was a carpenter, overseeing a team of builders and electricians who attended to all the UN construction and maintenance needs. He'd had the opportunity to learn the local language, but wasn't good with academic stuff, so got by with just a few basic words. Bethany was good with languages. In Albanian she was fluent. If she said they spoke Albanian, they were speaking Albanian.

Barry raised himself in his seat. A quick look confirmed no one had taken advantage of The Sheriff's offer for them to socialise. As Barry had expected, everyone sat still and mute. Satisfied he would be left alone, he fell back in his seat. What he was about to do needed to be done before some nosy passenger found the nerve to take a walk. On recent travels he had lost two money pouches and a phone to muggers, so on this trip he had followed his friend Jeff Bradley's advice. He had carried a smaller mobile phone and an extra credit card in a pouch strapped to his ankle. Jeff told him the credit card would get them money from an ATM, and the phone, help from the nearest embassy. Barry had told Jeff he wasn't a dumb-ass, but on this trip he'd followed the advice anyway.

He whispered to Bethany to warn him if any passengers came near. And keep an eye on the cops. Bethany leaned into the aisle and cast an eye to the front of the bus. The Sheriff still had his back to her and was speaking with his men. No passengers were walking about. Without turning, she gave Barry a thumbs-up.

Barry slid his hand down the side of his leg and under his trouser cuff, and found the pouch. He pulled on the Velcro flap. The ripping sound seemed almost as loud as a gunshot. He checked with Bethany. Her head still hung in the aisle. No one was coming their way. To remove the phone from the pouch, he gripped it between two of his fingers and slid it up his leg, setting it on his lap.

He put his thumb on the off-and-on slider and pushed the phone under his thigh to muffle any sound. He switched it on, and was relieved not to hear any noise. The phone back on his lap, he manoeuvred it until he could see the screen out the corner of his eye. He wanted to keep his head as straight up as possible. If his head was down, anyone looking his way might become suspicious. He clicked on Contacts. At the top of the list was Jeff Bradley's number. He tapped the screen.

He had first met the New Zealander in Kosovo. Jeff had introduced himself as a wine maker and said he had come to Kosovo to source bulk wine. Barry later learned Jeff was ex-Special Forces, and his real reason for coming to Kosovo was to find the men who killed a close friend. Barry had complete faith in the ex-military man. He and Bethany were only alive today because of Jeff. If anyone would know what to do right now, it was Jeff Bradley. And Jeff was not far from Turkey. He would be sitting in the house bar of his Rome hotel, swigging a beer and waiting for them to arrive for the wedding.

Barry typed with one finger: Bus hijacked. Heading for Syrian border. Need help. Forty passengers. Aussies and Kiwis. Two Yank women. Four men dressed as Turkish cops. Two of the cops Albanian. One civilian with them. Civilian shot driver. Right now halfway between Gallipoli and Istanbul.

Bethany nudged him in the side. She sat upright.

A bead of cold sweat dribbled down the back of Barry's neck. The Sheriff was looking directly at him. Bethany put her hand on Barry's thigh and patted it gently. Her stroking usually soothed him. Not this time. He risked a glance at the phone screen. The message needed to be sent, but he dared not make any movement. Then The Sheriff turned away and Barry, still not daring to breathe, tapped the Send icon. He switched the phone off and slid it back down his leg. He placed it in the pouch and refastened the Velcro.

Bethany snuggled into him. She kissed him on the cheek.

"My hero," she whispered in his ear.

Barry didn't feel like a hero. He wanted to pass out. He put his arm around her. There was nothing more to be done. It was now up to Jeff.

CHAPTER SIX

The only furniture in the room was a table and four chairs. On the tabletop, a notepad and a ballpoint pen. An interview room, Jeff assumed. It could serve no other purpose. He had been brought the back way to the Bari Police Station – or at least he thought it was the police station. The vehicle he'd been shoved into at the fish markets had driven through the streets and into the rear of a building. There had been no signage to indicate it was a police station. There were no police or personnel of any kind other than the men who had brought him.

They only spoke Italian. Jeff had asked for an interpreter, to see a senior officer, a lawyer, but the only response he received was a touch of the lips, and a shrug to let him know they did not understand him. He decided they either could not speak English for real or they were under instructions not to communicate with him. No fingerprints or photographs were taken. The question Jeff tossed around in his head was, why was he the only one arrested? Had he been arrested? They relieved him of his meagre possessions, then walked him to the interview room. And there he had been left.

The walls had recently been painted a light-pink colour. The faintest odour of fresh paint still hung in the air. He stretched out his legs, his hands behind his head. After a few minutes, bored, he fiddled with the pad. He pushed the point of the pen under the cover and flicked it open: blank pages. He reversed the pen in his hand and started tapping the tabletop. Jeff wasn't certain how many hours passed. They had taken his watch. The small window high on the wall told him daylight had faded and his grumbling stomach told him it was way past dinner time. And his bladder told him he needed to pee.

The door was pushed open and an overweight man entered. He was wearing a crumpled black suit and a knotted red tie that hung loose round the collar of his unbuttoned white shirt. He walked round the table and sat in the chair opposite.

"I am Captain Balboni," the man said.

Jeff relaxed a little. Captain Balboni's mannerisms suggested a friendly demeanour. Whatever was about to happen, it would not be an Italian form of torture. He noted the skin under Captain Balboni's eyes had sagged. His overall appearance was of resignation not tiredness, which was a look Jeff had seen in older cops who every day fought a never-ending battle against crime and had learned to live with the lack of success.

The Captain said, "You almost committed a serious offence in Italy today, Mr Bradley. If you had done so, I might not have been able to help you."

Jeff raised an eyebrow.

"I'm arrested because I might have committed a crime? Isn't that over the top? Even for Italy?"

"Yes, I agree, it would be over the top if an arrest had taken place, but this did not happen. You were taken into protective custody. Not arrested."

Jeff scratched the side of his face, confused and uncertain how to respond.

"The men at the markets were intent on killing you, were they not? Yes, it may have appeared you had the upper hand, but in Bari, Marius has soldiers everywhere. I know his gang well. Eventually, you would have lost. And if you killed one of them, you would lose again. I would have to charge you with murder. If you want to kill someone in Italy, at least do it in an alley and not in front of dozens of witnesses."

The Captain reached for the pad and pen. He folded back the cover and made as if to write something, but didn't. He tapped on the blank page instead.

"What did you do to aggravate Marius and his men?"

Jeff surmised that as Balboni had sent cars to his rescue, the Captain already knew the answer. But the Captain wanted to play games, and Jeff had little choice but to play along if he wanted to leave the station tonight.

"I was contacted in New Zealand by one of Marius's men. He said they had information on the whereabouts of a Kosovan Albanian named Avni Leka. Leka is a wanted international terrorist. He's responsible for bombings in Europe and recently New Zealand, and who knows where else."

The Captain nodded. "I am aware of the bombings in New Zealand. I saw them on television. Someone tried to blow up an American submarine. It was all over the news. And you say this man Leka was responsible?"

"Yes."

"And he is here in Bari?"

Jeff shrugged. "I don't know if he is even in Italy. I was contacted and told Marius had information on how to find him. The meeting today was to give me details. I walked into a trap."

"And if you found this Avni Leka, what did you intend doing to him?"

Jeff drummed the tabletop with his fingers.

The Captain said, "You do know it is illegal to visit foreign countries and murder people, don't you?"

"Yes."

"Just so you don't think us complete fools, we are aware of Avni Leka and we have been looking for him as well. Also, your presence in Italy has been known to us from the time you entered this country. And I have had men follow you from the time you arrived in Bari."

Jeff leaned back and his eyes narrowed. The revelation of a police tail surprised him. Was he on an international watch list? The Captain, perhaps thinking he doubted his words, stood, walked round his desk and opened the door. He rattled off orders in Italian and two men quickly appeared in the doorway. Jeff recognised them from the café at the port entrance.

The Captain said, "You know these two men?"

Jeff nodded.

The Captain waved the men away, closed the door and returned to his seat.

Jeff rubbed the back of his neck.

"I guess the obvious question, Captain, is why were you following me? And why have you not arrested Marius?"

Balboni threw up his hands in a gesture of surrender and grinned lopsidedly.

"To arrest a criminal like Marius is never easy, especially in the Apulian region. Organised crime has much influence. Money talks; especially when it is paid to corrupt public officials."

Balboni tilted his head on to the palm of his hand, his elbow resting on the table. He picked up a pen and drew a circle on a piece of paper.

"The circle represents organised crime in this region." He stabbed a dot in the centre of the circle. "The dot is me and my men. As you can see, we need many dots to fill the circle. It is hopeless, I know, but we have small wins and we try to satisfy ourselves with these nominal victories. It is enough to get me out of bed each morning."

Balboni dropped the pen and sat upright.

"And how is it you knew I was in town?" Jeff asked.

Jeff could sense the debate going on in Balboni's head. Should he be on the level, or keep the truth to himself?

Balboni dropped his two hands on to the table. He shrugged. "I guess it does not hurt for you to know. Someone from an American security intelligence service made contact with my bosses."

Jeff's eyes opened wide, and then Lee Caldwell came to mind. It had to be him.

"The Americans worried you might do something silly, and they wanted us to keep you safe. Not stop you, mind. It seems everyone wants Avni Leka. They, the Americans, think of you as a bloodhound. Is this how it is with you, Mr Bradley: once you have the scent you don't let it go?"

Jeff scratched his chin again.

"I don't see myself that way, but I can understand why the Americans do. And Marius?" Jeff asked. "How does he fit into this?"

Balboni said, "Marius is a small-time hood trying to become a big-time criminal." His eyes narrowed. "A peacock wanting to be an eagle, and this makes him dangerous."

Jeff nodded.

"As far as we know, Marius has no family and no known relatives in Italy. However, he might have changed his identity long ago and is using a false passport. Who knows? And, quite frankly, I don't care. The Marius of long ago does not concern me. He started out the way of all career criminals. Petty crime: breaking into houses, muggings, stolen cars, snatching purses off old ladies and tourists. The police arrested him many times, but he never spent more than a few nights in jail. It happens. No witnesses come forward, so many of these guys walk. But what worries me is recently our intelligence units have no record of him committing a crime. Not even a parking ticket."

Jeff raised his eyebrows. "And this worries you?"

"Yes. It might be he has climbed the ladder; only a step, but a move all the same. If he has been accepted into one of the families, it means he has committed a major crime. Murder or worse, if there is anything worse than murder? These crimes are like signing a contract for life. Now he is protected from people like me, so for you, if this has happened, Bari has become a very dangerous city."

Captain Balboni pushed a large brown envelope across the desk. "Your personal effects. I ordered for them not to be taken. What can I say? If my own men will not listen to me, why would Marius?" He chuckled at his humour. Then his eyes fixed on Jeff. "My advice: leave Bari."

Jeff placed his passport, mobile phone and wallet into his jacket pocket. He strapped his watch to his wrist.

Balboni said, "My men and I are a special unit within the Carabinieri. Our job is to fight organised crime in the Apulian region." He took a business card from his jacket pocket and pushed it across the table. "Next time you come to town, call me."

∾

The two men who had followed him to the café delivered Jeff back to the small park by the fish markets. Marius had long gone, they told Jeff. Sulla was still there though, leaning against his cousin's taxi. A beaming grin lit his face when he saw Jeff.

"How long were you going to leave it before you came to the station looking for me?" Jeff grumbled.

Sulla shrugged. "Only a few days. Remember, I am a Kosovan Albanian. Because of men like Avni Leka, the police are suspicious of all of us. But don't worry." Sulla slapped Jeff on the back. "Eventually, I would have come."

Jeff pulled out his phone and turned it on. The Text icon was covered by a large number three. He opened the first two texts, and they were from the phone company offering him free messaging for a special rate. The last message had no caller ID. He tapped it open and read the text. He read it again.

"Shit."

CHAPTER SEVEN

The bus entered the outskirts of Istanbul. Twenty minutes later, it turned off the main highway into an industrial zone. No bridges had been crossed. That meant they were still on the European side of the great city. Somewhere near the airport would be Barry's best guess, give or take a few kilometres. The factory/warehouse they stopped in front of was behind an uncut hedgerow. From his vantage point, Barry could not see the whole building, only the second floor of the administration block. One of the bogus cops aimed a remote at a square concrete-block pillar on the left-hand side of the driveway. An iron gate on two small wheels rolled sideways.

The bus drove into the compound.

Large blue and white letters were on a sign above the front entrance of the building. The words were in Turkish. Barry had no idea what they said, but presumed they were the name of a company. A flag hung limp on a pole protruding from the ground amidst an entanglement of weeds and flowers. From the street, in the fading light, it appeared the building's exterior walls were cream, but as the bus drew closer Barry saw the colour was light green. The building needed a repaint. Roof tiles had sagged where the framing underneath had collapsed, and the windows running the length of the wall beneath the eaves were all broken. This was an unkempt property waiting for a new tenant, a description that could be applied to many of the buildings they had only just now driven past. He bit the inside of his mouth as he searched for a more useful identifying marker. He saw none.

The bus moved down the driveway that ran past the side of the building and on to the car park at the rear. It half circled and stopped in front of a roller door. The driver gave two honks of his horn. A door in the left bottom corner opened. A head popped out. The man gave a wave and disappeared back inside. After a few seconds, the roller door rose. Before it reached full height, the bus drove under it and into the warehouse. Barry turned in his seat and looked back through the rear window. The roller door had already reversed and fallen. His gut churned when he heard the clunk of the metallic roller hitting the ground. Like birds flying into an aviary, the cage door had slammed shut and there was no escape. The outside world, and any hope of rescue, were gone.

He gulped when he saw armed men encircle the bus.

A big man in a dark suit waved his arms and rattled off orders. He was overweight, and the black satin waistcoat tight across his gut threatened to pop buttons. He spoke in a language Barry assumed to be Turkish, but could have been any language that wasn't English; Barry didn't have a clue. Not true – he could tell between French and German; not understand the words, but he knew the phonetic variations.

The bus door opened. Barry swallowed, and Bethany's hand returned to his arm. Her nails dug into his flesh. Not as hard as last time, but still hard enough for him to want to rip back her fingers. He would let her have her panic attack and rub the welts once she released her grip.

The four men in police uniform climbed off the bus first. The Sheriff followed. He gave no instruction to the passengers. No orders to obey. There was no need; everyone stayed in their seats. No one spoke.

Even so it surprised Barry no last warnings were issued. A fearful silence pervaded the bus. Barry had little doubt his companions were contemplating their immediate future and, like him, had concluded prospects were grim. But they weren't dead yet, and he wasn't about to act like it. The Sheriff said earlier they were free to wander and talk to each other. From Barry's perspective, that meant he could do what he liked. He took a quick look out the window. Why The Sheriff need not concern himself over his captives was obvious. The armed men encircling the bus meant escape was impossible.

The killer of the bus driver walked over to the fat man in the waistcoat. The big man flashed a half-smile and, as he moved forward to greet his guest, he ran a hand over his greasy black hair. There was no embrace or warm greeting of any kind. Whoever The Sheriff was, he was important, but not a long-lost buddy.

Bethany leaned against Barry, to better see into the warehouse. Her body was taut, but her hands had at least stopped trembling.

"What will happen to us, Barry?"

"For now, I don't know. But we will get through this, I promise," he lied.

Bethany rolled away from Barry and, closing her eyes, slumped into her seat. Barry could see his words of comfort had not worked. He decided against adding more lies to his original lie. What else could he say? He glanced across the aisle. Graeme Beattie had hardly moved. His wife sat rigid, hands on thighs.

Taking hold of the armrests, Barry lifted himself higher in his seat and cast an eye over his fellow travellers. As soon as he became visible, heads turned in his direction; like small children looking towards a teacher for help. They were seeking leadership, his leadership. Who did they think he was, the captain of a ship? What could he tell them? He gently pulled Bethany's legs to the side, enough to get past, and stepped into the aisle.

"Can everyone hear me?" he said, his tone a touch above a whisper, but loud enough, he hoped, for all to hear. At the back of the bus, Mildred, the wife of an elderly ex-soldier, a hint of defiance in her firmed chin, gave him a thumbs-up. "Good. For the moment, I think there is nothing to worry about. Just do as you're told. Nothing silly."

He eyed Graeme Beattie.

"Graeme, no heroics." Without lifting his head, Beattie nodded. "For those of you who don't know me well, I experienced a hostage drama not so long ago. I survived that, and we will survive this," Barry said. "Remember: keep calm."

He sat back down. He heard whispering. Good. They were now talking amongst themselves. Relieving the tension. Barry turned his attention back to the activity in the warehouse. A more relaxed Bethany leaned on his shoulder. She kissed the side of his neck. Barry reached out, placed his hand on her thigh and gave a squeeze in response. The head cop was in conversation with the big man. More than once, the big man ceased speaking, turned and snapped an order. Men obeyed without hesitation.

Bethany pushed her mouth near his ear. "That man giving the orders – he spoke to one of the policemen in Albanian," she said.

Barry studied the fat man in charge. He looked familiar. He couldn't yet place where they might have met, but he would. He was good with faces. Memories stored were images never lost. The boss man waved a hand at the cops standing a short distance away, and three of them walked towards the rear of the bus, then disappeared from sight. A few minutes of further discussion took place between the fat man, the police spokesman and The Sheriff. There was a lot of nodding of heads. The Sheriff walked back to the bus and re-boarded.

With the killer's presence, the whispering died and the oppressive blanket of dread returned.

The Sheriff offered his captives a reassuring smile.

He reminded Barry of a cat he once owned. The cat had a habit of tormenting the half-dead birds it caught, leaping in the air with joy; once he grew bored with the game, he killed them. The Sheriff was that cat. He had absolute control, and the callous manner in which he killed the driver showed he had no compassion. In Barry's judgement, The Sheriff was playing with his prisoners and loving every minute of it. What was going to happen to them when The Sheriff grew bored?

"In a few minutes, you will leave the bus," The Sheriff said. "My men will show you to the temporary accommodation. There is seating, beds, toilet facilities, food and coffee or water. Make yourselves comfortable. Please bring your passports – one of my men will take them from you." Hands of passengers rose, as if in school ready to ask the teacher an important question. The Sheriff raised his own hand, a stop sign. "I know some of you will have left your passports at the hotel; any form of ID will do. You can take your carry-on luggage. Bags stowed in the baggage compartment underneath the bus will stay where they are." Someone closer to the front raised a hand. "No questions for the moment. Please, for everyone's sakes, do as you are asked. The men outside are armed and they have orders to shoot." He turned to get off the bus, then stopped. "A reminder, but not of the friendly kind. Please don't misinterpret my accommodating manner as weakness. Remember the bus driver. If you step out of line or upset me in any way, you will be shot." The Sheriff paused to allow his captured audience time to fully grasp his message. "Talking is allowed. And until you disembark, walk about, comfort each other."

The Sheriff stepped down from the bus.

"What do you think, Barry?" Bethany asked.

"I think that asshole is a certifiable nut job." Barry took hold of Bethany's hand and kissed her fingers. "Outside of that, I don't know what to think."

She always believed in him. Who knew why she stayed with him, but she did, and he counted himself a lucky guy. Her birthday was the day before his, and he had her gift in his bag in the baggage compartment. He had organised a party for tomorrow night.

He turned his mind to the older members of his group. He did not know for certain, but he assumed some of them must be on medication. He would talk to everyone and find out if anyone had tablets they might need from the baggage compartment. If so, he would need to speak with The Sheriff and ask him to let them have their bags.

Images of the fat man in the waistcoat whirled around in his head, mixing with images from different moments of his life. Then the images settled, and he remembered where he had seen the big man.

And his heart sank.

CHAPTER EIGHT

Jeff settled into the back seat of the taxi. For the first fifteen minutes of the drive from the airport to Istanbul, little had changed. Green fields, high-rise apartments and industrial estates, and more green fields, trees, flowers, parks. But once across the bridge over the Golden Horn, traffic increased, footpaths became more crowded and his eardrums vibrated from the cacophony of car horns blaring from all directions. There were road rules, but Turkish drivers rarely obeyed them. The more maniacal attacked intersections as if red and green lights were the same. He asked his cabbie, after he ran a red light, if the citizens of Istanbul had a death wish.

The man behind the wheel, who introduced himself as Fati, said, "Allah decides on everything. If he wants me to die today, it is God's will. What can I do? My fate is decided."

The comment was a reminder to Jeff that he was back in the Islamic world. Istanbul as a city was more chaotic than he remembered. The metropolis was now ahead of Moscow and London as the largest city in the European region. It would always buzz with activity. More than fourteen million Turkish citizens lived within the city limits, and each year further millions of tourists helped cram the streets and sidewalks.

Before Jeff flew out of Bari to Rome, he phoned the New Zealand Embassy in Turkey even though he was reluctant to do so. His dealings with government departments in the past had not instilled in him a great deal of confidence. No one was ever prepared to make a decision that did not require fobbing off responsibility to someone else. When it involved an international incident, diplomacy would take precedence over concern for a New Zealand citizen. Not that this lack of governmental initiative was solely the domain of New Zealand; it was the same with all countries. Diplomats were diplomats. And there were always hidden agendas.

At any rate, he was unsure how helpful the embassy could be and decided, not a lot. A small nation such as New Zealand could hardly make demands on a country the size of Turkey. And if he was to help Barry and Bethany, he needed a lot more muscle than his own embassy could ever provide. From now on he needed to rely on his SAS training. In his head, he had become operational and, in the field, judgement calls went with the territory. Special Forces soldiers never considered themselves retired, and nor did the government. Because of this, his sense of duty overrode his reluctance to involve diplomats. He had an obligation to at least notify the embassy a kidnapping had taken place. Also, Barry's text said that, along with the Australians and New Zealanders, there were Americans on the bus. Once Jeff had alerted the diplomats, and while they bumbled about, he would follow his own course of action.

The New Zealand Embassy was in Ankara. Only a consulate office existed in Istanbul. Jeff got lucky. The Ambassador and his security officer were in Istanbul attending the Gallipoli commemorations. The woman working the phones in Ankara put him through to the security officer. Jeff told the civil servant he was an ex-SAS soldier and he was on his way to Istanbul. He needed an urgent meeting with the Ambassador.

"Yes, well, that is not going to happen, is it?" the security officer said. "The Ambassador is on leave for the next few days and I'm not dragging him off the golf course unless you can convince me the matter has extreme importance, and I'm highlighting extreme. Do you understand where I'm coming from?" He let the message sink in. Jeff waited. He'd been through military basic training courses. The training had given him the experience he needed to not react when treated like an idiot. "The Ambassador would be pissed off," the security officer continued, "if all that was wrong is a bloody Kiwi losing a passport."

Jeff didn't like the man's attitude, but understood it. He decided to keep the hijacking to himself. At the airport there had been no news items about a hijacked bus in Turkey. If it were known, it would be headline news around the world. Barry may have sent the text without the hijackers knowing. For the moment, his friend's safety might be reliant on keeping this secret.

Jeff's instinct told him no one was going to find the bus until the hijackers wanted it found. And that was not going to happen until they were ready to make their demands known. It concerned him there had been no more contact from Barry. It would have been helpful to have licence plate details, the model or manufacturer of the bus, or even the name of the bus company. If he had that information, how would he use it? He had to protect Barry's ability to continue to make contact. If the hijackers suspected information was coming from the bus, lives might be at risk. Of course, this was all conjecture, but he needed to make a plan, and he would build his plan on his best-guess scenario. Also, the hijackers had forty people. It might not concern them to kill a passenger or two if they thought someone on the bus was leaking information.

"I have reliable information that New Zealanders have been kidnapped," Jeff said to the security officer. That was enough for now.

"Do you have names?"

"I will provide details when I meet with the Ambassador."

A pause. Jeff had an image of a pissed-off security officer staring at his phone and thinking, 'Who the hell did this guy think he was to be stuffing him around?'

"It will take thirty minutes to contact the Ambassador. Call me back in an hour."

"Too long. I'm flying out of Bari to Rome in a few minutes. When I get to Fiumicino Airport, I'll have a couple of hours before my flight to Turkey. I'll phone between flights for a meeting time."

"How do you know about this alleged kidnapping?"

"You have enough information for now. I'll phone from Rome."

Jeff had hung up before the security officer could reply. News of a kidnapped New Zealand citizen should be enough to get him a seat at the Ambassador's dinner table.

Now, he was in Istanbul and had an hour to kill before his meeting. He wasn't expecting to get much sleep, but he needed a base, and booking into a hotel would fill some time. The Beyoglu district on the European side of the city would suit him best. He had stayed in the area before and was familiar with the streets. From what he remembered, the nightlife and cafés were open twenty-four hours. Jeff had spent more than one night while on leave from special ops drinking shots of raki in a late-night café on Istiklal Avenue. Not that there would be any heavy drinking on this trip, but he did his best thinking walking busy streets and sitting in late-night cafés. Beyoglu was in the vicinity of the Galata Tower, where his meeting with the security officer was to take place.

"Driver, I need a hotel near Beyoglu," Jeff said.

"Please, call me Fati."

"Okay, Fati, I need a hotel."

"I know a good place. And only a short walk to Istiklal Avenue. This street is very famous in Istanbul. Do you know it?"

"I know it," Jeff answered.

"Then you will like very much this hotel."

Jeff agreed to take a look. He held no fears for the quality of the hotel. Most Istanbul hotels were of a good standard.

Fifteen more minutes of heavy traffic and Fati said, "Here is the hotel." He stopped outside the entrance.

The English words above the Turkish on the brass plate to the side of the entrance read, THE OLD HOTEL. Good name, was Jeff's first reaction. The building looked as if it had been built in the time of the Ottomans. When it came to architecture, Jeff didn't have a clue and could not name the style or design of the five-storey building, but he did know it dated back to the nineteenth century. A taxi driver from a previous trip had told him this was the average age of buildings in the Beyoglu district. At street level, the hotel had its own café. From where he sat it appeared full. The patrons did not look like tourists. Locals, for sure. That could mean the state of the interior of the hotel might reflect the exterior's neglected façade. Did he want to rough it? He decided he didn't.

He was about to lean forward to tap Fati on the shoulder and tell him he wanted to be taken to the Marriott. Fati must have sensed his hesitation.

He said, "You will enjoy your stay. The owner and his wife and their daughter will look after you."

Jeff made to argue, then decided against it. He did not have the time.

"Is there a phone in the room?"

The cabbie nodded. "Of course. The hotel has five stars. Well, three official, but it should be five."

A man and two women approached the car. The boot popped, and his suitcase disappeared through the doorway. Fati the cabbie twisted in his seat and offered a grin. "Please, follow the manager. He will show you to your room."

It seemed Jeff was staying at The Old Hotel.

"Go nowhere," Jeff said. "Once I've unpacked, I have to go to a meeting. I need you to take me."

Fati nodded and turned off the motor. "I will wait in the café."

CHAPTER NINE

The New Zealand Embassy security officer had said, when Jeff called back from Rome airport, that he would meet him outside the Galata Guney Restaurant. The eatery skirted the plaza that surrounded the Galata Tower. He said it was easy enough to find. A black awning stretched out across the outdoor seating, and the name of the restaurant and the word GUINNESS were written in white lettering along the awning flap. The security man said to wait there for him. It was less than a two-kilometre drive from The Old Hotel to the plaza. Fati took a round-about route and drove it in three. He dropped Jeff and said he was not allowed to park in the area. He wrote his mobile number on a piece of paper.

"When you are ready to leave, phone that number," Fati instructed. "I will not be far."

Jeff had never been to the Galata Tower, but he had seen it from a distance. Close to seventy metres high, the six-hundred-year-old structure could be seen from many parts of the city. From a distance, it looked intriguing and worth a visit; close up, it was impressive. That it had been constructed that long ago made it more so. Jeff took a photo with his phone.

The restaurant was easy enough to spot. Jeff saw no one standing about. He checked his watch. He was early. In front of the tower, a small crowd had gathered to listen to a young female singer. A man playing an acoustic guitar accompanied her. She sang in Turkish, or it could have been another language for all Jeff knew, but it sounded okay, so he listened while keeping one eye on the restaurant. After fifteen minutes, and still no sign of anyone standing under the Guinness beer sign, he decided the security man might not step forward until he saw Jeff. Jeff couldn't think why that might be, but the men and women of the intelligence services were a quirky group, and most of them paranoid.

He elbowed his way through the busker's audience, then made his way across the grey paving stones. Thin lines of red stones mixed in with the grey jutted out from round the base of the tower, and the design made it look as though they were spokes on a wheel, with the Galata Tower the hub. There was a mini-market next to the restaurant. The shopkeeper in an apron stood beside a rack of newspapers. Plastic trays of bottled water sat on the pavement next to an outside refrigerator. Jeff was thirsty and bought a small bottle of water.

He had the cap part-way screwed off when a man in a navy suit, white shirt with blue stripes and a deep-red tie walked towards him. The neatness of the attire and his polished shoes suggested a man used to wearing a uniform. He had a solid look to him. Ex-forces, and not long out, if in fact he was out. Close to his own age, Jeff guessed; early thirties. When he stopped in front of Jeff, he stood shoulders back and hands clasped behind him. A soldier's at-ease position.

"Jeff Bradley," Jeff said.

He held out his hand. The security officer shook it, but did not offer his name. Instead, he asked to see Jeff's passport. He held the travel document at arm's length. Satisfied the photo and face matched, he passed it back.

"Follow me."

An order. Not an invitation. Jeff ignored the unsubtle stamp of superiority and obliged. What did he care if the guy had a carrot up his arse? Besides, he was the one who had asked for the meeting. After a five-minute walk they entered a small hotel.

"I have a room I use," the security officer said by way of explanation.

He waved to the concierge as he led Jeff through the foyer, and received a smile of recognition in return. It seemed the security officer was telling the truth and had been here more than once, not playing I'm-a-big-shot games to keep Jeff on the back foot. Why the hell would he do that anyway? Jeff admonished himself. He had to stop thinking the worst of everyone. But he had experienced the run-around from diplomats in the past and it prejudiced his attitude.

The room had once been a hotel bedroom and was now converted to a small interview or meeting room. Today, Jeff guessed it was an interview room. It had a kitchen and bathroom facilities, and a rectangular table and six chairs. One chair at each end and two either side in the middle. The security officer gestured Jeff towards a middle chair. He still had not introduced himself, and did not bother to do so now. Jeff perceived this guy was confusing him with the whiney Kiwi who had lost his passport he had accused him of being earlier.

"Can I offer you a drink? Coffee, water, fruit juice?"

Jeff raised his bottle of water. The security man sat opposite.

"Right then, Mr Bradley. Let's get started. You say there is an urgent matter for discussion; a matter of life and death, you said. A kidnapping has taken place. Okay, I'm all ears. Why don't you tell me why you think this might have happened and what evidence, if any, you have to support your claim? Let's hope to hell you're not wasting my time. The Ambassador is most concerned. He spoke with the police and they told him they have had no advisement of any kidnapping. The Ambassador was taken aback of course and is not happy."

Jeff tightened his lips, but controlled his emotions. The guy was pissing him off.

"I expected the Ambassador to be here," Jeff said.

The security man said nothing. He focussed on Jeff. Kept his mouth shut. Jeff knew the routine. Standard interrogation technique. Ask a question and then shut up. Sooner or later, the interviewee will open their mouth and fill the silence. Jeff wasn't here for an arm wrestle. Round one to the security man.

Jeff said, "Less than twenty-four hours ago a group of men hijacked a bus, loaded with New Zealanders, Australians and two American women travelling back to Istanbul from the Gallipoli commemorations."

The security officer stiffened. "You know this how?"

"A friend of mine is on the bus and sent me a text telling me so."

"And you've kept this to yourself why?"

"I was in Italy. It concerned me if this information got out before the hijackers want it known, they might figure someone on the bus is in contact with the outside world. My friend would be in danger. I kept the message to myself until I could deliver it in person."

The security man smiled.

"You have balls, Bradley."

The security man stood, walked round the table to the fridge and removed a bottle of mineral water. Jeff watched. The security man was taking a moment to assess the information and prepare how best to continue. A thinker, Jeff observed; he might have underestimated the man from the Embassy.

"Here is the deal," the security man started. "As you might imagine, we have little muscle in Turkey. Not any, to be honest. I have little choice but to hand this matter over to the Turkish authorities and let them handle it. I will need to tell the Australians and the Americans."

Jeff frowned.

"In the past," the man continued, "I have had dealings with the Turkish police. I've always found them efficient and competent. If a bus has been hijacked, they will give it a high-priority status. Tourism is an important industry. And the Gallipoli ceremonies are an important event. Kidnapped New Zealanders and Australians will make this a black day. When it gets out, and it will, the world will be watching, and Turkey will be well and truly in the spotlight."

"I was hoping to keep this quiet until my friend makes contact again."

The security officer shook his head.

"Can't be done. If we kept this information to ourselves and the Turkish government found out, then the political fallout between our governments would have dire consequences for the New Zealand government. Now, what can you give me?"

"There is nothing, other than the text," Jeff said.

"Can I see it?"

The security officer held out his hand.

Jeff was not about to give over his phone. He said, "Give me your mobile number and I will forward it to you." When the transfer was complete, the security man read it through several times. He turned his attention back to Jeff.

"Not a lot to go on, is there?"

Jeff shrugged. "The bus or phones should be easy enough to track on GPS. I'd have done it myself, but I don't have access to technical."

The security man stood.

"I'll get on to my police contacts. They might want to contact you. Where are you staying?"

The security officer slid a pen and paper across to Jeff and he wrote down his contact details before pushing them back across the table.

"Thank you for bringing this to our attention. We can take care of it from here," the security man said.

"You won't keep me informed?"

The security man shook his head. "No. I'll contact you when we have news your friend is rescued. Not before. That's it. However, if you hear from your friend again, I expect you to contact me. Enjoy your stay, Mr Bradley. Go sightseeing. Istanbul is an exciting town."

Jeff stayed seated. "You have got to be joking. You're not prepared to communicate with me? Bring me in on the inside and let me meet with the cops and anyone else you think you need to tell. I am ex-SAS and I have security clearances that will last forever. So what the hell is this shit?"

"You're a civilian now, Bradley. Turkey is under my jurisdiction, and what happens is my call." He shrugged. "I need not explain myself, but I guess your active service background deserves respect, so I will. Once I have reported this information to the Aussies, Yanks and Turks, from there on, they will make all the decisions and it will be out of my hands. I'll receive a progress report from time to time, but they won't be contacting me seeking permission before they take the next step. They will get on with whatever they might think of to do. That is the real world, I'm afraid."

Jeff put two hands on the table and pushed himself out of his chair. "I guess that's it," he said.

The security man's voice softened, sympathetic, but not friendly. "I know who you are, Bradley. I had you checked out. My assessment is, you're a loose cannon. Don't go off half-cocked. Not here in Turkey. We could pull your passport and have you sent home."

The security man opened the door, and when Jeff stepped into the corridor it shut behind him. Being told to get lost had not surprised Jeff; the security man was right: what could he do to help? And he was a civilian. The threat of pulling his passport didn't bother him.

It wouldn't happen, but even if it did it wouldn't be a hindrance. He knew ways to gain false travel documents and travel through countries without ID.

He had no intention of leaving Barry and Bethany's fate in the hands of someone else, and sure as hell not in the hands of a politician. In a hostage situation, the politicians would sacrifice the passengers if it suited. He had found that out to his cost in Afghanistan. He was trained to work alone or with a small team. If he was to save Barry and Bethany, he needed to go after them himself. To do that, he needed some muscle, and he knew where to go to get it.

CHAPTER TEN

"Lee Caldwell."

The American voice answering the phone sounded as calm and as unflappable as ever. Jeff first met Caldwell in Kosovo. In the beginning, Jeff suspected Caldwell worked for the CIA. The American had never denied it, but after working together on two missions Jeff had changed his mind. Caldwell wasn't a spy, but perhaps he was much more. Who he worked for, Jeff was still to discover. On the business card the American had given him in Prishtina, it said he was a Technical and Management Consultant for Devon Securities. Right off, Jeff had not believed a word of it; men from the agency labelled themselves with many bogus identities. It went with the territory. He had used similar covers himself at various stages of his career, but Caldwell differed from the spies he had met. Caldwell had power that CIA agents he associated with never had. In the end, who the American worked for didn't much matter to Jeff; Caldwell had always been there to support him, and that's all that counted in his book.

"It's Jeff Bradley, Caldwell. I'm in Turkey."

"And you have a problem? I should never have given you my private number."

"Yes, I have a problem. We both have a problem."

"Really?"

Jeff related the details.

"I see. Not good for Barry and Bethany. I like them both. And how has this become my problem?"

"There are two American women on the bus."

"Is this confirmed?" Caldwell asked.

Jeff heard the scepticism in the American's tone.

"In his text, Barry said the bus was full of Kiwis and Aussies and two American women."

"Not Canadians?"

"He said Americans."

"Do we know their identities?"

"Of course not. For Christ's sake, Caldwell, Barry was sneaking out a message on a hijacked bus. He didn't ask for passports. But he can tell the difference between a Yank and a Canadian. He's in the UN in Kosovo. He works with you Yanks all the time, as well you know."

"Indeed, I do. Why are two American women on a bus full of Aussies and New Zealanders?"

"That I can't tell you," Jeff answered.

"Why are you contacting me? You have an embassy in Turkey. Go to them. They will contact the American Embassy and the good old USA will give the problem to the CIA. It's more their domain than mine. They'll know what to do."

"I want to make sure Barry and Bethany come out of this alive. You Yanks have told the world you won't do deals with kidnappers, so sending a truckload of CIA agents is not going to be worth shit as far as I'm concerned."

Caldwell laughed.

"Okay, Jeff, I hear you. I guess you're going it alone, and I take it you want to be on the inside. Get fed intelligence as it becomes available, and have some big boys' toys available should you need them."

It was Jeff's turn to laugh.

"You've got it right."

"I'm caught on a project right now, but I'll sort something out for you. Give me thirty minutes."

"One last item," Jeff said. "Thanks for the heads-up to the Italians. You might have saved my life."

Caldwell laughed again. "Glad to help, Jeff. I need you around. You've become the stick I poke into the hornets' nest to stir up the bad guys. If I can keep you alive, who knows how many you'll scare my way?"

Without so much as a 'talk later' or 'goodbye', Caldwell rang off. Jeff stared at his mobile, then tapped his finger on the End Call icon.

CHAPTER ELEVEN

Caldwell phoned back within the hour.

"I've spoken with Devon Securities and someone will make contact in the next few hours. You were right to phone. My organisation can't tell the Turks what to do, but we can bring pressure to bear to ensure it is done the way we want it done. Once the bus is found, if it's possible to free the hostages, my colleague will make that happen. But you know how the world works, Jeff. Most times when shit happens, by the time we hear about it, it's too late to save the day."

Jeff said, "Give me backing and I'll keep on top of it."

"You've got the help."

"Thanks, Caldwell. I appreciate it."

"Jeff, whoever it is that makes contact, don't put them through the third degree. Accept this person has the same authority as I have, and work together. You won't be let down. Keep in touch."

And Caldwell hung up.

The conversation heartened Jeff. Caldwell said his colleague worked for the same organisation as he did. Caldwell could walk into embassies and demand cooperation, and he could issue orders to military officers of any rank. Jeff had seen it first-hand. Whatever government agency it was he really worked for, it gave him a great deal of authority. Another reason for Jeff to believe it wasn't the CIA.

He opened the room's fridge and removed a fruit juice.

There had been no further texts from Barry. It worried him, but the implications of no communications might only mean that the hijackers had confiscated his phone or, if he did still have his phone, that he had been unable to use it. Jeff had sent a text message to Barry to let him know he was in Istanbul. If he knew what vehicle to look for, it could be tracked. Barry was smart; he must have known how important those details were, and if he had not given information on what type of bus, the name of the bus company or the registration plates, then it was not possible to do so. When Jeff thought about it, the reason became clear. All that information was on the outside of the bus.

A day had gone by, and whichever bus company owned the bus must have reported a driver missing, or at least tried to make contact with him to find out where he was. If the driver was a private contractor, it might not happen until a nervous wife missed her bus driver husband and raised the alarm.

Somewhere in Istanbul, a hotel manager would have sent staff to check rooms. The manager would know Barry's group was due to fly back to Rome today. The hotel would contact the police and ask what had become of their guests. In all likelihood, before they found the bus its disappearance would go public. When that happened, the game would change. If Jeff could find it before that occurred, he might pull off a rescue. But without access to intel, he had no idea where to look. He might as well throw a dart at a map of Istanbul and use that as a start point.

He opened his bottle of fruit juice and gulped half of it.

A knock on the door intruded on his reverie. He placed the half-empty fruit juice bottle on the bench over the fridge as he made his way to the door. It was his taxi driver, Fati. He had rubbed oil over his bald head. It glistened under the hall lights.

"Mr Bradley, a message has come for you." He held out a folded piece of paper.

Why was Fati delivering the message, and not the hotel staff? Jeff glanced at the note, knowing Fati had already read it.

"This café, do you know where it is?" Jeff asked, not giving Fati the opportunity to deny it.

"Yes, it is not far," Fati answered. No sign of embarrassment at being caught reading someone else's mail. Jeff reached behind the door and plucked his jacket off the hook.

"Take me there."

৩৩

Jeff finished his espresso.

The stocky waiter, dressed in a white jacket and black trousers, cleared away the coffee cup and wiped the table. In his fifties, was Jeff's best guess; he could have been sixty. He had a distinct limp, favouring his right leg, a scar on his lower chin, and what looked to be a permanent sneer. It must be a family restaurant; in Jeff's opinion, the man was in the wrong profession and only family would hire him. The table now cleared of his cup and water bottle, the waiter hovered. Jeff knew the routine. He'd had his fill of it in Bari and now it was happening in Istanbul. Fair enough. Staff made the bulk of their wages from the income earned from the tables, and Jeff occupied a table with four chairs and had stopped buying.

From where he sat, he could see Istiklal Avenue in the distance. One of the most famous avenues in all of Istanbul, Fati had informed him on the drive over. Three million people per day visited on the weekend, Fati had stated. Today wasn't the weekend, and yet it was packed. Jeff watched a steady stream of pedestrians cross the bottom of the street. He needed a few essentials. Istiklal was a place to find everything, from what he remembered.

Potential patrons peered through the window looking for empty seats. When one fixed an eye on Jeff, he stared them down and they moved on. The irritated waiter continued to tend the other tables, but always returned to stand beside Jeff. He shifted from one leg to the other, his eyes fixed on the back of Jeff's head. When he moved off to serve another table, he glared in Jeff's direction.

Jeff didn't need the irritation. He dropped some notes on the table.

"Bring me water, when my guest arrives."

The waiter scooped up the money and thrust it in his pocket. He didn't need to count it to know it was more than he'd make selling coffee to a new round of guests.

She caught his attention as soon as she entered the café.

A brunette, her hair swept back in a ponytail, head held high and each movement balanced like a dancer or a gymnast, with the sleekness of a black panther. She stood near the door and scanned the crowded café. Jeff's eyes widened when her gaze fixed on him. She made for his table and stopped in front of it. He yanked his six-foot-plus frame out of his chair. She was tall. Another few inches and she could've eyeballed him.

His mouth dropped open a touch; he had expected a Caldwell look-alike. She was younger than he was; late twenties, he guessed, but her flawless skin made it hard to tell. He put it down to good genes and not regular applications of night lotions. A number of heads had followed her.

"You must be Jeff Bradley? I'm Reason Johanson."

Jeff shook the American's offered hand. He couldn't place which part of the States she came from. Her accent didn't have the drawl of the Midwest or a dialect associated with the southern states.

Reason was all business, the mannerisms of a CEO about to sit at the head of a corporate table. A charcoal trouser suit hung loose on her, but the canary-yellow T-shirt not well hidden behind the jacket was moulded like a second skin to her sculptured body. Tight abs. If nothing else, his new companion was fit.

"Please, take a seat," Jeff said. "Can I get you anything?"

"Water."

Jeff waved and the waiter hobbled away to fetch the water Jeff had already ordered. He turned his attention to Reason Johanson.

"Was I that easy to spot?"

The café was full. Maybe fifty patrons.

"Lee Caldwell sent me a photo. You're sitting alone," Reason said.

Jeff nodded.

Reason said, "I spoke to the intelligence officer at my embassy a short while ago. They've been in touch with your embassy, and the Australians and the police."

"So they do believe a hijacking has taken place? They don't think I'm a crazy man?"

Reason shook her head. "I can assure you they are taking it seriously."

"Okay. Good. Glad to hear it."

"I do have some news," Reason said. "They have identified a bus that may be missing. A woman reported her father, who lives with her and her husband, had not returned from work. He is a contract driver, and his company has confirmed he drove tourists to Gallipoli. And yes, he also confirmed they were New Zealanders and Australians, but then most of the people transported to Gallipoli on the memorial day are New Zealanders and Australians."

"That is a good first step. What are the Turkish cops doing about finding the bus?"

Reason said, "My read on the situation so far is the Turkish police are still not convinced a hijacking has taken place. They have difficulty believing a bus full of tourists can disappear for twenty-four hours and not be reported missing. But they are looking into it. They think it more likely the group on the bus decided to party it up somewhere and neglected to inform anyone. They have sent out a description of the bus to police patrols and to police stations between Istanbul and Gallipoli. For them, it is now a waiting game."

Jeff drummed the table with his fingers.

"I know these guys, and rest assured the initial investigation will be as thorough as they can make it. But they don't have a lot to go on. My contact told me, first off they will phone the hotels," Reason said. "As you can appreciate, that is a lot of ground to cover; there are lots of hotels in Istanbul. When you think about it, looking for missing guests will be an impossible task. Let's face it, tourists don't stay in their hotel rooms; they go out and sightsee."

Jeff asked, "Do the police have any ideas on who might gain from hijacking a bunch of tourists? I've always viewed Turkey as a safe country to travel in, even with the odd terrorist bomb going off from time to time. And Australians and New Zealanders have been attending ANZAC Day at Gallipoli for decades. There haven't been difficulties in the past; not that I'm aware of, at any rate."

Reason spread her hands palms down on the table.

"There is something I've been told that might have a bearing," she said. "Until the bus is found, it cannot be confirmed the link is there, but I think it's worthy of consideration."

"Sounds ominous," Jeff said.

"At the time the buses were leaving Gallipoli, a group of men dressed in Turkish police uniforms broke a prisoner out of the cells of a police station near the village of Sarkoy. Six Turkish police officers were killed. The buses returning from Gallipoli pass close to Sarkoy." Jeff's eyes narrowed. "It makes sense if they were looking to use hostages on a bus to aid their escape that one of the buses from Gallipoli could have become a target."

Thoughtful, Jeff leaned forward.

"If that is the action they've taken, to me it doesn't make sense at all. You and I are reasonably intelligent people; well, I know I am and assume you are," Jeff said, smiling at his attempted humour. Reason remained straight-faced. "They plan an escape down to the smallest detail, like masquerading as police. And their escape vehicle is a bus. And they wait at a bus stop for it to arrive. It does stretch credibility, doesn't it?"

Reason gave her head a slight tilt.

"As I said, it is only a theory, but your friend said they had been kidnapped. And you are assuming the jail-breakers ran out of the station and waited at the bus stop, as you put it. What if it wasn't like that? What if the bus was part of the escape plan from the beginning?"

Jeff was about to respond, but hesitated; he leaned back in his chair and interlocked the fingers of his hands behind his head. The waiter placed the two bottles of water on the table. Jeff took up his bottle and twisted the cap off; Reason ignored hers.

"I think the bus being part of the escape plan could be considered a logical assumption," she said.

Jeff nodded. "I don't disagree there is a certain logic to how you have set it out. But if what you say is true, I'm thinking there is something else going on. I mean, why not steal an SUV or something faster? They could have been in Bulgaria before the alarm was raised and, given the amount of elapsed time, now, well hidden somewhere in Eastern Europe. But they chose not to do this; they chose instead to kidnap a busload of tourists. That means they are preparing for a standoff with the police or the military, or whoever."

"It looks that way," Reason said. "On the positive side, the Turkish government will not be happy. If these men have taken the bus, the authorities will be as keen to find it as you are. But for the moment, it is all conjecture."

"Not conjecture," Jeff said. "Barry sent the text and they have been kidnapped. Until I hear different, I will assume the men who helped the prisoner escape in Sarkoy have taken it."

Reason nodded. "Nothing wrong with theorising."

"I was thinking," Jeff continued. "The phones have trackers, do they not? Do you have access to the technology? Maybe we can get a fix. Pinpoint where they are?"

"I can tell you it was the first step taken by the Turkish police. They checked for a phone signal from the mobile number you gave your embassy. And the bus has a GPS system, but there was no response from either the phone or the bus GPS. Wherever the bus is right now, no signals are being emitted. My advice," Reason said. "Go back to your hotel. I will contact you when I have news."

Jeff took a swig of his water. He kept his eyes on Reason Johanson, searching for a flicker of a sign she might be holding back information. He saw none. His thoughts switched to Barry and Bethany. Where were they, and were they still alive? And what the hell was going on?

CHAPTER TWELVE

The section of the warehouse that had become a temporary prison for Barry and the rest of the passengers matched the shabby exterior. Exposed beams were visible where suspended ceiling panels had fallen away. Some hung from wires, other panels had disappeared. It was cold and the air damp. But there was light, and because they had worn clothing to stave off the cold at Gallipoli everyone was comfortable enough. As promised by The Sheriff, the food and hot drinks provided also helped to ward off the cold and lift spirits a little. Their confinement area, including the bathroom facilities and beds and bedding, could have housed up to a hundred people. Barry's initial thoughts were it might have been an army barracks of some sort. But he dismissed the idea. The quarters looked too sloppy and disorganised to be military. It was more like a school dormitory without the cleaners.

Barry made a trip to the toilet every half hour. It concerned him making so many visits might attract attention, but there was no cause for worry. The guards had no interest in anything the hostages did, and the other tour group members were too distressed to have any interest in anything Barry did either. Each time, he tried sending a text, but there was still no signal. The battery level on the mobile phone had reduced.

Not yet to a level where he risked losing it altogether, but he would need to be careful to keep it switched off. The only reason he could think of for the lack of signal was the hijackers had installed jammer devices. He had seen them used in Kosovo. Jammers weren't big, and they were cheap. Two or three would be enough to blanket the warehouse.

The treatment of himself and the other passengers had puzzled Barry. He had seen videos of hostages held by Islamic terrorists just like everyone else had done. Usually the captives were tied up and bags placed over their heads. But this had not happened. So why not? Why hadn't they been strip-searched and the women's handbags and the carry-on luggage emptied and checked? Barry had thought them lax, but he knew they were smart. So what was their agenda? At the same time, he was not about to complain. They had shown how ruthless they were; they had shot the driver. Thankfully, a day had passed, and to everyone's relief there had been no further violence.

Even though the uncertain future kept everyone on edge, the para-lysing dread had waned. Some of the passengers had begun to look upon the hijacking as an adventure with a few hardships. One couple had discussed how much money a television station might pay for their story when it was over. But mostly everyone sat, and clung to a part-ner where a partner existed, and whenever the outer warehouse door opened, lips trembled and faces turned ashen.

Two guards stayed in the room at all times, but they kept their distance. They chatted and smoked cigarettes that smelled like camel dung. From time to time, shifty eyes gave the passengers the once-over before returning to their conversation.

An exhausted Bethany lay asleep on one of the bunks.

The two American women sat on a bed in the corner, arm in arm, nervous eyes staring into space. One rested her head on her friend's shoulder. They weren't much older than twenty. Barry imagined they were thinking that, when it came to hostage-taking in the Middle East, the Americans always drew the short straw. Barry decided he would chat with the two women. Comfort them, if needed. He walked across. His movement caught their eye. Two pale faces watched him sink down on to his haunches.

"Hi, I'm Barry," he said. He received a small flick of the hand as a welcoming wave. "Are you guys okay? It's bad enough being kidnapped, but being stuck here with a bunch of boring Kiwis and Aussies makes it worse."

This brought a smile.

"I'm Marcia, and this is my friend, Catalina," Marcia said.

"Call me Cat," Catalina responded.

Marcia had cropped blonde hair. Catalina had the same short hairstyle, but her hair was red. The two friends were dressed almost identically in jeans, green woollen pullovers and white running shoes.

Marcia leaned forward. "Are they Islamic extremists? We've seen the beheading videos. Are we going to be beheaded?"

Her jaw was firm but her eyes moist; a gutsy young woman. Cat pushed closer to her friend, fearful of Barry's answer, but like Marcia her head tilted, defiant. They would face whatever adversity awaited them together and with courage.

Barry gave a vigorous shake of his head. "No, of course not. That is not going to happen." The two women weren't convinced. "The man who calls himself The Sheriff might be an Islamic extremist, but two of the men dressed up as cops are Albanians. I'm thinking some of the other guards are as well. I know their boss. They'll be in it more for the money, not religion. We aren't dead yet, which I think means their job is to keep us alive. At any rate, extremists don't treat their captives the way we've been treated, do they?"

Marcia and Catalina shook their heads.

"So no, I think for the moment we're okay. But, it is important to keep calm and not antagonise them. And if you need anything or want to talk, come get me. Okay?"

Two heads nodded. Barry stood up.

He made his way back to Bethany. Graeme Beattie watched him walk past. It crossed his mind he should speak with him. As he half turned, a glare from Beattie's wife was a clear message to stay away. Shaking his head, Barry continued on towards Bethany. Screw them.

A small group, gathered near the entrance to the showers, caught his attention. Barry sighed. His first thought was someone had discovered a heroic spark and was assembling a group to confront The Sheriff en masse. That would be suicide. He would need to talk them out of it. A few steps towards them and he could see between legs a shape on the ground.

He squeezed his way to the front.

Reg sat on the floor, his legs out in front of him. Mildred, his wife and the oldest member of the group, had her head resting on his thigh. Mildred was moaning and in pain. Her face was as white as a sheet, and a throaty, gasping, gurgling sound escaped between slightly parted lips.

Barry liked them both. Reg was an old digger and had fought in a war somewhere. Barry still had to find out where. Their son had been killed in Vietnam. Remembering soldiers lost in war made ANZAC Day special for them. At Gallipoli, they had separated from the group. They wanted to be alone to remember their son, and everyone had respected their privacy. When the hijackers took the bus, Mildred had shown spunk. A younger Mildred might have let The Sheriff have a piece of her mind. Barry was thankful she hadn't.

"What is it, Reg?" Barry asked, a hand on Reg's shoulder.

"I don't know for certain, Barry. She said she had a pain in her arm and her head was spinning. She grabbed at her chest and I caught her as she collapsed. Her skin is all clammy. It's bad, Barry. She needs a doctor."

Barry knelt beside them. He reached out and touched her hand.

"Easy there, Mildred. You hang on. I'm going to get you a doctor. Okay?"

Mildred's eyes didn't open. She squeezed Barry's hand.

He stood up. "I'll get help."

Those gathered round parted to let Barry through. The guards watched as he approached. One waved him back. When Barry kept walking, two Kalashnikovs pointed at him. Both barrels aimed at his chest. He stopped and raised his hands.

"Easy, guys. Keep cool. Do either one of you speak English?"

One of the guards nodded. "I do. What do you want? You are not to come near us. This is the rule."

Barry pointed towards Mildred. "One of our group is having a heart attack. She needs a doctor."

The guard nodded. "Go back there and wait. I will go for help."

"Thank you."

Barry returned to Mildred's side and knelt beside her. He stroked her arm. Reg looked at him, hopeful. "The guard has gone to get help."

"Thank God," Reg said. "The pain is getting worse. She needs to be in hospital."

Barry knew that was unlikely to happen. Heads turned as the door was flung open and The Sheriff entered the room. The guard pulled the door shut behind him. Both guards took up positions with their backs against the wall and their weapons at the ready. The passengers stepped aside to allow The Sheriff through. Barry stayed kneeling next to Mildred. Bethany caught Barry's eye and gave a slight shake of the head. She didn't need to worry; he was not about to do anything silly. Mildred's breathing was now in sharp gasps; her eyes stayed closed, her hands still clutching at her chest, and low moans followed the spasms of heavy breathing.

"What is happening here?" The Sheriff asked.

"My wife is having a heart attack," Reg blurted out, still cradling Mildred's head. "She needs a doctor and to be in hospital." His tone was pleading, his eyes watering.

"I am sorry for your wife. She is your wife?"

Reg nodded.

"Then yes, I am sorry for your wife, but a hospital is out of the question, and none of my men are doctors. There is nothing I can do."

Reg said, "She is in pain; please help her. She can't be left like this. Please."

"Yes, you are right. She cannot be left to suffer. I will help. Do not worry," The Sheriff said.

Reg bowed his head at The Sheriff's words, his shoulders slumped, relieved. He stroked Mildred's brow. Barry was as concerned for Reg as he was for Mildred. The colour had drained from the old man's face. It would be no surprise to Barry if Reg had a heart attack of his own at any moment. Most of the passengers maintained a sympathetic vigil over the elderly couple, but the others, Barry included, watched The Sheriff walk to one of the guards. Hands covered mouths to stifle gasps when The Sheriff snatched the Kalashnikov from the guard's grasp. The Sheriff pulled back the cocking mechanism. A 7.62 bullet flew through the air and another was pulled from the magazine and loaded into the breech. His hand on the pistol grip, and the butt on his hip, he made his way back. Barry climbed to his feet. The group of passengers crowding around Mildred clung to the nearest arm and eyes widened in horror at the realisation of what was about to happen. For an instant, Barry froze, disbelieving, but he knew what he must do. He made to step in front of The Sheriff, confront him. Barry felt a tug at his jacket sleeve. He tried again. Bethany held his sleeve tighter. With no fanfare, The Sheriff aimed the Kalashnikov and pulled the trigger.

Three bullets slammed into Mildred's chest.

"Fuck!" Barry blurted out.

Passengers screamed and fell to their knees. Eerie wailing bounced off the walls of the enclosure. Agonised sounds like wounded animals. Some sobbed; others were struck dumb and stood silent. Faces the colour of snow. Barry turned on Bethany, still trying to shake his arm free of her. She clung on. Their eyes met. He saw the determination. She was not about to let him do anything that might get him killed.

Barry looked down at Mildred. Her eyes sprang open and mouth widened. A gurgling sound from deep within rattled up through her lifeless body, a final spasm as death engulfed her, and then, her head, still in Reg's arms, slumped to the side. Accusing eyes stared at Barry. Reg, dumbfounded, looked down at his dead wife's bloodied chest. He slowly raised his head, and his eyes, alight with hate, fixed on The Sheriff. Barry noticed Reg had moved Mildred's head from his thigh to the floor. His fists tightened and his eyes narrowed. The Sheriff also watched Reg's reaction, and waited as the old man struggled to raise his arthritis-riddled body. Mildred's killer pushed the barrel of the Kalashnikov against Reg's forehead and pulled the trigger. Reg fell forward across Mildred's chest.

The Sheriff turned on his terrified audience. Those closest backed away a few paces. "I know what you are thinking: that I am a generous man. First I help the wife when she is in pain, and now she no longer suffers. The husband is angry at me; this is understandable, but mostly he is an old man and the loss of his wife leaves a big hole in his heart." The Sheriff tapped at his own chest to emphasise his point. "Now they are together. Allah will be good to them."

Barry made to step forward. Bethany's hold on his arm remained steadfast. He looked over his shoulder. She shook her head. Barry stayed still, held his tongue. Bethany was right. Now was not the time for a pointless display of heroism. The American women, Marcia and Catalina, had remained on the bed, still huddled together. So much for his assuring them there would be no beheading, no more violence. What was he thinking?

The Sheriff tossed the Kalashnikov back to the guard and strode out of the room, the door shutting behind him with a solid slam.

Barry went to the beds, pulled off two blankets and covered the bodies. Beyond the blankets a pool of blood continued to spread across the warehouse floor. Bethany, holding the cross at her neck, uttered a prayer. Other passengers stood beside her, exchanging words of comfort.

On the other side of the partition wall, a roar as a bus engine ignited into life. The time of solace cut short by noise, and the smell of fumes.

The door opened.

Weary heads swung towards the door, and frightened eyes watched the policeman who had done all the talking on the bus journey enter the room. Barry had dubbed him The Sheriff's second in command. The two guards stood to the side with their Kalashnikovs at the ready. There was a stiffness to the policeman's demeanour that made Barry straighten. The man's gait as he walked to the centre of the room was that of a reluctant messenger bearing bad news for the king.

"Time to leave," the policeman said quietly.

CHAPTER THIRTEEN

You promised me Bradley would be dead. Why does he still walk about? I have had reports. You had all your men with you at the fish markets and could not kill this lone man."

"He had help. He is smart."

"Well, Marius, now you know he is smart. And smarter than you, it seems. What do you plan to do about it? You have been paid a great deal of money to get rid of this man, and you have failed to deliver. Not only that, you have embarrassed me. I give you this opportunity because you say you are ready. But look what you have done. You have made me question my judgement. And if I question my judgement, others might too. They will say my brain is not as sharp as it could be. That I have become weak."

Marius bit at his lip.

"Should I find someone else? Is this task too big for you?"

"No, of course not," Marius said. "The New Zealander got lucky. It happens. The police arrived and saved him. But he will not be lucky all the time. Besides, he has gone for now. Maybe he won't come back. No more snooping. You have nothing to worry about."

Pietro Gallo slowly shook his head.

Marius was watchful of the old man. He needed to be cautious. This ancient, cadaverous human being, with sunken, blood-red eyes and tufts of grey hair clinging to a leathery scalp, held power over one of the largest crime families in the southern Italian region. The heel of the boot on the map of Italy belonged to the Gallo family. A snap of his skeletal finger and thumb and Marius knew he would be tossed into the trunk of a vehicle and driven into the hills and shot, his body left for wild dogs to eat.

The crime boss had built an army of two thousand men, mostly family members and extended family. Their empire spread from the region of Foggia down to Lecce and included the ports of Bari and Brindisi. Smuggling, drugs, weapons, extortion, prostitution, murder, money laundering operated with impunity. Nobody dared cross the Gallo family. Officials and police were well paid to look the other way. When Marius had been invited into the organisation, it was always understood he could run his own team, and he was given a certain amount of leeway, but as an outsider he would never rise in the ranks. The organisation belonged to the cadaver and his family.

Marius hadn't cared. He made money, and lots of it.

The smuggling operation he ran with Osman Gashi was lucrative even after paying a tribute to Gallo. He had made his reputation and made everyone money, and other family members gave him the respect he was due. But now and then, like at this moment, the boss had to let him know his place. In the tone and delivery of the message the underlying threat was clear, and Marius was not foolish enough to ignore it. If he wished, he could reach across the table and strangle the worthless piece of shit with one hand. But he could never outrun the rest of the family. They had tentacles all across Europe, east and west.

The old man hunched over the table, leaning on elbows for support. His head lifted. Red eyes fixed on Marius.

"I have been paid a great deal of money to have this Bradley man killed. You tell me you are capable of taking care of this matter for me. I pass the contract on to you. The job was not to scare him off, not to give him a ticket so he can return to his country and visit his mother. I wanted him dead. Which part of our agreement did you not understand?"

"Okay, okay, I've got it," Marius said.

"Really, Marius? Have you got it? I have taken my client's money, and your answer to me is that he will not bother me anymore. He never bothered me before." The cadaver dribbled spit out the side of his mouth. "You have made me and my family look very bad. It is our reputation that keeps us in business. If our clients believe we cannot carry out our contracts, they will not give us any money. And if our enemies think we have become pussies, what do you think will happen? Tell me that." The old man spat out these words, then pushed himself up from his seat. His face reddened and he emitted a gurgling sound caused by the exertion of the movement. "Should I look elsewhere?" the old man whispered. Marius grew cold inside.

"I will take care of it," Marius said. "I get it. No need to look elsewhere. One of my men followed Bradley from the police station. He went back to his hotel, collected his belongings and went straight to the airport. He caught a plane to Istanbul, via Rome."

The cadaver raised his eyebrows. "We have a depot in Istanbul. Could he know about it?"

Marius shook his head. "No. It is not possible." But a shadow of uncertainty from Marius brought a frown from his boss. A quick rack of his brain led Marius to dismiss Bradley's ability to know anything of his Eurasian/Balkan smuggling operation. "And besides, why would he even be interested? He was only here chasing after the Kosovan, Leka. And wherever the hell he is, I have no idea. Outside of that, Bradley has no interest in Bari."

The boss nodded. Satisfied, he relaxed and his relaxed manner relaxed Marius. But why had Bradley gone to Turkey? At any rate, what did it matter?

"Are you going to take care of Bradley for me?" the boss asked.

"I will send two of my best men, today."

"Make sure you do. But I want you to go with them. Make sure the job gets done. Whatever it is Bradley is up to in Turkey, I am certain once he has finished he will return to Bari and continue looking into matters of no concern to him. This would upset my client, and I do not want this to happen. I don't want him leaving Turkey."

Marius nodded. "I have a consignment coming through in the next day or so. Should I wait until after that?"

"You have men who can handle receiving the goods. Bradley is your priority, make it so."

Marius said, "My informant within the police station has said Bradley met with a member of the Carabinieri, Captain Balboni – the cop who heads up the anti-organised crime squad. He and Bradley had a friendly chat. Like comrades, I am told, and not like a policeman talking to a prisoner. I think Bradley has made a powerful ally within the Carabinieri."

"Another reason it is better he is taken care of in Turkey," Gallo emphasised. "I want this done quickly. The wedding of my granddaughter is about to take place. You are to be my guest. This is a great honour for you, Marius. The family has shown you great respect with this invitation. In return, please respect me and my family. Do not leave this matter hanging."

"Don't worry," Marius said. "Bradley will never leave Turkey alive."

CHAPTER FOURTEEN

Jeff had showered and was drying off. The hotel room phone rang. "Mr Bradley, it's Reason Johanson. I have news. Meet me at the café we met at yesterday."

"I'll be there in fifteen minutes."

Sulla Bogdani arrived in Istanbul. He parked his car in a secure lock-up and climbed into his friend's taxi. When Serbia invaded Kosovo, many Kosovans fled. The exodus of refugees flooded the neighbouring countries and after the war many returned to Kosovo, but there were those, like his friend, who started new lives in new countries. Sulla had re-established connections with many old acquaintances from his school days and with friends from his village now living in the various countries of the Balkans; a network of contacts for his business enterprises. He was thankful many of his friends drove cabs.

He didn't know his way around Istanbul, and it might be he needed to get somewhere in a hurry. His friend Zef was best suited to the task. Zef and he had lived on the same street in Kosovo and walked to school together. Sulla had witnessed Zef's parents being dragged from their house and shot, and the torching of their home. His friend would never return to Kosovo.

Jeff had sent a text to Sulla with his contact details should he need to get in touch. Zef knew the hotel, and as they arrived they saw Jeff getting into a yellow taxi and driving off. Sulla decided to follow and not to bother trying to flag him down. Now was not the time to get into an argument about why he had come to Istanbul; they could fight it out later.

He hated having deceived Jeff, but after returning to Kosovo he made the decision it was important he keep an eye on his friend. In Turkey, as it was with other countries of the region and as it was in Kosovo, many bad men lived in the shadows, and Jeff was vulnerable if he was alone. This was foreign territory to the man from New Zealand, and to find his way amongst the locals he needed to understand the mentality of the locals. This could not be learned in a few hours. The staff at the vineyard were capable and could look after business matters well enough without Sulla's input. The drive through Macedonia, Bulgaria and into Turkey had taken most of the night. Once across the Turkish border, he had pulled over and grabbed a few hours' sleep before continuing on to Istanbul.

Jeff's taxi stopped near Istiklal Avenue, and he continued on foot. Cars were not allowed on to the avenue. A small van blocked Zef. Sulla tapped his friend on the shoulder and jumped out of the idling vehicle and chased after the New Zealander. Jeff was walking at a fast pace and when he disappeared around a corner Sulla had to run to keep him in sight. By the time he made the bend, Jeff had crossed Istiklal and was walking up a side street. Sulla crossed to the opposite side of the street. When he saw Jeff enter a café he slowed until he was facing the window of the café. He was tossing up if he should approach Jeff now and explain why he was in Istanbul when he saw his friend sit at a table with a woman. He made the decision to keep his distance. If Jeff was romancing, who was he to interfere? He would wait until the liaison had finished. His attention drifted to a small gallery. It sold paintings and ceramics. Through the window Sulla eyed a large vase that looked the right size for the small table in his new apartment. The colours were the same as the leaves in autumn, his favourite season. At least it would blend in with his brown carpet. He entered to have a closer look. From inside the gallery he could easily keep watch on the café.

Then he saw Marius.

∽

Jeff entered the café, and the limping waiter with the scarred face followed him to the table. The big tip left on the last visit had worked wonders. Instead of a cock-eyed, glassy glare and belligerent manner, the waiter was now all smiles and over-the-top attentiveness. Reason Johanson, grim-faced, tilted her head towards the empty chair. Jeff ordered a coffee and sat.

Waking early, he had decided his body needed a workout. Over the years, he had developed an exercise regimen suited to the confined space of a hotel room. It was partly learned through PT training in the military and a few adopted moves from various gyms he had joined. He couldn't afford to lose his edge. In New Zealand, he ran a few kilometres most days and swam a few kilometres every other day. Twice a week, he went to the gym for boxing practice. The boxing he enjoyed. It was a good defence skill to have, and the training used almost every muscle in his body. Each session exhausted him, and his trainer Manny made sure of it. Manny said he could have made it as a boxer, but Jeff had never been in the ring, and never intended to. He was only interested in the fitness. "You could never go fifteen rounds moving like that," Manny would yell when he began to tire from smashing his fists into the punching bag, and he would increase the tempo.

Reason was wearing another charcoal trouser suit. This time, under the jacket, she had worn a plain white T-shirt. Her lips looked redder, a hint of lipstick.

"What do you have to tell me?" Jeff asked.

"The bus has been found, and it's on the move. The bus GPS flicked on again about an hour ago. Signals from a few of the phones have also been tracked. Wherever the bus has been for the last day, either the bus GPS and phones have been turned off or the signals have been jammed."

Jeff said, "My vote goes with the jammer. My reasoning: why turn them off and turn them on? It makes no sense." It suddenly occurred to him: if the phones were now active, why hadn't Barry sent him a text? Or had he? Jeff opened his phone. "I'll check if there is a message from Barry." There were no numbers on the Text icon. "Nothing." He closed his phone and put it into his jacket pocket. "Where is the bus now?"

"It's approximately fifty kilometres the other side of Istanbul."

"I need to get ahead of it. Where can I hire a chopper?" Jeff asked. He made to stand.

Reason held up her hand. "Hold your horses, cowboy, there's more." Jeff eased back into his seat.

Reason took a photo from her jacket pocket and slid it across the table.

"This man is known as 'The Sheriff'. I told you a man had been broken out of prison and it might be him and his rescuers who hijacked the bus. It turns out I was right. And the description your friend gave of the hijackers – four policemen and a civilian – confirms it. The Sheriff is a dangerous man. He is a key military leader in the PKK movement. You have heard of the PKK?"

Jeff nodded. "A Kurdistan rebel group wanting to establish a Kurdish homeland."

"You've got it in one. This man is said to have used landmines against Turkish military transport convoys, set off bombs in the border towns, and within the last year ambushed and killed a squad of Turkish soldiers near the Syrian border. More recently, two bombs in Istanbul shopping malls and a marketplace in Ankara have been tagged to his name. The police said they hadn't confirmed the malls and market in Ankara are The Sheriff's work, but until they know one way or the other, he wears it."

Jeff picked up the photo and studied it.

Reason continued, "Turkish border guards captured him trying to cross into Turkey from Bulgaria. The Turks claim he was in Europe raising funds. Whether that's true or not, I can't say. He had no money when they arrested him. I'm assured by the police they want him bad, and they will do everything they can to get him back. They are worried if he makes it to the Kurdistan strongholds he will disappear again and start another round of violence. My intelligence reports on the Kurds are not that up to date. Views on The Sheriff vary; the more conservative Kurds say he is not so much a respected leader as he is a feared gangster. The young guns and the extremists worship him like a god, and believe he is the man who will deliver them their promised land."

"Could he do that?"

Reason shrugged. "Anything is possible, but I very much doubt it. Kurdistan has no real borders and is spread across Turkey, Iran, Iraq, Syria, and maybe some of Armenia. I don't know the boundaries for certain; I don't think anyone does. Anyway, to achieve a homeland, it would need all these countries to cede them territory, and in my opinion that isn't going to happen."

"So we could have a few civil wars start up," Jeff said.

"That is the likely outcome, but there have been moves made to placate the Kurds that seem to be working. Turkey has offered to discuss an autonomous province, and Iraq has already established autonomous Kurdish territory. So far this seems to be working, and many Kurds are happy with the outcome. But the PKK want it all, and are happy to carry on fighting until they get it."

"I've met rebels in other countries. Some have fought all their lives. Starting out as boy soldiers. They keep fighting even when they don't need to keep fighting because they only know how to be fighters. Eventually, if they aren't killed they age and tire of conflict. There must be members of the PKK who fit into that category, who would like to go sit in a café and have a cold beer or cognac and not get shot at?"

There was the hint of a smile from Reason.

"You may be right. There have been fractures within the group. The Turks have dropped a few bombs on Kurdish villages. Attitudes are changing. And recently the PKK were labelled terrorists and Turkey has been given a green light from America and NATO to go stomp on them wherever they may be. Turkey still needs to take care. Any overreaction leading to a whole bunch of innocent Kurds being killed could see a hardening of Western attitudes. But overall this has influenced many Kurds to look for a peaceful solution."

Jeff nodded.

"And the thinking is that The Sheriff might tip the scales against the conservative Kurds and lead them into starting a new civil war?" Jeff said.

"What can I say? The Sheriff is a long-time fighter, with a fearless reputation."

"And now he's on a bus and going home. I have to ask, why is he called The Sheriff?"

Red lips widened as Reason smiled. Nice. Jeff liked the sparkle in her eyes that accompanied it.

"He's called The Sheriff because he likes watching westerns – you know, movies about cowboys. Wyatt Earp is his favourite character."

Jeff grinned and slowly shook his head.

Reason continued, "Amongst his own people his reputation has grown. There is money; lots of it. Dollars splashed in his name across the regions of Kurdistan like confetti. Cash given to schools, hospitals, food for the poor. My sources monitoring Kurdistan tell me the word is that The Sheriff has organised the cash, but no one has any idea where he got it from."

Jeff was thoughtful. "Robbing banks?"

"Who knows? The distribution of cash has been followed up by a pretty snappy media campaign. This guy has become an iconic figure within the Kurdish community, the equivalent of a saint. Even the neutrals believe he might be the man that can lead them to the promised land."

Jeff sipped his coffee as he mulled over the information. The more he heard, the more he worried. Nothing Reason had told him alleviated his concerns for Barry and Bethany. In fact, it was having the opposite effect.

"Okay," Jeff said. "This guy is placed on a pedestal, but even so, how much influence can he hope to achieve in the end? Surely amongst all Kurds there is the reality of the Turkish military and their armaments? Kalashnikovs can't shoot down fighter jets."

Reason nodded. "There is a legend that has floated about Turkey for many decades that a new caliph will emerge out of the remnants of the old Ottoman Empire. This is the banner someone is waving, and it has carried some weight because The Sheriff was in fact born in Turkey, and therefore it is right to think he might be this new Islamic leader."

Jeff laughed. "You've got to be joking. Every new looney Islamic leader calls himself a caliph. ISIS leaders have. They're becoming a dime a dozen."

"Many Kurds are uneducated village people. Superstitions and legends are part of their daily life. Throw in a few million disaffected and disillusioned young men who are ready to follow anyone. Like a rock and roll band, The Sheriff knows how to play the right music. The Kurds want a homeland. The Sheriff is promising to give it to them. And remember, Turkish politics are not all that stable. In fact, few of the countries surrounding the proposed Kurdistan state are stable. None of them needs The Sheriff throwing petrol on the sparks of discontent and turning it into a goddamn forest fire."

Jeff's eyes widened.

Reason raised her hands. "Okay, a little over the top, but I think you get the point."

"And Iraq?" Jeff asked.

"Northern Iraq is a little different. The Kurds are well established. They have a capital and a growing administrative infrastructure. Their own police and military, and the economy is growing. Northern Iraq is the exception. But it is all so fragile. Stability in the Middle East in general cannot be taken for granted. If Iraq ever gets its act together, it might decide it doesn't want the Kurds owning a big chunk of its country anymore."

Jeff was thoughtful. The history lesson was helpful and informative. But something was not right. His suspicions put him on to alert mode.

"You know a lot about The Sheriff, Reason. The detail and observations you've just made needed digging up. I've worked intel in the SAS. It takes time. I don't think the Turkish police sat round a table with you over the last few hours and filled you in on the history of Kurdistan, the PKK and The Sheriff. What's going on here? How come you know so much, and why?"

"Let's just say I have been following The Sheriff and his activities for some months. I am in Turkey because my investigations involving The Sheriff brought me to Istanbul. I was to interview him in a few days, but he escaped."

Jeff, both elbows on the table, put his hands together, his fingers forming a steeple. He rested his chin on the steeple top.

"What is your interest in him?"

"That I cannot tell you."

"Then why tell me any of this at all?"

"I promised I would keep you informed."

"No, there is something else. I'm nobody. You don't owe me anything."

Reason grinned. "Lee Caldwell said that to protect your friends you would bulldoze a mountain. I need you to back off."

"Why?"

"There are two American women on the bus. You know this already."

Jeff nodded.

"The US has an embassy in Ankara, and a consul in Istanbul, Stan Greenberg. One of the women is his daughter, and the other her friend visiting from the States. Nice kids. And Stan's a great guy. Hell, I've had dinner with them."

Jeff pointed his finger steeple at Reason.

"The hijackers have been in communication, haven't they?"

Reason nodded.

❦

Sulla's heart missed a beat when he saw Marius talking with two men. He knew the face, but from Bari not Istanbul, and it had confused him at first. But when it clicked where he knew him from, warning bells rang in his head. Why was Marius in Turkey? To finish the job he'd failed to complete at the fish markets was the obvious answer. If Marius looked through the store window he might recognise him. Sulla turned his back and continued to watch the Italian in the mirror on the back wall. Marius pointed at something further along the street. The two men left him and walked on. Marius waited a few minutes then followed without giving the gallery a second glance.

Sulla rushed to the door.

One of the two men had positioned himself behind a car, his arm stretched out across the vehicle's roof, a gun aimed at the café Jeff had entered. The second man had crossed the street and now made his way to the café door. Gun in hand, but hidden inside his jacket. Further along, Marius stood in a doorway, watching. He had hired himself some local hoods, and Sulla assessed the assassins weren't professionals. If they were professionals, both men would have entered the café and blasted Jeff to hell. These men didn't have those kind of balls. One was about to enter the café and shoot at Jeff, the other would give covering fire from behind the car. And from the distance Marius was keeping, it appeared he didn't have much faith in his gunmen either. Whatever the outcome, he was making sure he didn't get caught up in it.

Sulla reached into his jacket. He cursed. No gun. He had had to discard it before he crossed the Turkish border.

ࡇ

"The hijackers have been very talkative," Reason said. "The bus is heading for the Kurdistan, Turkish, Iraqi or Syrian border. Nothing definitive as yet, but I guess their intention is to keep the final destination secret until the last moment. But I'd say the plan is to join up with PKK rebels. They have asked for a clear passage. They have even given the route they will take to enable the Turkish authorities to keep the roads clear. They are taking their time. They will make three overnight stops. Today they are driving to Ankara and then tomorrow to Goreme in the Cappadocia region. And then to Mardin. From Mardin, it is only a few kilometres to a border. Iraq or Syria."

"And?" Jeff asked.

"They intend to spend the night at each destination. They want food and liquid provided to feed the hostages, and mobile toilets."

"And?"

"There are explosives planted in the baggage compartments in the front and the rear of the bus. They say any attempt to rescue the passengers and it will be blown. The Sheriff has said he is prepared to martyr himself for the cause. A new leader is waiting in the wings, but he will only be named to the world on The Sheriff's death. The new leader would have The Sheriff's blessing and should be treated as if he were The Sheriff. This statement has been circulated to the media."

Jeff said, "The Sheriff does have a good public relations team. But why all the publicity? Why make so much noise? Why take so much time to get to the border? None of it makes sense. And why go to all this trouble and then blow yourself up?"

Jeff rubbed his forehead. He was missing something. He glanced up. Reason's eyes were fixed on him. They shifted a touch. He saw the movement. She was hiding something.

Jeff straightened and said, "Why don't we cut the crap and you tell me what you're trying to avoid telling me?"

Reason glanced sideways. No one was close. She leaned forward.

"The Turkish government does not want any more conflict in the region. They do not want any more of their police and soldiers killed. It is their belief if The Sheriff is not stopped, many more people will die. They are not only concerned for the safety of their people, but the fragile economy, especially tourism, would be greatly affected. Jeff, there are those in the Turkish government who will never allow that bus to leave Turkey."

CHAPTER FIFTEEN

The waiter placed two bottles of water on the table. "Anything else?"
"Not right now," Jeff said.

The waiter produced a cloth to wipe the table. Jeff caught his eye. "Find somewhere else to clean, will you? My friend and I would like some privacy."

The waiter raised his chin, thrust his cloth into his pocket and limped away like a petulant child. Jeff turned his attention back to Reason.

"Are you serious? Turkey is closing its border," Jeff said. His raised voice caused heads to turn at nearby tables. He softened his tone. "What if these idiots are serious and The Sheriff really does believe there are seventy virgins waiting for him in heaven?"

Reason shrugged. "When crunch time comes, I don't know for certain what they will do."

Jeff nodded, grim-faced.

"I think that pretty much sums up the state of play," Reason said in a soothing tone.

Jeff sat back in his seat. His facial muscles tightened. His jaw set and eyes narrowed.

"I guess I have to find some way of getting the hostages off that bus myself if I'm to save Barry and Bethany."

Reason raised an eyebrow. "After what Lee Caldwell told me about you, I expected this response. Jeff, I don't want this bus blown up any more than you do, but I think right now the best way to stop that from happening is to back off."

"And if I don't?"

Reason shrugged.

Jeff was about to ask her what that shrug meant. The limping waiter approached the table, cleaning cloth at the ready. Jeff now regretted leaving him a generous tip on the last visit. He had enough on his mind and didn't need the intrusion. The waiter was pissing him off. Jeff scowled in the waiter's direction and drummed his fingers on the table. The waiter ignored Jeff's attempt at intimidation. Finally, Jeff held his hands up and surrendered. He didn't see any point in wringing the man's neck; better to let him get on with it. A white cotton shirtsleeve reached across for Jeff's cup. The waiter's head turned to Jeff. A grin. Jeff saw it as a victory smile and it irked him. Annoyed, Jeff drew in a deep breath. He was certain he heard Reason laugh. He almost laughed himself. Bullied by a waiter. What next?

He opened his mouth to say something. Out the corner of his eye, he saw the café door smash against the wall as it was flung open. A figure filled the doorway.

The waiter's head exploded.

Blood and brain splattered across the front of Jeff's shirt. The waiter's body slumped on to the table. It upended. Cups, water bottles and a small bowl holding sugar sachets were flung into the air.

"Get down!" Jeff yelled.

He dived to the floor. More bullets slammed into the wall and ceiling. Powdered plaster trickled down like a dusting of new snow. Reason had thrown herself sideways.

Shots exploded close to Jeff's ear.

His head spun left. Reason Johanson was shooting back. The street-front window shattered as bullets smashed into the giant pane. Glass flew through the air like diamonds fired from a shotgun.

Jeff looked through the now-glassless window frame. He was flat to the floor and it was impossible to see into the street; a metre-high wall beneath the window framing blocked his view. More bullets buzzed over his head and thudded into the wall behind. The man he had seen in the doorway had disappeared. Had he gone across the street? He didn't think so. More likely he had a partner.

"There are at least two," he yelled to Reason.

"No kidding," she called back.

Other customers screamed. There was the sound of scraping chairs and smashing cups as they scrambled for safety. An elderly couple lay under their table. The man cast a glance in Jeff's direction. Jeff gestured with his hand like he was patting a child on the head. "Stay down," Jeff mouthed at the same time. The old man nodded.

Reason had nothing to shoot at. Her visual would be as bad as his. The shots were to let whoever was outside know that she was armed; clever girl. Without the return fire from Reason, right now the gunman or gunmen would have stormed the café to finish the job. An armed defender would force them to hold off and re-plan. Not for long. Jeff figured they had a few minutes. How long before the police arrived? Not soon enough, was Jeff's best guess. Istanbul traffic was hopeless at the best of times. The police response would be too late.

Jeff crawled across to Reason.

"Have you another one of those?"

She shook her head. "Who have you pissed off, Jeff?"

"Why do you think they're shooting at me? Why couldn't they be shooting at you?"

"Call it a gut feeling. Lee Caldwell said someone is always trying to blast your ass off. He warned me not to sit too close."

Two shots slammed into the upturned table. Splintered wood ricocheted off the top of Jeff's head. He brushed his hand over his hair, and as a belated thought, checked his fingers for blood. There was none. The shooters were firing blind and couldn't see their targets any more than he and Reason could see them. Good. He scanned his surroundings. A man behind him held a string of brownish beads in his fingers, praying. A few others scuttled across the floor like crabs and into the kitchen. Did it lead to an alley?

He leaned against Reason's ear.

"I'm going into the kitchen. I think it might have a rear entrance. If it has, I'll try to get behind them."

Reason turned on him, alarmed. "Don't be foolish. You're not armed."

"I'll find something to use as a weapon. Keep them busy."

Jeff didn't wait for Reason to respond. Like the others, he crawled across the floor until he had passed beyond the swing doors.

The kitchen was empty. No cooks and no café patrons. He saw the open rear door. He hesitated. Should he alert Reason? They could both escape. He dismissed it. Whoever was shooting might have the rear covered. At least where she was, and armed, was more secure than what might lie in wait for him beyond the door.

Jeff made his way between the gas cookers to his left and the stainless steel benches and serving shelves to his right. Plates of food sat on the serveries. The gas cookers had been turned off, but a giant skewered lamb doner kebab continued to rotate on its spit; freshly hacked chunks of meat lay in a heaped pile on a stainless steel tray beneath. The aroma of spices filled the space and reminded Jeff he was hungry. He stuffed a piece of meat into his mouth. An array of varying-sized pots hung from hooks next to ladles, large serving spoons and forks. None caught Jeff's eye as a potential weapon. He saw what he had been looking for on the furthest bench: a chef's knife. If the chef was true to his craft, it would be honed sharp enough to cut through bone. As Jeff dashed past he picked it up. It had good weight and balance. The blade was not as long as he would have liked, but it was long enough to kill, and that was all he needed.

The door exited into a narrow lane. Directly opposite was a line of tables and chairs with people sat drinking coffee in the shade. The coffee drinkers, alerted and alarmed by the fleeing customers and staff from the café, were watching the door. Confused expressions turned to looks of horror when Jeff made his exit with the knife in his right hand. They remained seated, uncertain, immobile with fear and incredulity, watching on, like an audience in a theatre. Jeff had seen it before in Afghanistan, when the fruit markets had been bombed. In the first instance, passers-by denied to themselves the horror they were witnessing had taken place.

A small crowd had gathered at the end of the lane. None of the spectators had dared to step out into the main street. Instead, some were leaning forward to peer round the corner. Jeff sidestepped a motor scooter and nudged his way through the onlookers. A man standing in front of a trestle table, stacked high with shirts and trousers, saw the knife in Jeff's hand and stepped back. He yelled something in Turkish, and others turned then backed away. Whatever the man had yelled was good enough for Jeff. No one tried to stop him. He moved past the stall to the corner. Fabric rolls leaning against the wall provided enough of a hide for him to see through a gap into the main street without being seen.

There were two shooters. One hidden behind a silver Toyota sedan. The other was beside a sloping wooden board displaying beads and other trinkets. He was crouched down just a few metres from the café door. Reason would be caught in a crossfire. The shooter behind the car kept her pinned down. Once the second man got close enough he would be through the doorway and have emptied his magazine into her before she ever saw the danger.

The crouching gunman inched forward. The man behind the car was setting himself. At any moment, he would let loose a fusillade of covering fire for his friend. Jeff pulled out his mobile and tapped on the contact number for Reason. She answered.

"It's Jeff Bradley. Are you okay?"

"Never better."

"I'm in place. When I say shoot, stick your head up and target the car opposite."

"Okay," Reason's soft voice, almost a whisper, replied.

"Three, two, now . . ."

Jeff dropped his phone into his pocket. Reason opened fire, and he ran from his cover. The sound of gunfire muffled his footsteps, but the man he was stalking must have sensed someone behind him. A hesitant look over his shoulder. His eyes widened with fear when he saw Jeff. He tried to swing his gun arm around, but it was too late. Jeff was upon him. His lips parted, and he screamed as Jeff drove his knife into the assassin's throat. Before the dying man hit the pavement, Jeff seized the weapon from his hand, and in one motion, dived to the ground swinging the handgun towards the car as he did so.

The top of the shooter's head could not be seen. This told him Reason's shooting had forced the assailant to keep down. It would not be for long and Jeff was out in the open. Too easy a target. He crawled into the doorway of the carpet shop next to the trinket board. Two rolls of thick carpet leaned against the wall. An invoice pinned to one; ready for delivery. My lucky day, Jeff mused. Both rolls were almost a half-metre thick. No bullet would penetrate that many tightly wound fibres. He turned the confiscated weapon towards the car shielding the second man and fired. The bullet slammed into the mudguard. He wanted to direct the shooter's attention away from the café. It worked. Jeff could see Reason had crawled forward and was lying across the doorway, her gun hand outstretched. Her poise impressed him.

A plan developed.

Jeff shouted and waved to get Reason's attention. She looked his way. He pointed at her, then to his eyes with two fingers before stabbing the fingers towards the car. He aimed his handgun in the car's direction. Then he pointed at himself, upturned his hand and moved his two fingers to show walking.

Reason gave him a thumbs-up; she understood he wanted covering fire.

Jeff checked the stolen weapon. He recognised it as a Sig-Sauer P250. He had fired one on the range. It looked old and a little worse for wear. He would guess it had been bought on the black market. His concern was how reliable it was. He had fired a shot, but now he needed for it to fire many shots for what he was about to do. The man he had killed had fired shots into the café. It hadn't jammed. He removed the magazine, had a quick look: 9mm rounds. With his thumb he pushed on the top bullet. It depressed easily enough. Half full, at a guess. The Sig magazine held fifteen rounds. Half a magazine and one in the spout gave him about eight rounds. He would need to make them count. Like a Glock, the Sig had no safety; instead, it had a cocking mechanism. If it wasn't cocked, it could be thrown on the ground and would not accidentally discharge. Easy to use: just aim and pull the trigger. Jeff dropped his gun hand to his side. He crouched like an athlete ready to run a hundred-metre race.

He still could not see the head of the shooter. His companion dead, he was probably taking stock. The odds were no longer in his favour. Jeff waved at Reason. She began firing at the car. Jeff sprinted towards it. He was reluctant to move too far to the right. If the gunman was still there Jeff would make an easy target. He dived across the bonnet, his weapon aimed at where the man should be, and as he slid off the vehicle on to the pavement he squeezed on the trigger, then released.

The gunman had gone.

Sulla had a clear view of the café. With the front window glass missing he could see inside, but could not see Jeff or the woman. He was not going to accept that an asshole like Marius had got the better of Jeff. Jeff and the woman must be lying on the floor. The sound of shots fired from within the café surprised him. Had Jeff found a weapon from somewhere?

Sulla stepped back into the gallery. Rushing the gunmen without a weapon would be suicidal. Dead, he would be of no use to Jeff; and armed, Jeff could more than hold his own against Marius's hoods. He shuffled about, weighing his options. As long as Jeff was shooting, he was alive. To help him, he must remain patient and be ready when the opportunity presented itself. The gunman who had fired from the doorway had been forced to take cover from the shots fired from inside. Sulla watched as the killer positioned himself and waved to his companion. Seeking guidance, no doubt. Marius kept his distance. He was not going to get involved. The gunman behind the car gave a thumbs-up. Anytime soon, he would lay down covering fire and the second man would rush to the doorway and shoot into the café.

Sulla knew he had to stop the gunman.

He prepared himself to race across the street. He stopped midstride. Jeff emerged from a lane to his left. When Jeff stabbed his would-be killer in the throat, Sulla nodded approval. His friend never stopped amazing him. He saw Jeff pick up the fallen pistol and check the mechanism. Drop out the magazine, then reload. Sulla turned his attention back to the man behind the car. More shots came through the windowless opening. Sulla's eyebrows raised, his eyes flicked back and forth. If Jeff was outside, who was shooting from the café? Now, with two shooters against him and one of his men down, Marius decided he'd had enough. He waved to his man behind the car and they ran off. Jeff was safe.

Sulla chased after the Italian.

CHAPTER SIXTEEN

Reason advised Jeff to get clear of the café and to keep his distance. "Now's not the time to be caught up in a police investigation." He had killed a man, and the police might not care to ask whether it was self-defence. They might lock him away, and some time in the future get round to asking him questions.

"This is Eastern Europe," Reason said. "If you're thrown in a cell, you don't get let out."

"I don't need telling; I've had first-hand experience. How about you? Will you be okay?"

"I have diplomatic immunity."

Jeff offered no arguments, and with the crowd increasing in number, he shoved his way into the melee. The sound of sirens increased in magnitude as the police cars neared. Over shoulders and between heads, he glimpsed flashing lights atop vehicle roofs as the blue-and-white patrol cars rolled past and into the crime scene. The blue-and-whites blockaded the street thirty metres either side of the café. Sirens became silent.

Uniformed policemen, pistols drawn, stood beside their vehicles, not daring to move about the crime scene until ordered to do so. Other police officers pushed spectators back behind a quickly erected barrier of yellow tape tied to posts and stretched across the street.

Jeff's gaze fixed on two men in the crowd. They were brothers, by the look of them; both had the same rounded body shapes, a surly manner and round heads on fat necks. Local tough guys, Jeff assessed. One of the brothers was sent reeling backwards from a shove in the chest by a cop. He almost lost his footing. Crashing into his brother was all that stopped him tumbling to the ground. Two sets of brownish-black eyes fixed on the cop. One of the brothers' lips curled into a snarl. He swung a fist that brushed the cop's cheek. The cop's comrades, truncheons in hand, came to his rescue and the brothers were buried under uniforms. The beating left both men bleeding in the gutter, writhing in agony. There was no arrest. The beating was enough. The onlookers cheered. The humiliated brothers struggled to their feet and disappeared into the crowd. It was all over in seconds.

For Jeff, the lesson was clear enough. Don't screw with Turkish cops.

℞

Reason Johanson, her gun back in its holster, had waited inside the café for the police to arrive, and she now stepped through the doorway into the open. She used the time to ensure Jeff had not left anything behind that might identify him. Café patrons and staff who hadn't already exited through the rear did so as soon as the shooting stopped. Reason shooed them along. It would be best if anyone who had seen her talking with Jeff was not around. Given the reputation of the police department, onlookers were unlikely to want to speak with the lawmen and would be long gone.

Reason showed her credentials to a police officer; he gestured her to wait and went in search of his commander. Reason scanned the crowd for Jeff. She didn't see him. He got an approval tick for staying out of sight. He had shown himself to be capable and dangerous. Lee Caldwell had been right: Bradley was a man you could rely on in a tight spot. He had courage.

Like the other police officers, the senior officer wore a navy-blue uniform. There were silver stars on his lapel, but Reason had no idea what rank they represented. He was in his late thirties, possibly early forties. He did not immediately come across as a man who wore his authority in a benevolent manner. Bloodshot eyes, probably from a night of drinking raki, added to an air of slovenly malevolence. He studied her passport photo, then ran his eyes over her body, staring deliberately at her crotch and breasts. He closed the travel document and passed it back.

"I am Captain Orbay. What happened here?" he asked, his tone casual but firm.

"No idea. I was drinking a coffee at a table near the far wall," Reason said, and pointed in that direction. "And the shooting started."

"Show me."

The officer followed her inside, and they stopped in front of the upturned table.

"Shots were fired through the window," Reason said. "I dived to the floor and drew my gun. I have a licence for it. My shooting back must have put them off. They hightailed it. Probably didn't expect someone in the café to be armed. The waiter was the only one killed. I assume he is the one they were after. No one else was shot, and the bullets were only fired in his direction."

The policeman looked at the body. "It wasn't you they wanted to kill and the waiter got in the way?"

"No. I'm not aware of anyone I've upset that much."

The officer scratched at his head.

"And may I ask what you were doing in the café?"

"Having a coffee."

"I mean why here? Why in this part of town?"

"Oh that's easy, I came for the markets. I enjoy the markets. Decided I needed a coffee, wandered about and found this café."

"Our markets held little of interest for you?"

Reason's brow wrinkled. Confused by the question, she looked down at her shoe as it tapped the ground. Then she understood and her head lifted.

"Oh I see. No shopping bags. The choices are many and so confusing, Captain. I was going to continue browsing after my coffee."

The Captain nodded. He bent and picked up an unopened bottle of water from the floor. Reason waited while he unscrewed the cap and gulped the contents. He dropped the cap and the bottle back on to the floor. This surprised Reason. Avoiding the contamination of a crime scene did not appear high priority in Turkey.

"Were you alone drinking your coffee?" he asked.

"I never drink alone if I can help it. An expat came in and asked if I wanted some company. I said, 'Why not?' He was an Englishman, I think."

There was no point in lying about having company. Plenty of customers saw her and Jeff together.

"There is a body outside. On the pavement. Stabbed in the throat. I don't suppose you know anything about that, do you?"

Reason shook her head.

"No, I'm sorry. I was trapped inside here until the shooting was over. Was he one of the gunmen or a bystander?"

"Witnesses have already identified him as a gunman. They also said a man came from the back alley – the one the rear door of the café opens on to – and stabbed the man. Then he came back into the café and after a few minutes ran off. Did you see this man?"

Reason stared to the sky, thoughtful.

"It was chaotic. Maybe he did come into the café; I didn't notice. I was helping people up off the floor and to safety."

"The man you were drinking coffee with – he has gone?"

Reason nodded.

"I suppose you do not know his name or where he is staying?"

Reason shook her head. "No, I'm sorry. I was sitting at my table. The man came in and asked if I was alone and would I like some company. I said yes. He had only that minute sat when the shooting started. I never saw him again. I assume he escaped out through the kitchen like the others. Sorry."

"And why did you not escape out the back like the others?" he asked. Probing, not accusatory. "If it was not your fight, why fight?"

"Habit, I guess. I have security duties with the embassy. I've been trained to respond to aggressive action. Once I'd started, it seemed reasonable to ensure the people still trapped in the café were safe."

"Like a civic duty, that sort of thing?"

"Something like that."

The Captain shrugged. It seemed she might be free to go. In the States, they would have rounded up the entire neighbourhood and taken statements from everyone. But after a moment's deliberation, she understood. He knew she was attached to the US Embassy, and if he needed her he knew where to find her. Still, there were two bodies: a dead assassin and a dead waiter. She couldn't help pursuing the issue.

"You don't appear overly concerned," she said.

"Why be concerned? There has been a shooting and one of the bad guys was killed. Allah has done his work. It is unfair the waiter is killed, but if they were not after you, the waiter was the target. Hitmen sent to kill someone means the target was very important to the bad guys. Waiters are poorly paid; maybe he did things to supplement his income – drugs, contraband, who knows? – or maybe he owed some bad people money. Again, Allah has done his work. If this is not the way it was, and the waiter is an innocent, I will pray for him. I will investigate of course, but it is unlikely any real witnesses will come forward and tell me what happened, or even if it was them the gunmen were really shooting at." The Captain scratched at his unshaven face. "The patrons and staff have run off, just as your friend has done."

"He was not my friend," Reason said as she turned to leave.

"Before you go, Ms Johanson?"

"Yes?"

"I will need a statement from you." He pulled a card from his pocket. "Call me sometime over the next few days, whenever you have a free moment. If you are, as you say, a woman who does not like to drink alone, when you are ready we could have coffee."

The police captain gave a mock salute, then turned his attention back to his men.

❧

Reason walked two blocks before Jeff fell in step beside her.

"Now you can tell me what that was about back there?" she said. "I don't like being shot at."

"I was in Bari, Italy, a few days ago. Someone tried to kill me. They obviously failed, and I guess they've followed me to Istanbul. Unless someone else I don't know about hates me enough to want me dead. But I think it was the Italians. The dead guy was wearing denims and a black jacket, which is pretty much their uniform. What we do now is the big question," Jeff said.

"Firstly, Jeff, you should have warned me about someone trying to kill you."

Jeff said nothing.

"Sure, you didn't think the Italians might react as quickly as they did and turn up a couple of days later in Istanbul. But you've been marked. Of course they're going to come after you. There's probably a bag of money on your head. I have other problems to sort out. I don't need to be caught up in your shit. And just now I lied to the police on your behalf."

"Really? Can I ask why?"

"Caldwell said to look out for you. I'm doing that, as a favour. Don't put me in this position again."

"Okay, fair enough."

Reason said, "Good. Now that's cleared up, I think we lie low. Not a lot we can do. I need to think, and I want a shower." She looked at his shirt. "You could do with one yourself."

Jeff looked at the front of his shirt.

"Walking the streets covered in blood is a great way to attract police attention," Reason said. "Go to your hotel. I'll be in touch."

Jeff watched her walk away. This was some woman, and attractive to boot. Would she make contact again? He thought she would. But Reason was hiding something as well. He was certain of it. She was right about changing his shirt though. He waved a cab down.

CHAPTER SEVENTEEN

Osman Gashi listened, eyes fixed on the half-empty glass of cognac in his large, bear-like hand. The fragile tumbler threatened to shatter. Finally, he had heard enough and raised his free hand to stop Marius talking. The big man put his cognac glass aside, dragged himself out of the creaking chair and set his two paws on the desk. He leaned forward. Cold eyes settled on Marius. The Italian up to now had stood his ground, but with this monster of a man looming over him, he swayed backwards. Not enough to be forced into a backward step, but enough to convey to Gashi he had been intimidated. Marius gulped. The Kosovan Albanian had built a criminal empire across the Balkan region and reigned over it with a ruthless and merciless hand. He did not accept failure nor disloyalty; both indiscretions punishable by death.

Rumours had it he had been imprisoned in Serbia for mass murder. None of these stories had ever been verified, but Marius had few doubts the man before him was a psychopathic killer, and fully capable of the atrocities he was accused of.

"Twice you fail to kill Bradley." Gashi spat the words between clenched teeth. "I paid your boss a lot of money to have Bradley taken care of, and he gives the job to an idiot like you. Not only did you fail to do what you were paid to do, but you come here, to the warehouse. What if you had been followed? You have jeopardised our entire operation. If you worked for me, I would snap your neck and feed you to the pigs."

Gashi slammed his fist on to the tabletop.

Marius recoiled in fear, and this time he took a step back.

"I was not followed," Marius said. His voice almost a whisper, and he hated himself for his weakness. In Italy, surrounded by his men, he would have this fat asshole shot to pieces. But here, on Gashi's territory, he needed to be careful. The Kosovan was twice the size he was, and armed men were within shouting distance. Any thoughts of arguing with the big man, he dismissed. He needed to concentrate on leaving the building alive. "Bradley was hiding on the floor after the shooting started. He had not risen before my men and I were forced to leave. No harm done."

Marius was not about to tell Gashi one of his men had been stabbed by Bradley. But he was certain the New Zealander had not followed him. Bradley had re-entered the café, probably concerned for the woman.

Gashi said, "I have cargo coming through here tonight. I do not need trouble. Why aren't you in Italy organising your end?"

"You know the answer to that. I was sent here to take care of Bradley. But do not worry – in Bari, all is organised."

"It had better be. And Bradley. You are no match for him. It is not a task for children."

Marius bristled at the insult. His face reddened. He remained passive, but the sleeve of his jacket tightened round flexed muscle as his hands closed to fists. After he had disposed of Bradley, he would find reinforcements and deal with this sweating pig.

CHAPTER EIGHTEEN

It had been easy enough for Sulla to keep Marius and his companion in sight. The two men, after dropping their weapons into a city trash bin, walked in a casual manner, not hurried. Marius even stopped in front of a store window and pointed out something of interest. Sulla had guessed they thought moving quickly might draw attention to themselves, but posing as shoppers was carrying the charade too far, in his opinion. Dumping the weapons, he understood. Armed men stopped by police would find themselves in a great deal of trouble, especially a visitor from Italy.

Sulla had phoned Zef as he followed the Italian on foot, and by the time Marius was in his SUV, Sulla was sitting in the passenger seat of his friend's taxi. Marius continued to be careful, keeping to the speed limit and obeying all the road signs. Zef's taxi, perfectly blended amongst the hundreds of other taxis, kept to a respectable distance.

The SUV drove along the road to the airport for twenty minutes before turning off into an industrial zone. When Marius stopped in front of a warehouse, Zef continued on for another one hundred metres before pulling over ahead of a parked truck. Sulla climbed out of the taxi and crossed the street, then walked back along the uneven pavement until he was close enough to have a clear view of the entrance into the warehouse. He slipped into the doorway of a mobile phone wholesaler. Across the quiet, potholed street, between where he stood and the warehouse, was a small tree: large enough to give him cover, but enough space between the branches for him to see through without being seen.

A high hedgerow surrounded the building, partially blocking his view into the courtyard. But he could see enough to spot Marius climb out of the SUV and reach behind a block pillar. When he pulled his hand away the sliding security gate opened. Marius stood back to allow the vehicle to drive through. Sulla could see a small grassed area that might have once been lawn, but was now overgrown with weeds. A flagpole stood in front of the main entrance. The driveway ran to the rear of the building.

Then the gate closed.

A tap on glass drew his attention. The receptionist of the mobile phone company eyed him through the window and gave a 'come in' wave. Sulla shook his head. She looked annoyed and held her hands out in a 'what the hell are you doing in my doorway?' gesture. Sulla pointed to his wristwatch and shrugged, indicating he was waiting for someone. That seemed to appease her. She relaxed and returned to her desk.

After a ten-minute wait, Marius had still not come out. When Sulla thought it through, it occurred to him it might not be a drop-off point for his vehicle. Sulla had expected Marius to reappear in a new car and drive off as if the shootout at the café had never occurred. Now Sulla had a second thought. It might be a hiding place, and Marius intended to hole up in the warehouse for as long as he needed to. Were there more men inside? Were they now planning another attempt on Jeff's life?

Sulla made his way across the street and found a lane to the left of the gate that ran down the side of the warehouse. The sign on the pavement said PASTA. The pasta factory was behind the complex Marius was hiding in. Sulla made his way along the lane until he was at the rear of the warehouse. He thanked Allah when he reached the double gates into the pasta factory and saw they were bolted shut. There was no chance he would be seen skulking about and risk someone calling the police.

The hedgerow was too high for him to see over. He looked around and found a beer crate. He placed it against the hedge and stepped up on to it. The rear of the building was a sealed parking area big enough for twenty cars. The parking lot was empty except for two wheeled rubbish bins, a small panel van and Marius's SUV. There was a window on the second floor. The fire escape below it would allow him to climb high enough to get a look inside. The first rung of the ladder was over three metres from the ground. He would need to jump up more than two metres to take hold of the ladder. Not possible. He eyed one of the wheeled bins. He would pull it across and use it to climb up.

He made ready to fling himself over the hedge. A small door in the bottom corner of a large roller door opened. It crashed against the corrugated steel. Sulla ducked. He heard voices. Shouting. He strained for a view through the hedge leaves.

Marius and his companion stepped out. Squeezing through the doorway behind Marius was a giant hulk of a man. Sulla recognised him instantly: Osman Gashi, Avni Leka's ex-henchman. His mouth dropped open. What was Gashi doing with Marius? He was too far away to hear the words passing between them, but the big man was agitated and kept stabbing his finger into Marius's chest. Marius spun on his heel and climbed into the SUV. His companion climbed into the passenger's seat. The motor revved, the vehicle reversed in a half circle, and then spinning tyres spat small pebbles in Sulla's direction as Marius sped away. Osman Gashi went back inside, pulling the small door shut behind him.

Sulla now knew where to find Gashi when he needed to. He would deal with him later. As he ran down the lane he clicked on Zef's mobile number. Marius would need to stop and let himself out through the gate. That was enough time for Zef to have his cab at the end of the lane to collect him and chase after Marius before he was too far down the road. He needed to find out where Marius had gone before he made contact with Jeff and inform him that an old adversary of theirs, Osman Gashi, was in town.

∽

Back in his hotel room, Marius phoned his boss, Pietro Gallo.

"Marius, you have had more problems, I see. This man, Bradley, seems to be more than your match. I have been thinking that you should come home and I will send someone else to take care of this man."

"I can do this. I need more time."

A pause on the phone. Marius's mouth dried. He ran his tongue across his gums to produce spit.

"No, my mind is made up. I want you back in Bari. There is also my granddaughter's wedding. Remember, you are invited to this. It will be a good weekend. And you should be here to enjoy it with the rest of the family."

"I had forgotten about the wedding. Yes, I will try to fly out in the next few days."

"Good boy. Let me know your flight details; I will have someone meet the plane."

"Thank you. That is kind of you."

The phone clicked in Marius's ear as his boss hung up. Marius wanted to throw up. He staggered back until his legs hit the side of the bed and he fell back on to it. They were going to kill him. Returning to Bari was now out of the question. He needed protection. Although he shuddered at the thought of asking Osman Gashi, Gashi was the only man who might offer it, and he was the only man he knew more powerful than the Gallo family. What choice did he have? Gashi would want a payment. This did not concern Marius. He had valuable information to trade.

CHAPTER NINETEEN

The hostage crisis was on all major international news channels and most local Italian channels. Journalists concentrated on two aspects of the story: the hostages and the man responsible for their abduction, The Sheriff. It seemed each channel had managed to get its own photo of the man who would be the new Kurdish leader. Everyone had in-depth bios on the kidnapper, and within hours of the news release, The Sheriff had become an international superstar.

Live broadcasts showed the bus rolling along the highway. Turkish military vehicles and police cars, in front and bringing up the rear, kept their distance. Helicopters hovered above the convoy.

A smiling Avni Leka nodded approval. The hype around the hijacking was unfolding as he had envisioned it would. The media were lapping up the story and his media machine had kicked in to keep The Sheriff's star on the rise. Over the next few weeks, millions of disgruntled Islamic youths across northern Africa, the Middle East and Asia would be hailing a new icon from the ancient lands of the once-great Ottoman Empire. This is how Leka's media people would write it and the young, like all youth anywhere in the world, would believe it. In their eyes, any man who could thumb his nose at the West, in such a demonstrable way, deserved to be a hero. Many of them had little future. And for Leka, this endless resource of the disenfranchised was going to be good for his business. Wars meant refugees, arms sales and contraband, and destroyed cities needed to be rebuilt; his construction supplies and cement factories would be essential.

He was giving them a saviour.

Soon he would be selling them firearms.

He took a grape from a bowl and dropped it into his mouth. Not bad. He picked up the bunch as he made his way to the balcony door. The grapes came from the local village and he supposed were picked from the vines of one of the estates he could see from his balcony. He had bought a five-thousand-square-metre castle on a hilltop near Rome through one of his dummy corporations. The castle had two towers, one at the front and one at the rear. They had proved to be valuable observation posts, giving his men kilometres of uninterrupted views of the surrounding countryside. The nineteen bedrooms, cellars and offices provided all the accommodation required for the small army of guards Osman Gashi had provided for his security. And in the centre of the structure was a courtyard large enough for a helicopter to land and take off from without prying eyes overseeing its activities. No one could approach his fortress without him knowing, and he had escape routes in place should the need arise. He had ears in all police stations, and would be informed of an impending raid if the police lucked out on his whereabouts and came looking for him.

International intelligence agencies pursued him, and he was probably at the top of most terrorist lists. But he was off the beaten track. No tourists came his way, and in the small villages and towns that surrounded him new arrivals drew suspicion. To date, any agents who had found their way close to his hideout had been easy enough to spot and monitor. A trail of misinformation for them to follow usually ended up with their declaring it was a dead end and moving on to look for him elsewhere. Hiding in plain sight was much safer than in some fucked-up

Islamic country. No American drone would drop bombs on an Italian town. However, despite his precautions, he knew that eventually he would be found. His survival lay in creating a secure haven in an area safe from the tentacles of the international police.

And yet with each step he took, Bradley was right behind him.

He had been assured that this was to be taken care of. He had been told that not killing him in Bari had been bad luck, and that Bradley's luck would not last forever and he would never leave Turkey. Leka knew from bitter experience that Bradley's luck never seemed to run out.

When he received the phone call from Gashi saying that the second attempt to kill Bradley had failed, it did not surprise him. But he had lost his temper all the same. Losing it did not happen to him, not often at any rate; he had trained himself to have control over his emotions. But Bradley had again escaped harm. Leka had smashed his fist on to his oak writing table. He had picked up the dagger he used as a letter opener and had thrown it at the wall. The blade had buried into the canvas of an oil painting by Valentino Soldati, a highly regarded local painter. Gritting his teeth, he had leaned on the desk until he calmed.

Despair gave way to hope when he remembered he had a back-up plan. Fortune had smiled on him. Two friends of Bradley's were on the hostage bus. He had ordered that Barry Briggs and his girlfriend be watched, nothing more. He would separate them from the other hostages later. When the time was right, he would use the twosome to bait a trap, and Bradley would finally get to walk with God.

Leka looked skyward. He could not yet see the helicopter, but he could hear it. It would be coming up from behind his castle. Any moment, it would be overhead, hovering, then descending into the courtyard. He ate another grape and dropped the rest into the pot plant next to him. He needed to prepare for his guest.

Pietro Gallo did not like to be left waiting.

"I do not like to fly, and I especially do not like to fly in a helicopter, but I wanted to meet with you to discuss a serious matter, and it needed to be in person."

They sat at the dinner table. The tabletop was bare, except for a tray with bottles of whisky, cognac and grappa, and glasses. Coffees would be brought when asked for.

"What is it you wish to discuss?" Leka asked, already knowing why Gallo had called for the urgent meeting. The Italian wore a brown Armani suit. The collar of his silk shirt was buttoned, but it was not tight around the crime boss's skeletal neck. Leka wondered how he had not been blown away by the downdraft of the helicopter's rotor blades.

"The New Zealander, Bradley. You have paid for a service, a great deal of money, I might add, and he is still alive. The man I appointed to complete this simple task has failed me. I have appointed another. I came here to assure you Bradley will be taken care of. I also came to make you the offer that, if you wish it, the contract can be cancelled and your money returned."

Leka screwed the top off the cognac and poured two glasses. He pushed one across to Gallo.

"You aren't the first to lose out against Bradley. I've had this experience myself. It is why I hired you. Keep the money and get the job done."

Gallo raised his glass. "A toast to the demise of Bradley."

Gallo dribbled a few droplets of the cognac between his lips then placed the glass on the table beside him.

"Now to the next matter," Gallo went on. "The smuggling route through Turkey, into Asia. In this you have invested a great deal of our money. We have made money from the immigrants, but I have warehouses of weapons in Russia and the Ukraine. My drug supplies are low. How long before we have a secure passageway through to Asia and our business can resume? What are you doing about it?"

Leka sipped his cognac.

"I will show you."

He walked over to the flat-screen television hanging on the wall and switched it on.

The CNN channel was broadcasting images of the hostage bus.

"You have seen this?" Avni asked.

"Yes, I have seen it." Gallo frowned. He looked from the screen to Leka. "This is down to you?" He pointed a bony finger at Leka. "But why? I don't understand. And how does this help us?"

"It is called expanding your horizons, Pietro. We cannot grow within our own borders. You know this; we have discussed it, and as you have rightly pointed out we need a passage through Afghanistan and Pakistan into Asia. To do this, I need the right people in control. The Turks and the Americans and their allies have made it difficult and are using all their money and military muscle to block movement through these trade routes. Not to stop us. To stop ISIS recruits, and Taliban and Al Qaeda, and any other group wanting to stir up trouble in Iraq and Syria. But it does affect us indirectly. To open these routes, I need a man with an army to ensure access."

"You are talking of this man The Sheriff?"

Avni nodded. "The Sheriff is our man."

"Yes, but this – the eyes of the world are watching. International agencies are watching. What if they find out it is us behind it? I have survived by knowing my place and staying strong in the shadows. This – this is inviting the world into your house. How can this be good for any of us?"

Leka compressed his lips and stifled a barbed comment. He needed Gallo. His security in Italy was reliant on him. It seemed he might have misjudged the crime boss's ambition.

"To move freely across the borders of Kurdistan, Iraq, Iran, Turkmenistan into Afghanistan and Pakistan, the tribal leaders who control the crossings are demanding more and more money. And worse, they are all the time unreliable. We need one man to unite all the tribal leaders. He needs to be Islamic and he needs to be iconic."

Gallo was thoughtful. "And The Sheriff is the man they will respect?"

Leka said, "When The Sheriff was captured by the Turkish police at the Bulgarian border, he thought he would never again experience freedom. This made him the perfect candidate to be made an offer he had little choice but to accept. Straight off, he saw it as mutually beneficial. If he is nothing else, he is a businessman. The Sheriff controls a small army that has been fighting with the PKK, roaming the disputed Kurdish homelands and crossing the borders of his neighbours for years. Recently his passion for a new Kurdistan has given way to smuggling contraband, weapons and people out of Asia. He knows the territory better than any other man I am aware of, and he knows most of the tribal leaders.

"I sent word to The Sheriff that I would have him broken out of prison and provided with safe transport into Northern Iraq, Syria or wherever he wished to go, and I would also provide enough funds for him to increase his troop strength and buy the necessary armaments. In return, The Sheriff would open and keep open the smuggling corridor to Asia. Of course he agreed. What choice did he have? It took a few weeks to organise, but as you can see on the television, it has gone according to plan."

Gallo looked at the television before he turned to Leka, his face a mix of confusion and incredulity. He shook his head. "I understand that The Sheriff might do what you say he can do. His involvement makes sense, even to me. But this" – he pointed at the television – "this, I do not understand."

Leka slowly placed his cognac on the table.

"In the world we live in, finding those we can trust and rely upon is becoming harder and harder. International agents are looking to infiltrate criminal organisations such as ours. You, for instance – how do you maintain your security?"

"Only family members are allowed in the uppermost levels," Gallo answered. "We have soldiers like Marius, but they are not privy to all the business. They operate on the fringes."

"And even Marius has had to commit a criminal act, like a murder, observed by one of your family to be allowed on the fringe. Is that right?"

Gallo nodded.

"And it is the same for me and the people who work for me," Leka said. "I cannot operate my business if the Western authorities can interfere at will. To keep them away I need armies, not gangs."

"And The Sheriff will give you this?"

"By the time this is over, The Sheriff will be one of the West's most hated and despised men. The world will know he is a bad man. The Sheriff is a Kurd and he is Sunni, but it wouldn't really matter to the extremists what Islamic religious group he belongs to. The malcontents, no matter whether they are Shia or Sunni, will love him to bits. Posters will be hung on walls. From here on in, when The Sheriff's men come knocking on their door, the tribal leaders will welcome him with open arms. He will make them lots of money, and our business from Asia to Europe will make us a lot of money."

"And if he is killed?" Gallo asked.

"It won't matter. The idea of him will survive and our media will keep him alive; even if the West shows pictures of him dead, our media will say they are fake. We will show our own photos of The Sheriff very much alive. The Sheriff can be anyone I appoint The Sheriff to be."

There was a slight shaking of his hand as a nervous Gallo lifted his glass of cognac.

"*Salute.*"

This time Gallo drained all the cognac from his glass.

Avni Leka stood on his balcony and watched until the helicopter and Pietro Gallo disappeared from sight. All was going to plan. The Bari crime lord and his organisation controlled the port and ensured the smuggling operations into Europe ran smoothly. Gashi controlled the Balkans and beyond. Soon The Sheriff would open the gateway to Asia. And The Sheriff would become another one of his many lieutenants overseeing his growing empire. They reported to him through Gashi, and his bookkeeper hidden in Paris oversaw the distribution of money. Through Gashi, he had a squad of Albanian enforcers who took care of anyone who might try to double-cross him. It did not happen often, but it did happen.

His attention turned back to the television.

As he expected, the Turkish military and police had kept their distance, but when the border neared they would become more aggressive. Well, let them. If they got too close, the bus would be detonated and the Turkish government could explain to the international media and the various governments why they had caused the deaths of so many innocent tourists.

The Sheriff would remain a force, dead or alive.

CHAPTER TWENTY

Sulla. What the hell are you doing here?"

"I have a friend in Istanbul I have not seen for a time. He is from my village. I came to visit with him."

Jeff did not believe him for a minute. "Sure you did."

He stood aside to allow Sulla into the room. Sulla sat in the only chair. Jeff had little choice but to sit on the bed.

Sulla said, "I have a short time ago seen an old acquaintance of ours: Osman Gashi. He is still a fat man, and I would still very much like to cut his throat."

Jeff laughed. "Gashi could be visiting friends, just like you, Sulla. Maybe he too has a cousin."

"No, I do not believe this. Men like Gashi have no family. I do not think he ever had a mother."

"Forget about Gashi, Sulla. He's in the past and we need to move on. We made an agreement with him that if he gave up Leka he could walk free. He did, so it's over. Now, why are you here and not back looking after the vineyard in Kosovo?"

"I'm thirsty."

Jeff opened the fridge and stood back. Sulla perused the available beverages.

"Orange juice."

Jeff plucked a bottle from the rack on the fridge door and tossed it to him.

"I did not think it wise that you wander about Istanbul without someone to watch your back," Sulla said as he unscrewed the cap. "I got here as soon as I could. I have been watching from afar. I saw the men shoot at you in the café. Lucky for you, they missed. When I saw you were okay, I followed the gunmen to a warehouse. And, I might add, one of the gunmen was Marius, from Bari."

"I'd already suspected as much. Well, okay, now it's confirmed. It makes sense he would want to finish the job."

Sulla said, "Anyway, it is interesting that Marius would bother to come to Turkey just to kill you. He does not know you well enough, but I think the man he met with at the warehouse may have all the answers."

Jeff raised an eyebrow. "Gashi?"

Sulla nodded.

"He and Marius had an argument, and Marius stormed off. Again I followed, and this time to a café. Marius met with two men. My friend went into the café and sat close enough to listen in on the conversation. The two men are local criminals and Marius was hiring them to keep an eye on you."

Jeff stood and walked to his hotel room window. It was late afternoon. Peak-hour traffic blocked the street, and pedestrians clogged the pavement. The hotel café looked busy. All the outside tables had filled. He searched the doorways and corners of buildings, but saw nothing out of the ordinary. That didn't mean he wasn't being spied upon. He turned back to Sulla.

"If Marius is reporting in to Gashi, then I guess Gashi is still working for Avni Leka. Well, I suppose that should come as no surprise;

Gashi is a thug without a brain. He needs to be told what to do; the perfect marriage. This means Marius was acting on Leka's orders, through Gashi of course, and not looking to protect his boss's business, as he told us in Bari. And, if he has a contract to kill me, and that contract was given by Gashi, then after missing me in Bari he had little choice but to follow me here. Gashi doesn't accept mistakes. Now he's screwed up again. Marius will be a worried man about now, I'd say. However, Marius being here in Istanbul I get, but the big question is: what the hell is Osman Gashi doing here in Istanbul? And what the hell is he doing holed up in that warehouse?"

Sulla shrugged.

"I think we need to pay our fat friend a visit," Jeff said.

Sulla finished his fruit juice and jumped to his feet. "I was hoping you would say that."

⚬

Night had come.

"Are you certain this is the right building?" Jeff asked. "There are no lights on and it looks empty."

"This is the place."

"Okay, let's find a way inside. The front entrance is too exposed. Someone might see us climbing the wall."

"There is a lane. Follow me."

Sulla led the way to the rear of the building. He stopped at the spot where he had watched Marius and Gashi from earlier.

"This is where I was – see, the beer crate is still there."

Jeff stood on the box and looked over the hedge.

"Was the car park empty this afternoon?"

"Two big bins for rubbish and a small van, and Marius's SUV," Sulla said.

"The vehicles have gone. The two bins are still there."

Jeff pushed on to the hedge to test its rigidity. A foot below the top, he found concrete. The hedge had been grown over a concrete wall. He compressed the foliage with two hands and rolled over it, managing to land on the other side on both feet. He waited as Sulla scrambled over. He had tried to follow Jeff's actions, but his trouser leg caught.

"Stop playing games, Sulla," Jeff said as he untangled him.

They walked across the car park to the back of the warehouse.

A chest-high loading dock protruded out a metre from under a roller door. Two metres further along was a much larger roller door, floor to ceiling. Jeff figured when opened a truck could drive through. He bent and gripped the hand-holder at the bottom of the roller door. He grunted as he pulled on it, but the door wouldn't budge.

"It was worth a try," Jeff said.

Car headlights flashed down the driveway and lit the sealed area, and then came more lights from other vehicles behind. There was a rattle of the iron gate as it opened.

"Someone's coming," Sulla said.

CHAPTER TWENTY-ONE

From behind the two bins, Jeff and Sulla watched a white SUV circle the car park and stop, facing the rear of the building. Close behind were three buses, but they stayed nose to tail back up the driveway, motors running. Osman Gashi climbed out of the SUV and took a key from his pocket. He fiddled it into the lock of the smaller door in the left-hand corner of the larger roller door. He and a passenger from the back seat entered the warehouse. After a few seconds, light streamed through the open door and a dimmer glow through the glass of the upper floor windows. There was a groan and the larger of the roller doors vibrated upwards. When the door was high enough, the SUV drove in. The three buses followed. Each bus was filled with passengers. Once the vehicles were inside, the roller door rattled to the ground.

Jeff and Sulla waited until they were certain no one else was coming down the drive before stepping out from behind the bins.

"What do you think, Sulla?"

"I think this is not a tourist site. No need for busloads of sightseers to come visiting. I did not see any souvenirs for sale. And it is not a hotel. So I think these people are not tourists."

"You should be a detective."

"I think this too," Sulla said. "And I am good at crosswords."

Jeff grinned as he shook his head. He scanned the rear of the building. To the right, a fire escape ladder climbed to just under a line of high-set windows, which Jeff presumed belonged to offices rather than being simply to increase natural light to the warehouse floor. Also, the low-strength light emitted told Jeff it was filtered by walls and doors. No brightness from lights switched on upstairs.

"I'm going up that ladder. See if I can't get a peek inside," Jeff said.

"It is risky. If someone comes outside you will be seen."

"I don't think I can knock on the door and ask to have a look round, can I?"

"You go up. I will wait here and be on guard. If someone comes I will signal. If they see you and shoot at you I will unleash our full arsenal."

Jeff looked hopeful. Had Sulla managed to secure a firearm? Then he looked at the stone in Sulla's palm.

"Great."

Jeff moved off. Halfway to the ladder he looked back. "I need a leg-up," he called in a low tone.

Sulla crossed to him. He stood underneath, and Jeff bent a knee. Sulla grasped it with both hands. "Okay," Sulla said. "On three. One, two, three . . ." Sulla hoisted Jeff high enough to take hold of the bottom rung. The iron frame creaked under his weight. Hand over hand, he pulled himself up until his foot caught. Each step of the climb brought a groan from the ladder. He doubted the sound would carry inside, and if it did he doubted it would be heard above the din being made by the busloads of passengers chatting amongst themselves and louder voices he took to be Gashi's men yelling out instructions. But outside, in the still of the night, and far away from traffic noises, it sounded deafening.

At the top, Jeff wiped his sleeve across the grime on the window. He cleaned enough to be able to see inside. It was office only. An open door offered a narrow-angled view into the warehouse but only of the ceiling and hanging lights.

He needed to get inside.

He reached out and tried the hinged window an arm's length to his right. It opened. Lucky me, he thought. He signalled to Sulla, and gestured he was about to climb in. Sulla waggled his finger; a definite no. Jeff turned away. He pulled the window out as far as he could and then climbed on to the railing before launching himself through the open gap on to the sill. He wavered on his stomach until he balanced, and then crawled the rest of the way in.

The office door opened on to a small landing. A waist-high railing enclosed the space, a wooden staircase led down to the lower level. The railing was covered in. Jeff crawled from the office on to the landing. He found a crack in a floorboard. Now he could see most of the lower level. At a guess, he estimated more than one hundred people were milling about: men, women and children. Whole families, it appeared. An equal split between adults and children.

A man clapped hands to gain their attention. He spoke calmly as he waved his arms about. Jeff did not speak the language. Arabic of some type, he assessed. The passengers followed another man through a door in a partition wall that closed off the front third of the building. The passengers weren't terrorists, Jeff reasoned. Not at first glance anyway. Unless they were recruiting children, but he doubted even Gashi would stoop to recruiting children this young. Illegal refugees made more sense. If Osman Gashi was behind it, and he must be, it was about money and smuggling illegals into Europe. Why not? He had the network, at least through Turkey to Albania. But what the hell were they doing here? In the warehouse? It wouldn't surprise him if, now he had their money, Gashi took them out the back and murdered them. One of the stories whispered about the big man was that during the Serbian war he had killed families after they had paid him to protect them. The rumours had never been confirmed, but this was Gashi, and Jeff was prepared to believe it was true.

He opened his mobile to text Sulla he was okay.

There was no signal.

He went back to the window and popped his head out. Sulla emerged from behind the rubbish bins. Jeff waved he was okay. As an afterthought, he held the phone out the window. There was a signal. He pulled it back in and the signal had gone. Puzzling. He would think about it later.

He gave the office a quick scan. It was sparsely furnished: a desk, two chairs and a battleship-grey three-drawer filing cabinet. Jeff pulled open the desk drawers. Empty. The filing cabinet contained a half-dozen empty manila folders and nothing else. Osman Gashi was not leaving a paper trail. He was not using the warehouse for anything other than the refugees.

Jeff moved back to the door and looked through the crack. There was still no sign of the people from the buses. He would wait a little longer. He sat on the floor, his back against the wall.

An hour passed.

Half asleep, he was roused to full alertness by the sound of voices.

He moved back to his vantage point. The passengers were filtering back through the door towards the buses. They looked freshened and had changed clothes. From the styles now worn he could see these were wealthy families. Such people would pay top dollar to enter Europe. Up to five thousand US dollars per head, maybe more. Jeff did a quick calculation. If the group tonight was typical, it amounted to a half-million dollars per shipment. Jeff couldn't guess how many busloads per week might pass through, but Gashi would be looking to maximise his profits. It was a good business. The people had the money to start a new life, but could not get a visa. Maybe many of them did not have passports. Without a passport or a visa, they'd never get through an airport and they couldn't cross borders. So, step in Gashi. With his criminal empire spread out across the Balkans he could take them anywhere and, once close enough, smuggle them into Europe. Looking like wealthy tourists made the task that much easier, and a tourist bus was less likely to be stopped en route.

The passengers re-boarded the buses, and the roller doors rattled upwards. Jeff made a decision. He rushed to the window. He could just make out the top of Sulla's head. He wrote a text to the Kosovan. He held his mobile out the window until he found the signal and sent the text.

Get to your friend and his car and follow the buses, the text read.

Jeff waited in the window until Sulla raised an arm and gave him a thumbs-up. Good. Now that was taken care of, when the warehouse was empty, he'd take a look round. Later, it would be a long walk back to the main road and a taxi. The exercise would do him good.

CHAPTER TWENTY-TWO

J eff stood near the sea wall looking into the waters of the Bosphorus. There had been rain. The bitumen on the road glimmered in the morning sunlight. The only pedestrian he had seen was a man walking his dog. In the distance, he could see the lighthouse and the coat hanger bridge and Reason Johanson, jogging towards him along the pavement that bordered the sea wall. As she drew nearer, his eyes were drawn to the black tights that against the sun silhouetted a shapely pair of legs, not muscled, not thin. She wore a baggy yellow T-shirt: the style of top she might have selected as a gesture of modesty for running through an Islamic city, but not her usual dress style. She waved when she saw him, and sprinted the last hundred metres.

She pulled a water bottle from a holder on her belt and gulped down a mouthful then stood legs apart, the water bottle clasped in both hands and held against her breast.

Jeff waited.

Reason breathed in deeply, then exhaled.

"Okay. What is it you want to tell me? I'm sorry I dragged you to this spot, but I never break my morning fitness routine for anyone." She pointed her water bottle at him. "This better be good."

"And a good morning to you," Jeff said. "It surprised me when you said you were off for a run. I thought you might be at the embassy coordinating a rescue."

Reason scowled. Playful, not antagonistic. Annoyed at the intrusion, but professional enough not to let playtime interfere with work.

She said, "You have worked twice with Lee Caldwell, so you know how we operate. Not with the official services. We use them when needed, but I can't tell the marines what to do, and they don't come to me looking for advice. I'm interested in the men who are doing this. My role is to protect American citizens and chase down anyone who harms them. Hostage rescue is in the hands of the CIA and the military. However, if you come across information that might be of help, I will gratefully receive it and pass it on. In the meantime, I will do my job and that means staying fit and alert so I can find the bad guys who harm Americans. And, to get fit, I jog. Fair enough?"

Jeff nodded. "Couldn't be clearer." He paused. "I found the men that shot at us yesterday. One of my men followed them to a warehouse after the shooting. They met up with an old friend of mine from Kosovo. A very bad man who is responsible for a good proportion of the crime that happens in the Balkans. He was the second in command to Avni Leka, and I'm guessing still is. Anyway, I can confirm that the man that shot at us in the café is the same guy that tried to kill me in Bari."

Reason put a leg on the railing and stretched forward, running her hands along her calves. After a good stretch, she changed legs. Jeff couldn't help but admire the fine lines. She tilted her head towards him and caught him appraising her. He didn't look away, and she didn't admonish him.

"Is that it? You brought me here to tell me you've found the men trying to kill you?" Her eyes flared. "What do you want me to do? Take care of them for you?"

Jeff laughed out loud.

"No, Reason, I can take care of them myself. I spent half the night at a warehouse. Three buses came, full of families. If I had to make a guess where they came from I'd say Syria, Iraq or Iran. Somewhere in that region. The three buses parked inside the warehouse. The passengers were offloaded and taken into a room at the front. When they reboarded the buses, the passengers had changed clothes and were spruced up. Just like regular people going on holiday. After they left, I had a look round. Hidden in the back of the warehouse were beds, showers, toilets, and a kitchen and lounge. I figured it was some sort of staging site."

"So they are trafficking in illegal refugees – is this the big secret? Again, what has this to do with me?"

Jeff shook his head. "There is more."

Reason stopped her stretching and now concentrated on Jeff, hands on her hips. Not bothering to hide her 'I'm pissed off that you are wasting my time' demeanour. Jeff ignored it. He was not about to let the American agent rattle him. He had been up all night and was tired, and when he got tired he got grumpy. He breathed deeply. He wouldn't lose control in front of her, but he was close.

"When I tried my mobile inside the building, it wouldn't work," he said through clenched teeth. "But when I hung it out the window, the signal bounced in loud and clear."

Reason rubbed the top of her forehead. The kind of stroking indulged in when a headache develops. Jogging on the spot, she checked her watch. At any moment, she would turn and run off. Jeff took his time to infuriate her more.

Jeff said, "Albanians dressed as cops hijacked the bus. Barry Briggs gave me that much information when he sent me his text. Then, no more texts. We know that for a time the bus GPS and Barry and the mobile phones were off the grid. I surmise that if the hijackers were Albanians, probably Kosovan, and this depot is under the command of Albanians – and I know at least one of them is Kosovan and bringing people from God knows where into it" – Jeff paused and looked Reason in the eye – "I might be stretching credibility here, but it's my belief that the hijacked bus ended up in Gashi's warehouse."

Reason took another gulp of water.

"And why would a bunch of Albanians, or wherever they might have come from, help The Sheriff and the PKK?"

"At a guess, knowing the man behind it, it is all about money. The hijackers will have been paid a lot of money to take such a huge risk. They would have known from the outset it might not end well for them. The funds have probably already been paid to their families back in Kosovo or Albania, or wherever."

Reason held Jeff's eye.

She said, "That's one hell of a risk. No return tickets on that bus, not if it blows. And who is paying the money to your man Gashi, and why? What has The Sheriff got to offer to warrant such an investment?"

Jeff shrugged. "Who the hell knows? Look, Reason, if the bus did end up in the warehouse, then Avni Leka is behind the hijacking and whatever other shit is going down. This man has an endless supply of money and people. And whatever it is he is up to, there will be bodies and two of the bodies might include your consul's daughter and her friend."

Reason stopped bouncing.

"Okay, you have my attention. Take me there."

⟡

Sulla's taxi-driving friend had little trouble staying in contact with the convoy of buses and Osman Gashi's vehicle. At the Bulgarian border, they stopped at the control point. Bulgarian customs officials boarded the bus, and for the next hour all Sulla could do was sit and watch. When the clearance came, the buses crossed through the checkpoint. The SUV turned back to Istanbul. Osman Gashi had boarded the lead bus and departed with it.

"Nothing more we can do here," Sulla said. "Let's get back to Istanbul."

Sulla opened his mobile, found Jeff's number and tapped the icon.

CHAPTER TWENTY-THREE

A s always, from the first time driving Jeff from the airport into the hotel in Istanbul, Fati the taxi driver was not far away. Why not? Jeff thought. A foreigner with money was a reliable source of income for the otherwise poorly paid Istanbul cabbies. Fati would stay close to Jeff for as long as it lasted. On the way to the warehouse, Fati dropped them at Reason's apartment. Jeff waited in a café across the street until Reason had showered and changed. She reappeared in jeans, a cream T-shirt and navy linen jacket; under the jacket, a bulge. She tapped it.

"I never leave home without protection."

"And I'm a typical male. I never carry any."

The warehouse was as Jeff had left it. Closed up and no sign of life. The box was still against the hedge. He climbed over, but first revealed the concealed wall. Reason, using the concrete under the hedge growth as leverage, flung herself into the air as if she were leaping a vault in gymnastics and landed on two feet on the other side as delicately as a cat falling from a roof.

"Impressive," Jeff said, and meant it.

"How do we get in?" Reason asked, ignoring the compliment.

"There is the fire escape," Jeff said, pointing to it. "I'll scramble up and climb through the window at the top and let you in. I can use one of the rubbish bins to hoist myself on to the first rung of the ladder."

"Why don't you hoist me up and I'll climb in and open the door."

"Really?"

"In a former life I was a stuntwoman, and before that a gymnast."

"Okay, you've proved your point leaping the fence. You're the winner by a clear margin."

He stood under the ladder.

"How do you want to do this?" Jeff said.

"I don't want your hands on my butt. And don't look at it when I climb up," she said.

Reason's jeans were tight-fitting. He wanted to say, 'I'm only human', but kept his mouth shut.

"Right, okay. That's clear." His eyes settled on the rubbish bins. "I'll push a bin over. You can use that."

Halfway to the bin, he turned to gauge her reaction. Reason had managed to get herself up to the ladder and was already halfway to the top. Jeff laughed. This was some woman. At the top, she pulled at the window he had climbed through the previous evening. It swung open. After a few minutes, the small door in the corner of the roller door opened. He entered, pulling it closed behind him.

For the next thirty minutes, they went from room to room.

Jeff said, "This is pretty much as it was last night. Bring the illegals in, take them into the front where the showers are, clean them up and take them over the last part of the journey. Smart idea. Spruced up, they look like any old busload of tourists. Except none of them have visas or passports. But that's what they pay for, and Osman Gashi is just the man to take care of those details."

"I get the picture. They pay Osman Gashi big bucks. He arranges everything. A real bad guy, but apart from the connection to the man who wants you dead, this Avni Leka, there isn't anything here that tells us the hostages were here, and nothing that might help us rescue them."

Jeff nodded. "I agree, it does appear a dead end, but my gut tells me this is too much of a coincidence to not be connected."

"Okay, gut instinct I can work with. But, and it is a big but, there is still nothing here that can help us get the hostages freed. And given that we, along with the rest of the world, only have to turn on a television to see them live, where does that leave us? I say we've struck out. At the end of the day, Jeff, all we can learn from the warehouse is the hostages were here. I'm open-minded; I'll say I accept the hostages were here. Now what?"

"If the hostages were here, Gashi is behind it. Marius came to see Gashi and Leka hired Marius to kill me. I'd say it means Gashi must still be working as Leka's right-hand man, and he must still be in contact with Leka. If we can find Leka, we might be able to force him to get the hijackers to hand over the hostages. We could have a persuasive conversation with him. Hold a gun against his head and threaten to blow a hole in it if he doesn't; that sort of thing. Knowing Leka the way I do, no one outside of Gashi will have been anywhere near him. Osman Gashi is our best chance. I know Gashi: he has no loyalty to anyone, only himself. The last time a gun was stuck up his nose, he gave us Leka. I'm certain he'd do it again."

"And how do we find this Gashi guy?"

"I have someone tailing him."

Reason said, "I fear it will be all too little, too late. The hijacked bus will move again soon. In another day or so it will be at the border."

Jeff grimaced at the thought.

His eye caught something not right. A large Turkish flag was draped across one of the warehouse walls. Near the top of the flag it bulged out, as if something was poking out into it from behind. Jeff wandered across and pulled the flag aside.

"It's a door," Jeff said.

He pulled the flag right back until he had the door wide open and the flag trapped behind it.

Reason followed him into the room.

"Well, well, look here," Jeff said.

The room was the size of a small bedroom. On three walls were three tiers of shelving, and on the top two shelves were dozens of small arms: a mix of handguns and Kalashnikovs and an assortment of rifles. On the bottom shelf, boxes of ammunition, and on the floor, unopened crates and boxes of varying size. Jeff eyed a lidded box. He pulled it into the middle of the floor. It was heavy. He lifted the lid.

He held up a hand grenade. "At least six boxes of grenades. The longer boxes will be rocket launchers. In this part of the world, I'd guess RPGs. I don't think they're starting a war; that's not Gashi's style, but I think we can now add smuggling weapons to his business activities."

The sound of the roller door rattling alerted Jeff and Reason. They dashed from the room and looked to the rear of the building. Jeff closed the door and the flag dropped back into place. The groaning of metal on metal was unmistakable. The roller door was rising.

"Up the stairs," Jeff said. "We can't go out the front door. There might be men stationed there. They didn't use the office when I was here before. If we're lucky, they won't come upstairs this time either. Come on."

Reason took the stairs two at a time as she raced after Jeff.

Three SUVs drove in and the roller door closed behind them. Six men climbed out of the first two vehicles, and Marius and two men out of the last. Jeff and Reason lay side by side on the landing looking through the crack in the wooden floor Jeff had discovered earlier. As long as they stayed back from the edge they would not be seen from below.

Jeff whispered, "The man in the bright-red shirt is the guy that shot at us in the café. His name is Marius."

"You're not dead yet, Jeff. It could be the reason he is here, to discuss the next move. Isn't that why he came to Istanbul?"

Jeff nodded.

The men spoke loudly, laughing, relaxed. They used a simplistic form of English to speak with each other. Italians, Albanians, Turks, and who knew what other ethnic group might be represented. English would be a common language between them. One of the men opened a cupboard underneath a fire hose and produced two bottles of cognac. He placed them on a tray with enough glasses for everyone. He carried the tray back to one of the vehicles and set it on the bonnet. Glasses filled, the men took one each and raised them in a toast. The drinks were downed, and the glasses refilled.

Jeff whispered, "I hope they are not settling into a party."

"It's not even noon," Reason whispered back.

Jeff smiled. "Across the Balkans men drink alcohol for breakfast."

"I had a father like that."

Jeff raised an eyebrow.

"We can't stay here all day," Reason said. "You've already said the only man who can lead us to Avni Leka is Osman Gashi. If that is true, we need to find him. And fast. Remember we have forty lives on a bus not that many miles from the border."

Jeff crawled back into the office. Reason followed. They tiptoed across to the window. He could see two men in the parking lot standing next to the rubbish bins. Their manner looked casual enough but they were there as security. Jeff had little doubt both men were armed.

"Two outside and nine downstairs. How good a shot are you?" Jeff asked, looking at the two men.

"I'm a crack shot, but from this distance, no chance."

"And climbing down the fire escape ladder with them standing there is out of the question," Jeff said.

They moved back to the doorway, then crawled once again to their vantage point.

"Where are the weapons I asked for?" Marius was saying.

"Over there, behind the flag," one of the men said, and pointed in the direction of the mini arsenal.

Jeff had not closed the door properly. Careless.

"Hold on a minute," the man said.

He walked across and pulled back the flag. He turned on the others. "Any of you leave the door open?"

Shaking heads was the response.

Jeff watched the man's facial expression. Had the door been left open by mistake, or had someone been in the warehouse? He was taking stock. A scratch of his chin and a slow scan of the warehouse followed. His head tilted, and eyes fixed on the upstairs landing. Jeff and Reason froze. Barely breathing. The only muscle movement their eyes as they continued to monitor below, through the crack in the floor. Any moment now, Jeff expected to hear shoes pounding on the stairs. He glanced to the right. Reason had her Glock in her hand. He had left the Sig-Sauer in his hotel room. The man went into the room. Jeff closed his eyes as he remembered he had left a box of grenades in the centre of the room. The man came out, jabbering and pointing at the room.

Half-full glasses were placed back on the tray. Heads moved in all directions, eyes searching every corner of the warehouse. The man in charge issued orders. Weapons were drawn. They spread out and moved towards the partitioned-off rooms at the front of the building.

Marius and his two men stayed put. Jeff watched him. The Italian eyed the roller door. Jeff could guess what he was thinking. He had no desire to be caught up in Osman Gashi's troubles. It had nothing to do with him. He wanted to be well away.

Jeff turned to Reason.

"They're searching the front rooms first, but it won't be long before they come our way."

"What about the cop I spoke with at the café after the shooting? I could call him and ask him to send in the cavalry. What do you think?"

"How well do you know him?"

"I don't. I only met him that one time."

"It's not worth the risk. An operation the size Gashi is running has protection from local cops. I think it best not to trust any of them. If he is in with them, they will drag your ass off to jail."

"I have a diplomatic passport; I won't be going anywhere. You, however, could be in trouble."

"At any rate, you won't get a signal in here, and if you stick your head out the window you'll get it shot off. So, we're on our own. We need to turn defence into attack."

"What do you suggest?"

"We can't go through the window, so our only option is to fight it out here in the warehouse. There are lots of places to shelter when the shooting starts. And, when we're clear of the building and on the street, we can send an anonymous message to your cop friend and they can raid the place."

"Okay, I can go along with that, but the only weapon we have is this one." Reason held up her Glock. "We're outgunned and, as we have discovered, they have an arsenal for resupply if they run out. What did you call a situation like this when you were in the Special Forces?"

"Another day at the office."

Reason stared at him as if she were looking over the top of a pair of spectacles. "I sure as hell hope you're as good as your mouth says you are."

"The others are in the back. Only Marius and his two men below. Time to move. You cover me from here. Remember: height puts you in the superior position. How many rounds for that firearm of yours?"

"A mag in my Glock and a spare on my holster. Thirty rounds."

"That's enough. Make them count."

"What are you going to do?"

Jeff sprang to his feet and leaped over the railing.

"Shit," Reason blurted out. She wriggled forward, swinging her gun to cover him.

Jeff landed on the roof of Marius's SUV. The man next to Marius spun when he heard the thud. He instinctively swung his weapon in Jeff's direction. Two shots from above slammed into the gunman's chest. He slumped to his knees. Jeff didn't need to look over his shoulder to know Reason had scrambled to the edge. He leaped from the buckled roof to his right, his arm catching the second man as he hit the cement floor. He wrenched the man sideways, smashing his head on to the concrete. Jeff scrambled to his feet and yanked the man up, then slammed his head into the rear passenger door. The impact caused him to drop his weapon. Jeff pushed the groggy thug away and searched for the fallen handgun. It was a metre away. He dived for it and, as he scooped it up, turned on to his back, firing two shots. Marius's man staggered backwards clutching his shoulder. Jeff fired again and a small hole appeared in the centre of the man's forehead. He collapsed across the vehicle hood and slid to the floor. Jeff rolled on to one knee, his weapon directed to where his instincts told him Marius was hiding. He fired off two rounds.

Automatic rifle fire punched holes along the side of the vehicle inches above Jeff's head. Bullets ricocheted off concrete walls. A piece of shrapnel flicked his ear. Jeff fell to the floor, flattening himself across the concrete. He judged the shots were fired from the front of the warehouse and not from Marius.

Shots from above. Reason was holding the attackers at bay in the walled-off front part of the warehouse used by the immigrants. Jeff heard the small door in the roller door slam against iron. There were no tell-tale footsteps of reinforcements. He glanced over his shoulder, half expecting the men from outside to appear. No one had entered.

"Marius," Jeff muttered under his breath.

Staying low and keeping the SUV between him and the shooters, he moved towards the vehicle Marius had been hiding behind. The Italian was gone. Had the two men outside run off with him? Inside the warehouse it was a standoff, with the gunmen trapped in the immigrant processing area and he and Reason trapped between the gunmen and the outside guards.

"Reason, I can keep the shooters up front busy. Go into the office and check the car park. If Marius has run off, the other two guards might have too," he shouted across to her.

Seconds passed.

"All clear out back," she yelled to him.

"Okay, come down. I have you covered."

He heard a thud, and Reason slid off the vehicle and knelt beside him.

"I meant use the stairs," Jeff said.

"I told you I was a stuntwoman."

"Okay, let's get the hell out of here."

Jeff ran to check the driveway. Reason stood in the doorway, her Glock trained inside. When he returned, still no one had emerged from the front room.

"Marius and the two men have gone."

Sirens could be heard in the distance.

Reason said, "Someone has heard the shooting. We better get out of here before the cops arrive. I'm not certain I can explain away the bodies with my diplomatic passport."

They scrambled over the hedge and ran down the lane. Opposite, a smiling Sulla stood beside his friend's car. Jeff ran to him.

"Have you been here all this time?"

Sulla nodded.

"I thought I told you to follow Gashi."

"Yes, this is what you did tell me to do. You were very clear, and I understood you perfectly well," Sulla said, a sparkle in his eye. "But I had no visa to enter Bulgaria. Do not worry though, I have a cousin in Bulgaria. He is following Gashi and the buses."

"Okay, fair enough. Did it cross your mind that we might need help?"

"Yes, I did give this some thought, but I am not armed and therefore of no use. If I had come, I might have been shot. I know you would not want me to endanger myself. Besides, you are safe. You did not need me."

Jeff turned to Reason. "My friend, Sulla, has a very bad sense of humour, Reason; a regular comedian."

Reason smiled. "I think he is very funny," she said.

Jeff shook his head.

"Get us out of here, Sulla. I'll phone Fati to tell him we have a car and to find his own way home."

CHAPTER TWENTY-FOUR

Reason invited Jeff and Sulla up to her hotel suite: two bedrooms, a bathroom and a small lounge/kitchenette. She pulled open the fridge door and took out three cans of Budweiser.

"What now, Jeff?" Reason asked.

"Time to get after the bus. But I need to apply pressure elsewhere." He swallowed a mouthful of beer.

"Sulla, any news from that cousin of yours following Gashi? I think it's time for you to go have a talk to the fat man."

Sulla grinned broadly. Reason raised her eyebrows.

"Sulla has a history with Gashi," Jeff said, by way of explanation. "They tried to kill each other in Kosovo. Sulla let him walk." Jeff paused. "With justification, I might add. He gave up Leka to us. That was when we first learned Leka was behind the terrorist bombings in Europe and he was building an empire of terror. A smart man, our Leka. Anyway, Osman Gashi was his right-hand man and it appears all is forgiven between the two. He is our only connection to Leka. Whatever happens from today, the warehouse is shut down for good. And Marius won't waste any time informing Gashi I was involved. He will also tell Gashi about the big Kosovan Albanian helping me. In Bari, at any rate. Gashi will know it has to be Sulla and he knows we are friends. If Sulla can catch up with him smuggling his illegals to wherever, and spoil it for him, it might piss him off enough to bring him out into the open and have a go at Sulla."

Reason looked quizzically at Jeff. "Won't that be dangerous?"

"Sulla is a big boy. He can handle himself."

Reason looked at Sulla. He nodded.

"We need to grab Gashi." Jeff pointed his can at Sulla. "It's down to you, my friend."

Sulla digested the request. "You would like me to push his button."

"Get right up his nose."

"How far up his nose should I get?"

"I think the time has come to put a barrel against his head and pull the trigger if he does not give us the information we need."

Sulla stood, pulled out his phone and walked to the window. "I will phone my cousin."

"I need to use the bathroom," Reason said.

In her absence Jeff scanned Reason's room. It was bare of personal effects or personal touches. An open laptop on the small writing desk and the hint of scent were the only indications of occupation. He tapped Enter on the laptop. The screen filled with colour. A photo. Jeff leaned forward to take a closer look. The photo was of a happy family: two smiling children, a boy and a girl, and a woman sitting next to her husband, each adult holding one of their children on a knee. The woman in the photo was unmistakable. Her hair shorter than it was now, but he recognised her. Reason Johanson.

⁊

Avni Leka paced the room with his phone to his ear, his face reddening and eyes narrowing as Osman Gashi related what had taken place in the warehouse. He held his tongue until Gashi had finished. Two of

Marius's men were dead, and four of Gashi's men arrested. The police were now crawling all over the building.

"Will they have discovered anything that can lead back to us?" Leka asked.

"No, nothing. They have the weapons, but we can buy more. The warehouse is no longer usable, but I can find another. It will take time. Maybe a month."

"We have more shipments, don't we?" Leka asked.

"Yes, we do," Gashi answered. "I will arrange something temporary. I have options."

Leka nodded, relaxing a little, soothed by Gashi's reassuring calm. The big man might be an idiot, but when it came to his business, he was a master of control. This was good news. It appeared the risk to the smuggling operations was limited. Leka sat in his chair. The smuggling was an important part of his organisation. It brought in cash, and he needed the money rolling in to keep his Italian connections happy. His security relied upon happy Italians.

But Marius; what to do about Marius?

The man the Italian crime boss had sent to take care of Bradley was proving to be an incompetent moron. It seemed that, as well as Bradley, there was a man Marius had described to Gashi who had helped the New Zealander in Bari; the description left little doubt it was Sulla Bogdani. This was troubling. When Leka practised as a lawyer in Kosovo, before he agreed to become Prishtina's prosecutor, he had manipulated the legal system to have Bogdani sent to prison. He should have been in prison for a long time, but somehow Bogdani had won a release, and Leka knew if they ever crossed paths Bogdani would take his revenge. And with Bogdani came his brother-in-law and his mini army of ex-Kosovan Liberation Army soldiers.

"What has happened to Marius? Do you know where he is?" Leka asked.

"No, I have no idea. I am in Albania with the latest shipment. We will reach Vlore in a few hours. I am hoping to send a group across the Adriatic tonight. Once the deliveries are made, I will deal with Marius."

Leka hung up. He walked out on to the balcony and looked at the countryside. Somewhere out there, he imagined there might be a hole big enough to dump Bradley and Marius into.

∾

Marius booked in to a new hotel. As always, he travelled on false documents, and it was these he had used when booking a room and for the rental vehicle. If anyone went to his last hotel looking for him, the documentation would lead to a dead end. When the police checked the rental vehicle left behind in the warehouse, this too would lead nowhere. He had already arranged to get a new passport. He would have them by the time he needed to leave. He organised his new hotel room through connections and the management would not ask him questions.

His new room was comfortable. The hotel, hidden down a back street, was smaller and of a lesser quality, but it would do. He had left his bag behind. He needed to buy new clothes. Marius had little doubt Gashi's men had already informed on him. Gashi would be pissed off with him again, and that was dangerous.

How had Bradley found him? Had he been followed? He didn't see how that was possible, and Bradley had been in the warehouse before he arrived. Had he been followed earlier? It was the only obvious answer. Reality hit. Whether it was his fault or not, all fingers would be pointing at him. Gashi would make sure of it. His stomach churned and he almost vomited. If he was to survive, he needed to make amends.

He had to get rid of Bradley.

Bradley was destroying the reputation he had carefully built over the last few years. His future, and the lifestyle he had come to take for granted, were now in jeopardy. Marius paced. Until Bradley was killed, he had to consider himself a dead man. Either Pietro Gallo or Osman Gashi might have already dispatched a hitman, or maybe more than one. He needed to take care of Bradley as quickly as possible. He would hire more local hoods. Twice as many as he would normally need. When next he met with Bradley, he would surround him with a small army.

"Let's see Bradley walk away from that," he said out loud. "The New Zealander will not walk away next time," he promised the desperate image in the mirror.

CHAPTER TWENTY-FIVE

Jeff lay on his hotel bed thinking over options of how to rescue Barry and Bethany, but no matter how many ideas he came up with, nothing was feasible enough to consider seriously. It was now a waiting game. He walked down to Istiklal Avenue and found a Turkish restaurant he had eaten at the last time he was in Turkey. The ownership had changed hands, but the standard of the food was as good as he remembered. It was close to midnight when he returned to the hotel and his bed and fell asleep.

The sound of his mobile phone theme tune, 'Slow Coffee', woke him. He groped for the phone on the bedside table and flicked open the cover.

"Bradley," he mumbled.

"The bus is on the move again," Reason Johanson said. Jeff swung himself into an upright position. "The night in Ankara passed without incident. Its next stop is Goreme in the region of Cappadocia."

"I think it's time for us to get close to the bus," Jeff said.

"My advice is, stay right where you are until you hear back from your friend, Sulla. You might need to back him up, and getting to him from Goreme in a hurry will not be easy. Let the Turkish government handle it until it appears all hope is lost. After that, we can make our move. Although I still don't know what it is we can do. Not without resources. And if you switch on your television, you can watch it like the rest of the world. It's just like being there."

"I'll worry about what to do when the time comes. I don't need to worry about Sulla. He'll get the job done. I want to get to Goreme. Can I fly?" Jeff asked.

"I anticipated you might ask that. I've made enquiries," Reason said. "No helicopters are available for hire and no small planes. It wouldn't make a lot of difference anyway. The skies above the bus are off limits to any low-flying aircraft. They've even banned the media choppers. The military have established a no-fly zone. The Turkish authorities aren't taking any chances. If you want to get to Goreme, you have no choice other than to drive."

"How long will that take, and can I get there in time?"

"About eight hours' drive, I think, depending on traffic. And yes, *we* can get ahead. The hijackers will stay the night, so there is plenty of time."

"You're coming?"

"I'm not letting you out of my sight. I have a vested interest in this too, remember?"

"That's fine by me."

"I have an SUV if you prefer to travel in comfort, or you could hire us a car."

Jeff said, "I have a Turkish taxi driver called Fati. We should use him. If we need to get there quickly, I'm sure Fati won't concern himself with dodging in and out of traffic and breaking a few road rules. He might know of a back road or two."

"Okay by me. Pick me up in an hour."

❧

The man standing near the entrance to Jeff's hotel watched the taxi driver open the passenger door and the New Zealander throw his bag on to the back seat before climbing in after it. He heard Bradley ask his driver how far to Goreme. That was all he needed. He phoned Marius.

CHAPTER TWENTY-SIX

I t was dusk when the strange mushroom-shaped rock houses and freestanding skyscraper caves of Goreme came into view. Jeff's first thoughts of the rugged, weird terrain was that it was a landscape that might be imagined while under the influence of an hallucinogenic drug. Fati pointed at a roadblock ahead, manned by Turkish police, not the military. A policeman stepped on to the road and waved Fati to the side.

"Whatever happens," Fati said, "let me do the talking."

The officer leaned through the window. He gave Reason and Jeff a brief look, and must have decided they didn't warrant wasting his time because he stepped back and settled his attention on Fati. He spoke in Turkish. Fati nodded. The taxi driver turned to Jeff.

"Do we have a problem?" Jeff asked.

"He is saying the hijacked bus that is on all the news channels has stopped here in Goreme. The only people allowed into the town are residents and officials and media. Everyone else, he has been told, must be turned away."

"We need to get in, Fati."

Fati nodded and spoke to the policeman.

Fati said, "He is asking why it is so important that we have come to Goreme, and he has said it would be best for tonight to turn around and go to another town. He told me to tell you that the Cappadocia region has many wonderful tourist attractions and we would be much happier and a lot safer visiting these. Tomorrow, if it is clear, you can return to Goreme."

"Tell him it is important we see Goreme tonight. Tomorrow we must return to Istanbul to catch a flight. It has been a very long drive. We have come all the way from New Zealand."

Fati muttered something to the cop. The cop, stone-faced, leaned into the window. He lowered his voice. Whatever he said upset Fati. Jeff didn't need to understand Turkish to know Fati's response was a swearword. The cop held up his hands. A slight tilt of the head and a shrug followed. Jeff read the gesture easily enough. Take it or leave it, was the message. Fati turned in his seat and held out his hand.

"I need one hundred euros."

Jeff reached into his pocket and pulled off two notes from the concealed wad of cash, careful not to let the cop see, and handed over the two fifty-euro notes to Fati. Fati palmed them in his hand and held them out to the cop. The handshake took place, and the cop waved them on.

Fati shrugged. "The police are not well paid. Not local cops. This cop said, foreigners wanting to go where they should not go, can pay. He said you can afford it so why not." Fati spat out the window. "The thieving shit. I also told him you are staying at my cousin's hotel here in Goreme. Everyone knows my cousin. This helped make up his mind. Later, he will go to my cousin and ask for money for letting us through." Fati again spat out the window.

Jeff raised his eyebrows to Reason. He said, "I'm starting to believe everyone in the Balkans is related."

Reason nodded.

As they drove into the bottom section of Goreme and slowed near the mosque, Turkish Air Force helicopters could be seen hovering in the distance. The bus wasn't far away; Barry and Bethany so close. He had an image of Barry consoling his fiancée, telling her Jeff was on his way and would rescue them.

Jeff clenched his fist, frustrated.

Reason had been right. There would be no getting near the bus. Not in the air, at any rate. Traffic was heavy. Mostly press vehicles following the convoy. Jeff reasoned hotel rooms would be scarce. He was grateful for Fati and his relatives. The town swept back up into the hills and whitewashed homes sat in between the pointy-topped rock formations. They rounded a bend; the SOS restaurant was on the corner, and a sign in English a little way past it said, BATH.

Reason said, "The restaurant reminds me I need to eat and the bath sign, I need a soak."

"Later," Jeff said. "We have work to do."

Reason frowned at him.

Fati parked on the street a few metres from the hotel entrance. Jeff looked through the rear window. A man, almost the spitting image of Fati, came to greet them. Fati spoke to his cousin.

Fati said, "He has only one room. But the room has two beds."

Jeff looked at Reason.

"I'm a big girl," she said.

CHAPTER TWENTY-SEVEN

Reason and Jeff walked the streets until they identified a slope that would suit their purpose. It took another ten minutes before they found the road that would take them to the foot of the hill. They climbed the white rock face until they were high enough to get a good view of the temporary encampment. The bus had stopped a few hundred metres off the main road and parked on a flat, grassed field, or as flat as rolling terrain would allow.

The bus stood alone.

Military and police vehicles formed a circle round it, but had kept a good distance away. The equivalent area of two football fields was Jeff's best guess. Poles embedded in the turf had floodlights attached at the top. At night, the area would be lit up like day. No movement would go undetected.

Jeff had bought a pair of what were claimed to be US Army wide-angle binoculars from the markets in Istanbul. He had used US military-issue binoculars before and these were nothing like them. The only other pair for sale would have done for a night at the opera and little else. He rotated the focus ring until he had a sharp image. A nod of approval. They would do. He swept the lens across the bus and outer area. A canvas had been draped along the side of the bus to shield the door, and more canvas had been used to create a small secluded courtyard. Portable toilets, at the request of the hijackers, had been placed in the courtyard, along with trestle tables for food. He did not see food, only empty containers and a number of pizza boxes. The canvas wall blocked the goings-on from ground view. But anyone prepared to climb a hill, as Jeff and Reason had done, had a clear view of the hijackers' inner sanctum. Jeff gave the hijackers a begrudging grunt of respect.

He said to Reason, "Whoever is in charge of this has thought of everything. What I still can't get a grip on is why are they taking so much time? They could have made the border from Istanbul in a day. Why spread it out over three?"

"That has puzzled me as well," Reason said. "All I can think of is that they are using the press to build world pressure. Maybe The Sheriff was fully aware the Turkish government would never allow the bus to cross the border."

"That makes sense. Whether or not it works is another issue."

At least Barry and Bethany were being fed. And for now they were safe. But how long would that last? The next stop was the town of Mardin and that was only a few kilometres from the border. Less than twenty minutes, Reason had said. She also said the Turks would not allow the bus to cross. He had little hope the government would soften its stance. Politicians were politicians. When it came to making a tough stand with other people's blood they were always heroic. He clung to the fragile lifeline that, because the American consul's daughter was a hostage, the Americans would muscle up on the Turkish government and make sure they didn't do anything stupid. And he did not believe for one moment the Turkish military would be swayed by world opinion. He had less than twenty-four hours to attempt a rescue.

❧

As Jeff and Reason walked back to the hotel, Jeff gave thought to their sleeping arrangements. He was about to share a room with a beautiful woman, an interesting woman. As yet, she had not shown him any come-ons, and had not led him to believe they were anything more than soldiers fighting side by side in the same battle. He and Reason had experienced combat together, and in the military, after the shooting was done, soldiers would find the nearest bar, have a few drinks and bond. He had a feeling that Reason was not the boozing or the bonding type. For all they had shared, they were still strangers. But they were also adults, and different sexes, and about to spend the night together.

Reason pointed to a restaurant on the other side of a small foot-bridge. Halfway across she held on to the wrought-iron railing and looked into what appeared to be a storm drain. There was no rushing torrent that Jeff could see. He stood beside her.

"It is very pretty, don't you think?" she said without looking at him.

"Yes, it is," Jeff said, though he didn't really mean it. It was an empty drain. He looked at her and found she wasn't looking at the drain but along the street and up the hill. Evening had come. As lights turned on, the village brightened and neon signage above the cafés and restaurants added sparkle. They moved on across the bridge and stopped on the pavement outside the restaurant. The aroma of spices and roasting kebabs wafted through the open door of the eatery.

"I'm hungry. Will you buy me dinner?" Reason asked.

Jeff said, "Anything you want."

Through the window, the restaurant looked full. He stretched to look over diners' heads and spot a spare table. He hesitated, and fixed on a spot on the glass. In the window's reflection, he caught sight of a man standing in the doorway behind him. There was no mistaking the man was watching him. Jeff scratched the back of his head, and as he did he looked left and right. He spotted a second man further up the street. In the SAS, he had been trained to spot a tail. These guys were amateurs, and easy to spot.

He then gave consideration to an obvious alternative: maybe they weren't trying to hide.

"We're being followed," Jeff said, without turning towards Reason. "No prize for guessing who by. If nothing else, Marius is persistent."

"What do you want to do?"

"I want you to go back to the hotel. They have no interest in you. Order room service and if they have a bathtub, have a relaxing bath. Get some sleep. Tomorrow we have a big day. It's a long drive to Mardin."

"You're kidding, right?"

"Not at all," Jeff said. "Look, Reason, I know you're more than competent and can hold your own. I've seen you at work. But my gut tells me Marius has arrived with enough men to overwhelm me. This time he is taking no chances. Good tactics on his part. The only way to overcome those odds is for me to keep moving. This is a small town, but it has lots of narrow streets and alleys and lots of hideouts, especially in the cave houses. Two of us looking out for each other will have no chance."

Reason eyed Jeff. "I can't give you my weapon. Agents don't hand over their firearms. Not to anyone."

Jeff tapped his side. "I have the gun from the warehouse, and an extra magazine. Now, let's walk. At the next corner, we say goodbye. I'll catch you back at the hotel. And don't use my towel."

Reason stopped. Jeff frowned. "We need to keep moving, Reason."

Reason said, "Jeff, this place is full of police and military, and I'd say, right now, they're trigger-happy. If there is a shootout, they will be over you like a swarm of locusts."

"What do you want me to do? Roll over and let them kill me?"

"No, but remember why we are here. We have a busload of hostages to rescue, and you can't do that as a dead man. We could give them the slip. Stay out of sight until morning. You said yourself there are plenty of hiding places. The bus will be on the move again, and so will we be."

"This is not a big town, Reason. Sooner or later, the hiding places would be found."

They walked the next thirty metres in silence. At the corner, Reason slowed, while Jeff kept walking. Without turning, he raised his hand as a farewell wave, and continued on. He did not want the men following to believe he and Reason were anything other than acquaintances.

Right now, he knew Reason would be struggling with having walked away. She was as much a warrior as he was. And no warrior would ever leave their comrade. In the SAS he wouldn't do it. He'd sooner cut off his leg. Would he have left her behind if he was in her shoes? No, he wouldn't have.

The men Marius had tailing him looked Turkish. He would have hired them in Istanbul. The Turks were an unknown quantity but, if they were like the men from the café, not competent. In the end, this might give him a slight edge. If Marius acted the same as he did during the café shooting he would stay back. Jeff had no doubt the Italian was copping flak from whoever had hired him to make the kill. The fear of failure was driving his persistence. In Marius's world, failure led to a shallow grave in a forest, or a weight tied round the ankles before being dumped in the ocean.

Two men were in front of him now, and two behind. They were keeping their distance. He couldn't see Marius anywhere. Had he sent the gunmen on their own to do his dirty work and stayed back in Istanbul? The paved streets had filled. Tourists and locals mingled with the media and government officials and police and military personnel. Reason was right: a gunfight in the open was out of the question. He needed to draw them into an environment that gave him an edge or at least balanced the odds.

Marius stepped out of the shadows.

CHAPTER TWENTY-EIGHT

Marius watched as his Turkish hoodlums moved into position. Finding Jeff Bradley's hotel as quickly as they had he had put down to luck. The cop at the roadblock had been only too willing to give news of a taxi transporting an American woman and a New Zealander. He knew the hotel they were staying at and gave easy-to-follow instructions. Marius had gladly given over two hundred euros for the information. He considered the cop greedy, but what the hell.

At first, the hotel manager was deliberately vague, and said he did not know the couple.

"Goreme is a busy town. There are many guests and the hotel is full," the manager had said.

One of the Turkish gunmen had shoved his pistol into the manager's ribs. He immediately told them Bradley and the woman had gone sightseeing. Marius told his men to spread out and wait. He would signal when he saw Bradley and the woman return. Why had Bradley come to Goreme? It puzzled Marius. Was he connected in some way to the hijacked bus? Should he inform Gashi? What did it matter? Tonight the New Zealander would be dead and his secret could die with him. Then Marius would return to Italy and relate the details of how he had hunted his prey and killed him to his boss, Pietro Gallo. Of course, he would talk to him by phone first. He would be able to tell by his boss's tone if all was forgiven. If the danger was still there, he would run. Go to another country. He had money stashed in offshore bank accounts. Enough money to ensure he never need return to Italy.

Jeff kept walking. Each step brought the assassins closer. The net was closing and his options for survival lessening. With the bus in town, the streets had a heavy police and military presence. Curious locals, buoyed by the excitement of the occasion and unconcerned for their safety – they could see on the television the hijackers were surrounded and did not pose a threat – had poured out of their apartments and blended in with tourists and media. The business people, especially the restaurateurs, were not about to miss out on the opportunity to cash in on the unexpected out-of-season bonanza. Goreme was bustling with activity.

Jeff was confident Marius and his men would not fire their weapons in front of so many spectators. The cops and military were armed. Jeff tossed about a variety of offensive scenarios in his head. He rounded a corner, and saw the perfect site to make his stand. A hotel built into one of the upright caves.

From where he stood he could see it had a roof terrace. Did it have an easily accessed stairway or was a guest key needed? He had little choice but to take the risk. Once inside the hotel there was no turning back. Marius and his men would have him trapped. He estimated the height of the building to be at least three storeys, maybe four. As he made his way to the hotel, he used the reflections in store windows to keep track of his pursuers. Thirty metres from the hotel, he turned and caught the eye of the closest of Marius's gunmen. He feigned nervousness and increased his walking pace. As he neared the entrance one of his pursuers drew his handgun and aimed. Alarmed, Jeff ran for the hotel entrance.

A helicopter passed overhead. Surrounding heads turned upwards. As Jeff jumped on to the first step of the stairs leading to the hotel entrance a bullet splintered a wooden sign screwed into the block wall.

"Bloody hell!"

A shot. And a miss. The miss did not surprise him. Hitting a moving target in dim light from a distance was not likely to happen unless the shooter was a marksman. He gambled that Marius's hired guns were not sharpshooters. The helicopter had drowned the noise of the shot. No one near him looked startled. No one gave the gunman a second glance. It had surprised him Marius's man had fired. Now it was clear. Marius wanted him dead, and it didn't matter how it was done, as long as by the night's end his bloodied body lay in a heap.

Jeff had avoided drawing his own weapon. He needed Marius's men to believe he was unarmed. His plan depended on it. He stepped into the foyer and eyed the desk. Reception was busy attending to a queue of a dozen guests. Unnoticed, he ambled across the grey slate floor in a relaxed manner so as not to attract attention. Nice hotel, he observed. It was more up-market than the one he and Reason had booked into. An arrow at the bottom of the stairwell pointed up. A sign in English read, TO THE ROOF, HOTEL GUESTS ONLY. Jeff waited on the bottom step until one of Marius's men entered. The pursuer blinked when he saw Jeff watching him.

Jeff turned and ran up the stairs.

❧

Marius joined his men at the bottom of the stairwell.

"It goes to the roof balcony," one of the men said.

Marius looked up. The stairwell had been carved out of rock. There was no way he could see all the way to the top. It was like looking into a spiralling cave. Bradley could be waiting round any bend with a gun in his hand. He glared at his hired men.

"What are you waiting for? Get after him," Marius said.

"What if he is armed?" one of the men said. "We would have no chance."

Marius turned to their appointed leader, who had advanced up the stairwell a few metres to peer round the next bend. He returned to the second step.

"What do you think?" Marius asked.

"He saw me draw my gun and aim. He reached into his pocket, I think for a weapon, but his hand came out empty. A little panic set in and he ran for the hotel door. I think that he is not armed. But I cannot say for certain. We have him trapped. The stairs are the only way out. We can wait him out. It is much better to do it this way."

Marius shook his head. "No. Waiting is out of the question. The hotel staff will grow suspicious. What if they call the police? Then he will have an escort to safety." The six men had gathered round him. Marius pointed to two in the rear. "You two go outside and keep watch. There might be another way out, and if any police walk this way, come and warn us."

The two men nodded.

"Now, the rest of you get up the stairs. I will be right behind."

He saw the hesitant looks. No one wanted to be first into a potential tunnel of death, even if the man they were trying to kill did not have a firearm. Marius did not trust that Bradley had no weapon. If nothing else, the New Zealander had proved resourceful on a number of occasions. If Bradley did have a weapon, in the stairwell, even with his eyes closed, he couldn't miss.

"I'm paying you guys, remember. And there is a bonus in it for you. I will double the payment to the man who fires the fatal shot. Now, do your job."

❧

At the top of the stairwell was a steel door that opened inward. When Jeff stepped through the doorway, he pulled the door closed. An advantage to him. Whoever opened the door could not do so without being fully exposed. If they thought he was armed it would make them hesitate.

The owners of the hotel had utilised all the roof area for their balcony garden restaurant. It would be a popular spot in summer, especially with tourists. The rooftop offered a panoramic view of Goreme and the brightness of the city's lights allowed him to see all the way to the main highway and back to the surrounding white hills. Off-white and cream homes constructed of tufa blocks stood amidst the giant toadstool cave hotels and retail stores and restaurants.

In one corner of the terrace, there was permanent overhead cover and, to provide extra shade through the summer months, canvas awnings. The awnings, now rolled up, hung from walls, ties holding the rolls in place. In the heat of the day, the awnings could be stretched across the exposed area to hooks on poles embedded in the cement surface. An ornate wrought-iron safety railing encircled the rooftop. A stack of tables and chairs stood in the corner next to the bar. Behind the bar was a small fridge. Jeff opened the fridge door, looking for anything he might use as a weapon instead of his gun. The fridge was empty.

Marius and his men would be making their way up the stairwell. He ran to the railing and looked down into the street. Two men were shuffling about a few metres in front of the entrance. Even in a crowd of pedestrians, they looked like men up to no good. It was obvious they were Marius's lookouts. Good. It was two fewer gunmen for him to worry about.

He made another check of his surroundings. There was nowhere to hide. He took note of how high up the terrace rooftop was. If a gun battle took place, the gunfire would be heard at a distance and the gun flashes easily seen; they would quickly be targeted by the military and the police. He needed to keep the fight undercover. Any police or military involvement and they would all be arrested and thrown in a cell until the hostage crisis was over, and that would not help him save Barry and Bethany. If he tried to shoot it out in the stairwell, the fight would end in a stalemate. The gunmen could stay where they were and he would be trapped on the rooftop. Eventually, the hotel manager would call the police. And a foreigner with a gun would have a lot of explaining to do, especially if there were bodies. This needed to be over, and quick, and without shooting anyone if possible.

The noise of men coming up the stairs alerted him. They would argue about who should go first. The local hoods weren't going to get themselves killed over a few bucks. Jeff had little doubt if Marius was with them he had taken up a position behind them and was not leading from the front. He had a minute at most.

An image sprang into Jeff's head.

His would-be killers would be lined in single file. The stairwell was too narrow for two men on a step. He took another quick check of his surroundings. His eyes narrowed on the half-fridge. He dashed to the bar and pulled the fridge out from under the bench. It was light-ish. He grasped hold of two corners and tried to lift it. He easily raised it above his waist. He jostled it until he held it firmly, then stepped back into the centre of the terrace.

Satisfied he had the perfect weapon, he readied himself.

The doorknob turned to the right. A faint click as the lock released. A gap appeared as the door was carefully pulled back. That was the signal. Jeff, holding the fridge to his chest, charged at the door and smashed against the metal panel. It swung on its hinges, and crashed back. A cry of pain came from the man behind the door as his head slammed back against the stone wall. He crumpled to the ground like a bundle of wet laundry. Jeff stomped his legs, the extra force driving his body forward as he rammed the fridge against the line of men; they fell like pins in a bowling alley. He ran over the top of the first three and then Marius was in front of him. The last man had stumbled backwards against the Italian gangster as he was raising his weapon. Marius was knocked off balance, and they both fell on to the stairs. Marius was pinned by the man on top of him. He looked up at Jeff. Eyes wide open. Jeff smashed the fridge on to Marius's head. Marius grunted, eyes clouded over with fear. His head rolled to the side, dark blood pumping from the gash on his temple and running down his face.

Jeff pulled his handgun from his pocket and spun round to movement behind him. Without taking his eyes off the downed gunmen, Jeff reached across and placed two fingers on Marius's neck. There was no pulse.

The man who had been close behind the door and borne the brunt of the impact when Jeff smashed it open had recovered enough to be searching for his dropped weapon. Jeff stepped back from Marius and aimed his handgun. The assassin reached for his pistol and managed to wrap his fingers round the grip.

"Don't," Jeff ordered. His gun aimed at the man's forehead. The man stopped moving, his weapon halted halfway to targeting Jeff. Eyes widened as they focussed on the barrel of Jeff's pistol. "Do you speak English?" Jeff asked.

The man nodded.

"Your boss is dead. Has he already paid you for this job?"

The gunman nodded. Nervous. His eyes danced about, looking for an escape. Deciding there was none, he refocussed on survival. Beads of sweat formed on his brow. He licked his lips. Death was a fraction of a second away. Jeff's knuckle whitened on the trigger.

The gunman's chin jutted out. Eyes narrowed. Jeff read the sign. The asshole was going to try to beat him to the draw. He sighed and held up his free hand, waggling his index finger. "Do not be an idiot.

Drop the gun," Jeff said. "You have your money. That means no more money for you and your friends no matter what happens from here on. Your boss is dead, so what happens doesn't matter, does it? Do you understand?"

The man nodded, and let the gun fall from his fingers.

"Good. Do you want to die tonight, or are you happy to call it quits?" Jeff said.

The man said, "You will have no more trouble from us."

"I'm leaving now. If you follow, I will kill you," Jeff said, his voice steady.

The man responded with a slow nod.

Jeff, keeping his pistol trained on Marius's men, backed away. He needn't have worried. No one moved. Once round the bend and the gunmen gone from sight he made his way down to the foyer. He wiped the gun clean of prints, and placed it on the last step. If there were police outside, now was not a time to be stopped and searched. He no longer needed to worry about Marius. The Italian assassin was gone, but that did not mean it was over. Leka would send someone else.

The hotel management paid him no heed as he made his way towards them. The rock walls must have muffled the sounds.

"There are men in the stairwell with guns," he said. The blonde behind the desk looked confused. "I think one of them is dead. You'd better call the police."

The startled concierge standing next to the blonde peered across the top of his glasses. Not believing.

"Men with guns," Jeff repeated. "Call the police."

The concierge, with one eye on the stairwell, reached for the phone. Jeff turned away. A couple stepped through the door ahead of him and he followed after them, keeping close behind. As he walked past Marius's two sentries, they scrutinised him and frowned. They looked at each other and back at the hotel. When Jeff glanced over his shoulder they had entered. Sirens could be heard, and as he entered the street of his hotel a flashing light swept past.

Someone emerged from the shadows a few metres in front of him. Reason fell into step beside him as he walked past.

"I see you didn't go to the hotel," Jeff said.

"I thought I'd better hang about. Just in case. Any bodies?"

"Only Marius. I'm hungry," Jeff said. "How about you?"

Reason nodded.

Jeff said, "I need a shower and you want a shower, and we both need to relax for a bit. I think we order room service. How does that sound to you?"

Reason shrugged. "Why not?"

CHAPTER TWENTY-NINE

Sulla drove into Flag Square, the main plaza of the Albanian port city of Vlore. His brother-in-law, Blerim Basholli, was standing next to a knee-high hedgerow that fringed the mosque. Sulla had flown to Tirana, the Albanian capital, collected the car Blerim had organised for him and driven the coast road to Vlore. The trip had taken too long. It was early evening. Blerim had been in Vlore for the day. Sulla hoped he had news of Osman Gashi and his busload of illegal immigrants.

Blerim crossed the road to meet him.

"Have you seen Gashi and his people?" Sulla asked, as he locked the car.

"Yes, they left an hour ago."

Sulla's shoulders slumped. He spread his hands and leaned on the bonnet of the car.

Blerim patted Sulla on the back. "Do not be downcast, my brother, we are not too late. They have three boats. Fast boats, but not as fast as my boat. First, they will go to Sazan Island. It is about half an hour into the Adriatic Sea in my speedboat. For them, maybe it takes longer. Italian naval vessels and planes patrol the Adriatic, especially between

Sazan and the Apulian Peninsula. This is the main smuggling route to Italy from Vlore."

Sulla nodded. His brother-in-law should know what he was talking about; he was one of the major smugglers. At first, it had upset Sulla when he learned heroin, cocaine and other shit drugs were fed into Europe through Vlore, but Blerim swore his men never touched drugs. Sulla had not believed him and had him investigated. To his relief, he found out it was true. What it was Blerim smuggled, he wasn't certain. Cigarettes were once high on the list, and commodity stolen goods like cooking oils and sugars that he could turn a quick profit on in Kosovo. Sulla didn't care what the goods were as long as they weren't drugs. During the Yugoslav and later the Kosovan war, Blerim had traded weapons, but this market had dried up when the war finished. Besides, he was only interested in bringing goods into Kosovo, not taking them out. Sulla had heard most of the high-quality perfumes and make-up on Kosovan retail shelves came via Blerim.

Blerim said, "Gashi and his men will wait behind the island until they have an all-clear and are certain the Italian navy is not about. We have time. You said there were more than one hundred people on the buses."

"Yes, give or take ten or twenty."

"They will need to do two trips. If we miss them tonight, we can catch them tomorrow. This is good, yes?"

"No, Blerim, it is not good, we might not have that much time. The hostages will arrive in Mardin tomorrow. This town is only a few kilometres to the Iraqi and Syrian borders. It has to be tonight that we find Gashi. I need him to lead me to Avni Leka. Now, where is this boat of yours?" Sulla asked.

"Leave the car. I will drive us to the port. The boat is moored there."

"The car will be safe?"

Blerim laughed.

"Look at the rust. It needs paint. The tyres are worn. This car is a heap of shit, Sulla. Who will steal it? There are much better cars."

Sulla had not been in the resort town for years. In June and July, the promenade and beaches bustled with holiday-makers and the restaurants and nightclubs partied into the night, but right now the chill air had sent everyone off to the warmth of their homes, and the streets were empty.

Blerim parked near the port gates. Not really a port, in Sulla's opinion. It comprised a single jetty, and he doubted there was enough room for two or three small ships. He followed Blerim along the shoreline. Anchored boats rocked back and forth as small waves rushed past them. Blerim pointed into the bay.

"It is the one with the white hull."

Sulla squinted into the dark. A street light gave some illumination. "I see it."

"A twenty-seven footer, and all the luxuries needed to travel in style. It is very nice on board. Most important for you, it has 450 horsepower; more than enough to catch up to Gashi's boats. You know what Gashi is like. Caution will lose out to greed every time. He will have overloaded his boats with people. Too much weight will slow them."

Sulla scratched at his day-old stubble.

Blerim led Sulla along the shoreline for fifty metres before scrambling down the embankment. They strode across the sandy surface to a rowboat sitting in a foot of water and held steady by one of Blerim's men. The three pushed it out into knee-high water and climbed in. A short row and they were alongside Blerim's speedboat.

"You own this boat?" Sulla asked, as they climbed aboard.

Blerim nodded.

"Smuggling must pay well; I think that is an expensive boat."

"Yes it is, and if I ever meet the owner I will negotiate a price. In the meantime, I think we can say it is borrowed. Come on, let's get under way."

"We're gaining."

They had closed the gap. Sulla could clearly see Osman Gashi's giant frame. From this distance, he could shoot him and be done with it. He would like that very much. But Jeff wanted him alive, and that was all that would save the Balkan crime lord on this day. But Sulla might need to control Blerim. Gashi had murdered Blerim's father. Blerim had already forfeited an opportunity to avenge his father's death not so long ago, when Jeff needed to keep Gashi alive. And now here they were, crossing paths again, and Sulla knew it would be difficult to calm his brother-in-law a second time.

"More throttle, Blerim," Sulla yelled.

"That's it, all we've got, but we will catch him, don't worry. The Adriatic Sea is very big and there is nowhere to hide," Blerim shouted back.

Blerim had mounted a floodlight on the cabin roof. Sulla kept it trained on Gashi as Blerim steered. What puzzled Sulla was why Gashi was on the boat at all. It was not like him to take such risks. He had men to do the dying and the going to jail for him. He paid them well, and they were loyal; they all knew the consequences of betrayal and failure. A lack of mercy was behind Gashi's criminal success. The loyalty his men showed was whether they liked it or not. And, Sulla knew, in a country like Kosovo, where there was eighty per cent unemployment, well-paid jobs, even if illegal, had a queue waiting to take them on.

Gashi's three boats had been side by side, but now two slowed. Gashi's boat moved ahead of them. The two rear boats split: one to starboard and the other to port.

Sulla yelled to Blerim, "Gashi has no idea it is us after him. He thinks we are the police, and that, by splitting, he will make the police chase one of the other boats."

They closed to within fifty metres. Blerim pulled out his gun.

Sulla tapped him on the shoulder. "Remember, we need him alive."

Gashi threw bundles of rags into the water.

Blerim said, "Look at that: he is lightening his boat by dumping the possessions of the immigrants. This will not work."

Another bundle brought a reaction from an immigrant. Sulla watched as a man rushed at Gashi. Then gunshots. The man fell from sight. "He shot one of the migrants."

Two more shots were fired.

Sulla bit at the inside of his cheek. "Something is wrong." He squinted into the darkness. "There." He pointed and swung the lamp round until he found a bundle of rags. It was splashing. "It is a child!" Sulla screamed. "He's throwing the children overboard."

Blerim twisted to look at Sulla. Horrified. "Are you sure?"

Sulla pointed to where the beam of his searchlight was directed. Blerim saw the movement. "I'm sorry, Sulla, but we can't leave the children to drown."

Sulla tightened his lips. He turned away and kicked at the wall of the boat. He turned the light one last time on to Osman Gashi. The big man had moved to the stern. He waved. Sulla turned the light away to search for the children. Gashi's boats disappeared into the darkness. A defeated Sulla opened his phone to send Jeff a text. No signal. He would have to wait until they returned to Vlore. He had failed Jeff. Without the information to find Leka, the last opportunity for Jeff to save the hostages was gone.

CHAPTER THIRTY

A knocking on the door woke Jeff. He flung his legs over the side of the bed and stumbled across the room. He pulled the door open. It was Fati. The cabbie pointed at the watch on his wrist. Jeff took hold of Fati's arm and turned it towards him.

"It's only six-thirty," Jeff said.

"We need to leave by seven-thirty. It will take the whole day to get to Mardin. We must be on the road before the bus. If it leaves first we will never be allowed to overtake it."

"Okay, Fati, we will meet you downstairs before seven-thirty."

Jeff closed the door. Reason was sitting up in bed.

"Good morning," Jeff said. Reason lifted her hand in response. "Fati says we need to be on the road early. It is going to be a long drive."

"I heard," Reason said, not fully awake.

She peered at him through half-closed eyes, entangled hair falling around soft features. She looked alluring and vulnerable at the same time, and not the strong, capable woman of the last few days. If he said what he thought out loud, she would probably leap from the bed and toss him out the window. But they had spent the night together. Not intimately, but the dynamic between the two of them had changed; at least in his mind it had. He found her appealing; more than that, if he was honest.

Jeff said, "Why don't I take a walk for twenty minutes and you can use the bathroom, get yourself organised? When you've finished, I'll do my ablutions and we can eat."

"Thank you, Jeff. I'd appreciate some time alone."

૭૦

The hotel breakfast was a smorgasbord of cold meats, cheeses, fresh buns and plates of Turkish traditional dishes that Jeff did not recognise. He would have liked an English breakfast; in his mind, nothing was as good as bacon and eggs, but the cold dishes filled a hole. And Reason, freshly showered, agreed the coffee was drinkable. She ordered a second cup. Jeff shook his head when the waiter looked his way.

The previous evening had been a pleasant distraction. When Jeff and Reason made it back to their hotel they had showered, and while Reason used the bathroom, Jeff ordered food and wine brought to the room. They sat on the floor. Reason, clothed in a T-shirt and shorts, looked as sexy as hell. Only a thin layer of cotton had covered her toned nakedness, and the aroma of her perfume heightened the sexual tension. He had wanted to hold her, and she was less than an arm's length away. Would Reason resist? Relaxed, her attitude towards him had softened. It was a natural reaction. The excitement and thrills and fear experienced through conflict were life-changing, and shared with another often formed the foundation of a lasting camaraderie. For a man and a woman, the ordeal might lead to intimacy between strangers.

They had agreed not to discuss business while they ate dinner. The events unravelling around them were out of their control, and the frustration borne of bashing their heads against an immovable political stance needed to be put to one side. Reason had laughed at Jeff's stories of his struggle to establish his vineyard, and she had told him of her training as a Hollywood stuntwoman and some of the stunts she had performed. While Jeff thought he had been open about life and life experiences, after an evening of chat Reason had not revealed anything truly personal about herself. Not that it mattered. Whatever she told him was her choice, and beyond that it was none of his business. When she laughed, she touched his arm. He liked her touch. The wine had loosened their moods. Once or twice, their eyes met and held a fraction longer than would happen between friends. Jeff sensed Reason would not resist if he leaned across and kissed her.

But the photo on the laptop in her hotel room was an unassailable barrier. Reason had a family. Danger and circumstance had brought them together, but the moment would pass and it would be unfair of him to take advantage and have Reason regret it later.

Across the breakfast table, as if reading his mind, Reason said, "You were the perfect gentleman last night, Jeff. By choice, or do you not find me attractive?"

Jeff raised an eyebrow.

"What can I say?" she said, teasing. "I'm a woman. We're sensitive."

"Okay, fair enough. In your hotel room in Istanbul I saw the photo on your laptop. Call me old-fashioned, but married women are off-limits. However, for the record, I find you very attractive."

Reason looked down into her coffee. She fiddled with the ring on her right hand. On the wrong finger and the wrong hand, but from Jeff's observation the ring was a wedding band. When she glanced up her eyes were moist.

"My family – my husband, my two beautiful children – are dead, Jeff. Killed, two years ago."

Jeff remained still.

"I am so sorry, Reason."

He was about to ask her what happened, but waited; if Reason wanted, she would elaborate.

"You can't have known, but it's something I have learned to live with. I have moved on. It was either that or go insane or do something silly, like try to join them."

Jeff opened and closed his mouth, uncertain how to respond. His phone bleeped. He tilted the screen until he could read the sender's name. He glanced across at Reason.

"It's from Sulla."

Reason nodded. "Go ahead and read it. I'm okay, really."

Jeff gave the text a quick scan. His lips tightened, and he shook his head. "Damn it." He looked up at Reason. "Osman Gashi escaped."

"Then it's the end of the line, I guess?"

"Yes, it is. I've run out of options."

Reason glanced at the television over the café bar and behind Jeff. "The bus is about to move again."

Jeff looked back over his shoulder. The TV showed that the canvas was down. Jeff swung back to Reason. Her eyes had cleared. The moment between them was gone and it was back to the business at hand. He would ask about her family another time.

He gulped the last of his coffee.

"We need to leave. Fati will be waiting."

"I'm eating."

"It's a bun. Bring it with you."

CHAPTER THIRTY-ONE

F ati sped down the sloping lanes and on to the main road out of Goreme. Traffic was heavy, and after a hundred metres it had ground to a halt. Like the other motorists, Fati beeped his horn at no one. The bend in the road prevented Jeff from seeing whatever it was that was causing the hold-up. To the right, in a small field, a man stood beside a box selling motor oils and hubcaps. Near the seller was an inflated hot air balloon. The wicker passenger basket was pegged to the ground to stop it rising. The balloonist was inside the basket operating the propane burners to keep the balloon filled. The giant, brightly coloured balloon swayed back and forth in the breeze. A banner hung down over the front of the basket.

"What's that all about, Fati?"

"Goreme is very famous for hot air ballooning. The press is here. The balloonist is getting free publicity. On the banner is his company name and phone number."

"Good for him. With the traffic going nowhere, he now has the fastest mode of transport in town. Something is up," Jeff said, stating the obvious. "I'm going to have a look."

"I'm coming with you," Reason said.

Jeff opened his bag and pulled out the binoculars. When they reached the corner at the top of the slope they could see a roadblock was in place a half-mile before the hostage bus encampment. Military vehicles sat parked across the road. Jeff raised his field glasses.

"The bus hasn't moved," he said to Reason. "And the tarpaulin is back in place."

Two military officers stood beside the bus speaking to one of the hijackers in the shadows of the canvas wall. The military men waved their hands about. One of them placed his hands on his hips and shook his head. He kicked at a rock. The second officer pointed to the shadows like he was stabbing holes in the air. They both turned and stomped off.

Jeff lowered the field glasses.

"I have no idea what the hell the soldiers and the hijackers were talking about, but whatever it was, the soldiers are not happy. With the cover back up, my assessment is, I don't think that bus is going anywhere, and nor is this traffic. There is another roadblock further ahead. More armoured vehicles. The road is blocked both sides."

He passed the binoculars to Reason.

"I hope what appears to be happening is not happening," Jeff said.

Reason looked across at him. "You mean, have the Turkish government drawn a line in the sand?"

"Looks like it. I have a feeling this is the end of the journey for the bus."

Reason said, "Two army trucks are circling the bus dropping poles and giant bags of something. Soldiers have run forward and are opening the bags. It looks like more canvas. Huge rolls of it. Now we have soldiers picking up the poles and one of them has a handheld post-hole borer. I'd say they're building a screen round the bus to block it from the media."

"Do you still think the Turks will blow it up?" he asked.

"I don't know," Reason said, scanning the activity with Jeff's binoculars before passing them back. "I don't know if they will blow it up.

Not yet anyway, not with their soldiers so close, and not with those military officers standing next to it. My fear right now is The Sheriff and his men will blow it."

"I say that won't happen, not yet at any rate. That will be an act of last resort. I think it will only happen if the army attack the bus and attempt a rescue."

For the next hour, they watched as the Turkish soldiers encircled the bus with a canvas wall. Portable toilets were brought back and smaller trucks offloaded trays of food. When the wall was complete, all activity within the enclosure was gone from sight.

"The soldiers have set themselves up inside the compound. A discussion could be taking place with the hijackers," Reason said. "It could be a negotiation to hand over the hostages," she added, hopefully.

"Or it might be the soldiers are about to blow the bus themselves and don't want the public or media to see," Jeff said. "There are many ways a government might choose to bring an end to a crisis, and one of them is to bring it to an explosive end no matter how many innocents are killed. I've experienced it first-hand." Reason gave Jeff a sideways glance. He caught the quizzical look. An explanation could wait. "A blown bus now, without anyone able to see, will ensure it's blamed on the hijackers. The military could be setting their own explosive charges along the side of the bus as we speak."

"I hope you're wrong, Jeff, for all our sakes. I want The Sheriff. He is no good to me dead."

"Can I ask what is so important to you about . . . Hold on a minute."

Jeff had had the binoculars fixed on an area in the hills south of the encampment.

"On the hills in the distance I'm watching a vehicle, a type of military jeep. The vehicle has stopped. The terrain is too steep." Jeff paused, still watching. "Two men are climbing the slope on foot, and one of them is carrying something over his shoulder. I can't make out what it is. It's covered with a cloth. The other guy is holding on to what looks like a packing case of some type. Something tells me this picture is not right."

"Not right how?"

"I don't know."

"You are not becoming just a touch paranoid?"

"Absolutely I am. I was trained to be paranoid. I work on the basis that everyone is an enemy until proven otherwise, and right now two men climbing a hill carrying something hidden has piqued my interest."

"Jeff, if you can see them, the military can see them."

"Maybe not. We are higher up, and these guys are behind a ridge."

"Not for long," Reason said. "A helicopter is swooping in their direction."

Jeff raised his glasses. "I can't see them now." He watched as the chopper passed over where the men had been and continued on before banking away. He brought his glasses back up. "There they are. They were hiding. I have no idea what they're up to, but whatever it is, they don't want the authorities to see them."

"Or they could be goat hunters and they are carrying hunting equipment."

"Hunting is illegal in Turkey," Jeff said.

"And that will be why they hid when the helicopter came their way."

"Whatever is under that cloth is not a rifle." He looked through the glasses again. "The men look military. Neatly trimmed hair. Tidy clothes. I can't quite make out the faces, but I'll bet they shaved this morning."

"Now you've gone loco."

Jeff shook his head. "You said it yourself. The Turks might draw a line in the sand."

"Yes, I did say that, but there is still a long way to go to the border. The next stop is Mardin. A lot can happen between now and then."

"I haven't been to Mardin," Jeff said. "But it's the Mesopotamian Plains all the way to a number of borders. Take your pick: Syria, Iraq, Iran. There is nowhere to set an ambush. This is the last ideal spot. I think if they are going to blow the bus, now is the time. Besides, Mardin has a Kurdish population. I think a car bomb blew up a police station there a few days ago. No, Mardin is not the place for the Turks to bring this to an end."

Reason nodded. Thoughtful.

Jeff said, "They've stopped climbing. Whatever it is they are carrying is now laid on the ground. And off come the covers. Fuck." He lowered the binoculars. "They've got a Javelin anti-tank missile. An FGM-148 Javelin to be exact."

"How can you be so sure?"

"I trained on one. The Javelin launch tube is a metre long and exactly the shape of the tube these guys are holding. It can be fired off the shoulder. Besides, these are the most advanced anti-tank weapons. There is nothing else like them. Anyone who has ever used one would recognise it right off. They have a Javelin – trust me on this – and that means the day is about to turn to shit."

"Aren't they too far away?" Reason asked. "If they are going to hit the bus, won't they have to get closer? I've seen a few RPGs fired from a few hundred metres and none ever hit the target."

"These things have an infrared guidance system. Lock it on the target, pull the trigger and off it goes. It won't miss. And I'll bet the other guy has an extra missile. That is what will be in the container he is carrying, but they won't need it. One will be enough unless the first malfunctions. It happens."

"The big question is, who are they?" Reason asked.

"I would have said the Turkish military. But the soldiers down in the camp have had plenty of time to clear out and they haven't." Jeff checked the encampment again with his binoculars. "They are still blabbering away down there." He switched back to the men on the hill. "They're setting up to fire. We need to warn the soldiers."

"It's too far away," Reason said. "We can't drive it."

He scanned the surroundings. "No cops or soldiers about." His eyes set on the balloon. "Follow me."

Jeff ran down the slope and weaved his way between the cars, Reason at his heels. Fati followed when he saw them rush past his vehicle.

∾

Jeff ran on to the field. The balloonist was now standing beside the basket. Jeff stood in front of him and pointed to the sky. "I need to get up there."

The balloonist looked at him. A blank look. Fati was now beside Jeff.

"Tell him I need his balloon. I need to get in the air right now."

Fati spoke in Turkish.

"What's the idea, Jeff?" Reason asked. "How is a balloon ride going to help? What are you planning to do – zoom across the sky and jump out on to these guys? It's a balloon, Jeff. They don't zoom."

"He said it is not allowed to take the balloon in the air," Fati explained to Jeff. "No aircraft in the sky. This is the order from the military."

"I know this," Jeff said. He turned to Reason. "I only want to get high enough to attract that military helicopter circling the bus. It has missiles. If I can point them in the right direction they could fire a missile and blast those two men to hell."

Reason nodded agreement. "Sounds like a plan to me."

Jeff said to Fati, "Tell him once that's done, we will turn the balloon around and head back home."

"They can't turn around, Jeff," Reason said. "A vehicle follows below, and when the balloon lands, wherever that might be, the vehicle drives you back, to the hotel normally."

"You've done this before?" Jeff asked.

"Of course I have, I'm an ex-stuntwoman, remember; we have to give everything a go. I can't believe you haven't. Aren't you an adventure man? I would have thought a hot air balloon ride might have been top of the list."

"I'm not good with heights."

"You were in the Special Forces. Didn't you have to do parachute jumps?"

"Yes, but I didn't like doing them."

Reason put her hand on his shoulder. "Don't worry, cowboy. It's a safe way to travel."

"Fati," Jeff said as he bent down and pulled up one of the pegs anchoring the basket. "Tell him I am taking this balloon with or without him. Bad men are about to blow the hostage bus and I need to stop them."

"He says he will call the police," Fati said.

"I don't care," Jeff said as he pulled the next peg. Reason climbed into the basket. "Where the hell do you think you're going?"

"Where you go, I go. Besides, those men in the helicopter might decide you are the enemy and want to shoot you down. A lady on board might cause them to hesitate."

"Good point," Jeff said as he pulled the third peg.

The balloon now lifted the basket on its end. The balloonist shouted at Jeff and then climbed aboard.

"He said it is his balloon and only he will fly it," Fati yelled.

Jeff looked at the balloonist. "Good man." Jeff pulled himself into the basket. "Fati, take that last peg out."

Fati pulled it and fell back as the balloon rose into the air.

Jeff turned to the balloonist and gestured a lifting motion with both hands. "Get us as high as you can. Quickly."

"It is a bit breezy," Jeff said to Reason. The balloon rose. "Now, where the hell is the chopper?" he said, searching the sky.

Reason pointed. "Over there."

"A fair way off." He turned to the balloonist. "Higher." He brought up the binoculars. He could easily see the two men on the hill. "The guy is kneeling and checking the launcher. It won't be long before he fires."

"The helicopter pilot has seen us," Reason said. "They're heading this way."

The helicopter banked to the right.

"It's a pity it's an Iroquois, but it will do," Jeff said to Reason.

"What does that mean?"

"An attack helicopter like an Apache has a laser guidance system and could fire their frigging missiles between the eyes of those two assholes on the hill. See those pods under the machine gun?"

"I see them."

"2.75 mm rockets. A whole bunch of them. Not accurate at this distance, but it should be enough to either wipe them out or at least turn the ground around them into a mini-volcano. Hopefully, if they don't get killed outright, the dust from the explosions will be enough for them not to see the target until the Iroquois gets to them. The machine gunner will do the rest."

An airman strapped to a harness leaned out the door opening and pointed to the ground. Jeff and Reason pointed in the direction of the two men with the Javelin missile launcher. Jeff mimed an action of holding the missile launcher, and Reason kept pointing towards the two men. The man in the harness ignored them and again pointed to the ground. The barrel of his machine gun now aimed in their direction. Jeff and Reason again pointed to the hill, and again Jeff mimed firing a launcher. The man in the harness hesitated. He reached across and tapped the shoulder of the pilot. Jeff saw a helmeted head turn his way. Jeff and Reason pointed. The pilot looked away. After a few moments, the chopper banked away in the direction Jeff had pointed.

The man in the harness gave Jeff a thumbs-up, then disappeared from sight as the Iroquois lined up its target.

Reason touched Jeff's arm. "Well done, Jeff. It's worked."

Jeff looked over the side of the basket, binoculars focussed. He guessed they were now at about five hundred feet, but drifting over the hostage bus.

"Can you see inside the compound?" Reason said, her mouth close to his ear.

The sound of the helicopter motor was making it difficult to hear.

"Yes, I have a good view. There's a long table. Three military officers are sitting on one side, and two hijackers wearing ski masks on the other. I'm searching the side of the bus for any sign of explosives. Nothing yet . . . nothing . . . yes. There they are. Two black packs attached to the front half, and another two near the rear above the wheel."

He passed the binoculars to Reason.

"I see them." She passed the field glasses back as the balloon drifted past. "It's a negotiation with a gun to the head."

Jeff nodded. "Don't you just love politics? I think you Americans call this a double play or something."

"I think you mean a Mexican standoff," Reason corrected. "Why has the chopper not fired its missiles?"

"It will. Any second."

The *whoosh, whoosh* was barely heard above the din as the helicopter unleashed its deadly payloads. Jeff followed the vapour trails.

Then his eyes widened in horror as a plume of white from the hill passed under the balloon's basket. Jeff spun round towards the encampment. A bright light flashed from below. He brought his arm up to cover his face. He reached out and grasped Reason's upper arm and dropped to the bottom of the basket, pulling her with him. Almost instantaneously, a low growling sound from the blast of the exploding rocket built in a deafening crescendo as the shock waves thundered past them like a tsunami of sound. The balloon's basket was flung upwards into the skirt. Shrapnel thrown up from below ricocheted off the woven wicker covering and ripped through the balloon's nylon panels. In seconds, the basket dropped back to the length of the suspension cables. The balloonist moved quickly and checked for damage. Jeff, following the man's actions, saw flames from the propane-fuelled burner had not set the envelope ablaze. Jeff could never work out why they called the bag that carried the balloon aloft an envelope; it looked like a parachute to him. But no matter what it was called the shrapnel had done its damage. The torn fabric flapped and tore into bigger holes. Hot air escaped at a faster rate than it could fill.

Jeff gripped the side of the basket and pulled himself to his feet. Reason grasped hold of the offered hand and allowed herself to be pulled up. They stood side by side looking towards the explosion site. Smoke billowed into the air. As it cleared, Jeff stared in disbelief. He could make out a black circle and a hole in the blast centre. The bus had disappeared.

"Where the hell is the bus?" he said, more to himself than to Reason. "The blast of the rocket must have set off the extra explosives on the bus." His eyes focussed on the ring of flame.

Reason pulled at his arm. "Jeff, we're in trouble."

Jeff ignored her. "Barry and Bethany: where the fuck are they?"

The ground was looming, the balloon dropping too quickly.

"Jeff!" Reason screamed into his ear. "We're dropping!"

He looked at her, still uncomprehending. She punched him in the chest. It snapped him out of his shock.

"Sorry. Okay. Got it. I'm with you."

Her eyes cast around, alert. He could tell her mind was assessing the danger and seeking options. "We're drifting towards that gorge. It's still too high to jump."

Jeff checked the balloonist. He seemed calm enough and was concentrating on working the controls. His lack of panic gave Jeff cause to think that maybe their position was not as precarious as he feared. The balloonist turned and looked over Jeff's shoulder. He saw the danger and started pointing towards the gorge and babbling in Turkish. From a distance, it had looked shallow; now, up close, Jeff could see the gorge was more a canyon and the side of the abyss a sheer cliff face. If they were in the basket when the balloon crashed into it, the drop was a long way to the bottom. They wouldn't survive it. Jeff turned to Reason. She hadn't moved.

He placed a hand on her shoulder. "Are you okay?"

She looked at him. "Yeah, I'm okay. We only have two choices: jump to our deaths, or go into that bloody great hole and the cliff face will kill us. Why wouldn't I be okay?"

CHAPTER THIRTY-TWO

Jeff hesitated, but managed to overcome his trepidation, and followed the balloonist out of the basket as Reason had instructed. They copied her exactly, clinging to the frame as she had done. Reason nodded approval when the two men looked at her. Now Jeff, Reason and the balloonist stood on the small protruding ridge that ran round the bottom edge of the basket. They gripped the upper frame poles attached to the cables. The ground was getting closer. The balloon gained momentum as it neared the earth, and was racing towards the gorge. To Jeff, the craft was falling to the ground faster than a car speeding along a highway.

"Here we go," Reason yelled. "Don't worry about a thing. Remember to let go when I say. You have a choice of three ways to die: crashing into the ground or smashing into the cliff face, and if that doesn't kill you, the fall to the bottom of the cliff will."

"Are you sure this is a stunt you've done before?" Jeff asked.

"Of course," Reason laughed. "Trust me, and do as I say."

Jeff shook his head. "If I get killed, I'll never trust you again."

"It's going to be like jumping out of a moving car," Reason yelled. "Roll as you would if you were parachuting."

"You call it, Reason," Jeff yelled.

"Okay, get ready." She held up her hand so the balloonist could see, and with each call of the number she pushed out a finger. "Three, two, one, jump!"

In the SAS, Jeff had parachuted many times, and he adopted the standard landing stance as he fell through the air. He allowed his legs to collapse as he hit dirt and rolled, stopping twenty metres short of the gorge. He bounced to his feet and looked for the others. Reason lay on her back and waved she was okay. The balloonist was wailing and holding his leg. Jeff ran to him. He pulled the man's trouser leg up and grabbed where the man had been holding, and squeezed. The balloonist screamed and pushed at Jeff's arm.

"Sorry, my friend. I'd say you have a broken leg," Jeff said, gesturing for him not to move.

Reason came across and stood beside him. The helicopter passed overhead. Jeff could see smoke where the two men with the missiles had been. He had heard machine gun fire and the two men had either survived the missile blast and had now been finished off, or they were dead and the men in the chopper were making sure of it. The helicopter banked and turned back to the bus encampment.

"I'd say the two men are definitely dead," Reason said.

A military jeep leaving a trail of dust sped towards them.

"I think I'll leave you to explain what happened," Jeff said.

Reason nodded. "Yes, I think this is one of those occasions where I can be of some use. I'm sorry you lost your friends, Jeff."

Jeff looked towards the blast area. He clasped his hands together on the top of his head and looked to the sky. He had failed.

"Me too."

❦

Fati dropped Reason off at her Istanbul hotel before driving Jeff to his. They had not bothered to stay the night in Goreme. Jeff wanted to get as far away as possible from the bomb site that had killed Bethany and Barry and Reason wanted to escape the pervading sense of dread and darkness that surrounds violent death. Her reaction intrigued him.

She worked with Lee Caldwell's company, and that company was all about death. Caldwell searched the world for terrorists who killed Americans, and whenever a suspect was found, Caldwell left behind a high body count. Devon Securities was all about bringing a day of reckoning to the assassins. They did not go after the planners, only the men who did the shooting or blew up the bombs, or whatever hare-brained way they had devised to kill. However, if the terrorists killed themselves, which was a common occurrence, the planners would be next on the list. Given this background, two murdered American women should have filled Reason with vengeance, and she should be hot on the trail of whoever initiated the attack. Instead, she was flat. Preoccupied.

On another day, he might have questioned her, but today he didn't care. He'd failed Barry and Bethany, and he had a single-minded focus. He knew who was ultimately responsible. Tomorrow, he would go hunting for Avni Leka. Tonight, he needed a beer to unwind and refocus.

The Turkish military officer who had come to check on them listened as Reason explained why they had been in the balloon. She said Jeff was an acquaintance, and when she had seen the two men with the launcher, she had guessed what they were up to. As an employee of the American government, she had little choice but to try and help. Jeff had insisted he come along, and the balloonist was a patriot helping his country. She showed him her diplomatic passport. Their story, corroborated by the helicopter pilot, was accepted. The officer thanked Reason, and drove off. An hour later, Fati and his taxi appeared. Jeff told Fati to tell the balloonist he would buy him a new balloon.

"I think the US government can pick up that tab," Reason said. "I'll arrange it," she told Fati, who translated the good news to the grateful balloonist.

"I want to leave for Istanbul today, Fati," Jeff said. He turned to Reason for agreement.

"Let's get out of here," she replied.

The drive back to Istanbul had been in silence. Reason stared out the window. Her body upright and determined, but with her hands clenched together. Jeff knew the signs. She was experiencing guilt for not saving the dead. He was drowning in the same emotion himself. Reason was a warrior as much as he was, and today they had lost comrades. As soldiers, they wanted payback, but first they needed to mourn and bury the dead. But this would not happen. They could only mourn. The explosion had vaporised the vehicle and the passengers.

Back at his hotel, instead of going to his room, Jeff asked Fati to have his bag sent up. He sat at an outside table and ordered a beer and whisky chaser. The evening was chilly and the other tables were empty; patrons had chosen to sit inside where it was warmer. He downed the whisky and asked the waiter to bring him another.

Fati stood by the table, his hands in his pockets, and his head down. He shuffled and cleared his throat. The attempt to attract Jeff's attention did not go unnoticed, but Jeff didn't glance up and make it easy for him. Fati could go and rot in hell for all he cared. He wanted to be alone.

Instead of taking the hint, and leaving Jeff be, Fati said, "Would you like company, Mr Bradley? I can join you, if you like?" He sat before Jeff could answer.

Jeff's eyes narrowed. A frown appeared on his brow.

Jeff eyed the taxi driver. He had wanted to be left to drown his misery in alcohol. But, what the hell, he could get drunk with or without Fati, so where was the harm in letting him sit?

"Let me buy you a beer?" Jeff said.

"I do not usually drink, but after so many deaths, what does a drop of alcohol mean? Allah will forgive me under such circumstances. I would prefer raki."

"Raki it is."

Jeff waved to the waiter, held up his can to indicate he needed another and asked for a raki. He sipped more whisky. Another few mouthfuls and he'd be ready for another. He had given thought that he might need to phone someone on Barry and Bethany's behalf, but he didn't know any family members. The embassies would contact close relatives. By tomorrow the list of passengers would become front-page news in all the world's newspapers and the lead story on television networks. As photos of the New Zealanders, Australians and the two American women became available they would be added. Sadly, anyone who knew or cared about the hostages had known where they were at all times. And now the families, along with the rest of the world, had witnessed their deaths. The news item of the explosion would be replayed over and over again, and they would witness the deaths and experience the loss over and over again. Jeff finished off his whisky and ordered another.

He watched as Fati took a sip of raki. If any of the alcoholic liquid had passed between Fati's lips, it would surprise him.

"What do you make of all this killing, Fati? All the fighting with your neighbours. You're Turkish, but the whole region is all from the same bloody stock, aren't they?"

Fati tilted his head, shrugged a little. "Some would say this is true, but for me I think we are all different. But Allah – he thinks we are all the same."

Jeff held Fati's eye. "There you go, so maybe you can tell me why these followers of your god fired rockets into the bus and killed all those innocent people? Two of them friends of mine."

Fati shifted in his seat and looked away. Uncomfortable.

"Are you married, Fati?" Jeff said, changing the subject. Taking his bitterness out on Fati wouldn't resolve anything. He hated that he had done it.

"I was, some years ago. But no longer."

"I'm sorry to hear that," Jeff said. "None of my business."

"It was a bad marriage. My wife was from a small village. She did not like it in the city, and in the village I could not make enough money for us to live. She went home to her family, and I stayed in Istanbul."

Jeff now wanted Fati gone. He wanted to be alone, and he wanted to get drunk. He wanted to hit someone and there was no one to hit. A hopelessness overwhelmed him. In the end, all the training that made a Special Forces soldier had proved useless. Everything he had ever done with his life now had no meaning. He called into question his ability to make decisions. So many had died because of the bad decisions he had made. And now Barry and Bethany too had paid the ultimate price. Had they blown the bus because he was too close? Was this all about his battle with Avni Leka? How did he get so arrogant that he thought he had the skills to help his friends? His past victories had been luck, that was all. Not cleverness or skill. He had failed to recognise that he never really had abilities. Had he become hooked on adrenalin so badly he had become addicted to it? His thirst for adventure overrode common sense and discarded any regard to how his actions affected those around him.

❧

Jeff held his mobile to his ear as he listened to Sulla relating the information from Kosovo.

"Gashi is nowhere to be found, Jeff. My brother-in-law says the word on the street is that he has stayed in Italy. I even went to his village of Fushe Kosove and spoke to one of his men. They know nothing. There is a guard at his home, but no one has heard from the fat man."

"Okay, Sulla, thank you, my friend. Go back to the vineyard. There is nothing more you can do."

"What are you going to do, Jeff?" Sulla asked.

"I'm going back to Bari. That's where Leka's trail ended. I'll try to pick it up again. Marius is dead. So no leads from that quarter, but there are others, his boss for one. I will speak to Captain Balboni. He will know which criminal was Marius's boss."

"I will give my brother-in-law your mobile number. One of his men will be in touch with you. Jeff, be careful. Do nothing silly."

"You know me better than that, Sulla. Just keep an eye out for Gashi."

"Should I come with you?"

"Sulla, who knows how long this will take? You have a business to run. If I need help, I'll be in contact."

∽

Reason parked her SUV opposite the hotel. She had dressed in her charcoal trouser suit and an emerald-green T-shirt. Her hair was in a ponytail. She was back in business, and wanted to look the part. She had little doubt Jeff had used the night to grieve and then had let it go, as she had. And now, as she was doing, he had refocussed. The New Zealander was a handsome man, and she was attracted to him. For a time in Goreme, she had let her feelings for Jeff cloud her judgement and had let him lead her. She worked alone. Had this weakness cost the consul's daughter her life? No. When she thought it through, there had been nothing more that she could have done.

Jeff stood on the pavement, suitcase at his feet. His face was passive, devoid of emotion, and there was a coldness in his eyes. It was a look she had seen before, on the day Marius had shot at them. Someone was about to die. She had expected sadness, a sagging of shoulders, a physical reflection of guilt from having lost his friends and not following through on his promise to make good their rescue. Lee Caldwell had told her Jeff was a man who seemed to bear responsibility for everyone. How was he able to shoulder such a burden?

"Morning, Jeff."

He nodded.

"Going somewhere?"

"The airport. Fati is getting his cab."

"What are you going to do, Jeff?"

"Find Avni Leka."

"Not on your own. You cannot do that. They will expect it."

Jeff shrugged. "Little choice, Reason."

Fati's taxi came into view and stopped alongside. Jeff opened the rear door and threw his bag in. He turned to Reason.

"I guess this is it."

He took a step towards her. Did she want him to reach out and take her in his arms, kiss her? If he did, she would not resist. In his eyes she saw the indecision. The unspoken message: now was not the time. He turned away, climbed into the taxi and pulled the door shut after him.

Reason lifted her hand to wave as Fati depressed the accelerator. Jeff did not look back.

༄

Halfway to the airport, there was a bleep from his phone. A text. Jeff looked at the screen. Unbelieving, he read the text from Barry Briggs again.

Where the hell are you, mate?

CHAPTER THIRTY-THREE

Reason read the message on Jeff's phone again.

"How is this possible?" she said. "We saw the bus blow up. There were no survivors." She paused. "I don't want to kill any hope you have that your friend is still alive, Jeff, but could this be a delayed message? The text is sent, but it is delayed in the system. This happens often. It happened to me. I received a text I know my friend sent the day before."

Jeff nodded. Grim-faced.

"There's always that possibility, but I'm going to accept the message is for real until proven otherwise. Can you get the message tracked and find out where the phone is that sent it? I've sent a reply, but as yet no response. Barry is a smart boy. If he is still alive, he may not leave it on all the time. He'll want to save the battery. He might switch it on every hour for a few minutes. Long enough to check or send a message. We need someone to listen for the signal. Anyway, I've sent him a reply and told him to keep safe and that I'm on my way."

Reason reached out and touched Jeff on the arm. "It might also be someone found Barry's phone and is setting a trap."

Jeff drummed the fingers of his left hand on the table.

He nodded. "Yes, that possibility also crossed my mind, but for what purpose? To get at me? Unlikely, I would think. I'm easy enough to find as it is, and if this is a trap, it's not a good one."

Jeff stood and paced. He looked out the window. A tram stopped on the opposite side of the street. Passengers offloaded and loaded and it moved on, smooth and silent. He turned back to Reason sitting on the end of her bed.

"The only way we can find out if this text is for real is to find out where the signal came from. And to do that, we need hi-tech gear. That brings in the military or some higher form of intelligence agency. But, to be honest, I'm not certain I want the military or police involved – and let's include NATO in that list. If any of these organisations find out the hijackers are still alive – and we can't ignore the possibility that if the hostages are still out there, so are the hijackers – the military might order a bombing raid, and Barry and Bethany would be blown to hell. I've lost them once, in my head at any rate; I'm not going to lose them twice."

"I can follow your logic," Reason said. "But you are drawing huge conclusions based on what might be a delayed text." She sighed. "Look, okay, I'll play along. If not the military, who do I get to track the signal?"

Jeff shrugged. "I have no idea. Somewhere you must have a phone company connection. If it wasn't the hostages blown up on the bus, it was their own people. All that says is, when the time comes, they won't hesitate to kill Barry and Bethany."

Jeff rubbed the back of his neck.

"I would like to know how many were on the blown-up bus," Jeff said.

"I can tell you that," Reason said. "The head count was exact: forty passengers, plus the driver and the four cops and The Sheriff. They ran infrared scanners over the bus. No one could be identified, but the body heat count registrations are accurate."

Jeff paled.

"So much for my theories. If the body count is accurate, then I guess I was wrong."

He opened Reason's fridge and took out a fruit juice. He held it up.

Reason said, "Go ahead. I'll have one too." She held out her hand. He uncapped a bottle and passed it to her. "I'm only debating the theory. You received a text. What if you're not wrong?"

Jeff's head tilted, his brow furrowed. "Then I guess the big picture just got scary."

Jeff stepped back to the window and leaned against the wall.

"If I'm not wrong, the implications are staggering. It deserves the wow factor award. Imagine the planning, the attention to detail of such an elaborate ruse, right to the exact number of stand-ins to match the passenger list. We believed it, because seeing is believing, as any professional illusionist will tell you. We have some very, very clever bad guys. The question is, who was on the bus? And what is so important that so many needed to die to keep it secret? And the bigger question that frightens the shit out of me is, what the hell are they going to do with the hostages now?"

Reason said, "It's got me beat. It might also be that Barry escaped and is on his own."

"If he was free, why not go to the nearest authorities? And I'm certain he would have said it in his text. At any rate, if the body count on the bus is correct, if Barry had escaped, it would show one less."

"Yes, it would have."

"Yeah, well, we can dwell on it later, I suppose. First thing is to find out if Barry *is* out there, and where he is. We need someone to track the phone signal."

Reason said, "Give me the mobile phone number. Someone in the embassy will have a connection in the phone company. And there's always a techie ready to do covert work just for the hell of it."

"Good. And don't forget: no police, no military, and don't give your embassy any details. Not yet. The Turks were going to blow the bus, remember, and it might be that your government was aware – or the CIA, at any rate. Leave them out of it for now. It also might be the hostages are no longer in Turkey. If they are out of Turkey, which

I suspect they are, there is nothing the local police or military can do anyway. If it's made public, another group of politicians will step in and their bluster will send the hijackers underground. Or worse, make them kill the hostages for the hell of it." Jeff paused. "We also have to protect Barry's phone connection to us. If I am right, and the hostages are still alive, we need the hijackers to believe the rest of the world thinks they are dead. If it's revealed they aren't, the hijackers will conclude someone from the inside has given their game away."

Jeff passed Reason a slip of paper with Barry's mobile number on it.

"Give me an hour," she said.

 ❧

Jeff went for a walk and returned to Reason's room ten minutes after the hour.

"The signal is coming from across the border in Northern Iraq," Reason said.

Jeff's face burst into a broad grin.

Reason said, "We have troops on the ground in Iraq, Jeff. As does New Zealand and Australia; we should use them."

"We don't talk to anyone. Not until I find Barry. After that, you can call in the reinforcements. If Barry is alive, I'll bet the others are too, and right now the hijackers don't know we know. That might be all that will keep the hostages alive. Let's keep it that way. I want no one poking their nose in."

Reason said, "For the moment, I'll go along with you. But I also have an obligation to a higher power: the US government."

Jeff paced. "Let's go over what might be happening here; wildest notions allowable."

Reason rested her butt against the desk. Arms folded.

Jeff said, "If the hostages weren't on the blown-up bus, where were they? The obvious answer: on another bus."

"Yes, and that is the aspect of this incident that's been bugging me. Why did they take so much time to drive across Turkey? And why tell everyone where they were going?" Reason said.

"And now we know why. They were covering for the second bus, which was taking an alternate route . . ."

"And it needed time to get to its destination," Reason finished off for Jeff.

He nodded.

Reason said, "It makes sense. It also means The Sheriff is still very much alive, and safely inserted within the Kurdish province of Iraq."

"That's what the signal from Barry's phone says," Jeff said. "I think The Sheriff took the long route to Turkish Kurdistan. Once there, it would have been easy for him to go anywhere, especially crossing the border into Northern Iraq. There is no way they could stay on the Turkish side; the Turkish military would send in a kill squad once they found the location. It doesn't matter what the Kurdish people want to call that area, it is still Turkey. Northern Iraq is different. Not only do the Kurds have well-established strongholds in the mountains, but the autonomous Kurdish government will not let Turks anywhere near the place. And there is no love lost between the Iraqis and the Turks."

"What is the next step?" Reason asked.

"I think I need to get to Erbil, the Kurdistan capital of Northern Iraq, and find some PKK members to have a chat with, see if they can't point me in The Sheriff's direction. I wish I had an SAS team here. This is what we're trained to do. Track the enemy for hundreds of kilometres into no-man's-land without being seen. Observe and destroy. Well, okay, it's not quite like that. We find the enemy, radio through the coordinates and get someone else to destroy them – same thing."

It was Reason's turn to smile. A twinkle in her eye.

Jeff looked at her, eyebrows raised, waiting. "What is it?"

"I can tell you that some of your old SAS buddies are here. Staying at a five-star hotel: the Marriott."

"Really? How the hell would you know that?"

Reason said, "The CIA tracks all ex-Special Forces personnel. Sometimes they change sides. As soon as the passports show up on a terminal, it links to a computer somewhere. I made an enquiry at our embassy. I expected you might look for a comrade or two."

Reason passed Jeff a slip of paper. He glanced at it.

"I don't recognise any of the names on this list," Jeff said. He shrugged. "No matter. Once you join the squadron, you never leave."

"A brotherhood of men," Reason said.

Jeff grinned.

"Well, I too can leap tall buildings," Reason said. "At least, climb up fire escape ladders and leap from crashing hot air balloons. You better not keep your brothers in arms waiting."

CHAPTER THIRTY-FOUR

The silver Alfa Romeo sedan pulled to a stop in the centre of the courtyard. Two men rushed to open the door. Leka watched the arrival from his balcony. He had no intention of rushing downstairs to greet his visitor. If wishes could come true, Gashi would be at the bottom of the Adriatic Sea with the bodies of the immigrants he had dumped from his boat. Within a week, he had lost the warehouse, the smuggling route, Marius the assassin sent to kill Jeff Bradley and the confidence of the Puglia crime family. He paid a lot of money to the Italians to provide his security, and that included payment to the Rome crime families. They kept the authorities from his door. Pietro Gallo had failed to kill Bradley, but the smuggling routes were Leka's responsibility, and now Gashi had brought it all crashing down. Could he find an alternative source of income to compensate? Of all his enterprises smuggling was the most lucrative. It brought in millions. The Italians would not be happy.

What was he to do?

Leka heard footsteps at the top of the stairwell, and then the slow lumbering thuds of Gashi walking along the hallway. He opened the drawer to his cabinet and pulled out a bottle of cognac. He banged the bottle on his desk and took two glasses from his drawer. Gashi would demand a drink because he loved to drink. Leka would have a drink because the bumbling buffoon was driving him to drink.

Osman Gashi appeared in the doorway.

Leka filled two glasses. He took one for himself, and sat in his chair behind the desk. Gashi pushed aside the steel-framed chair Leka had placed for him, and, uplifting his glass, stepped across to the burgundy-coloured leather sofa and flopped into it. He raised his glass.

"*Gazeur.*"

"All right, Osman, you lose the warehouse, you lose your immigrants and the second payment along with them. Marius is dead. And the smuggling has come to a halt. I now have disgruntled Puglia gangsters to deal with. Have you been in contact with The Sheriff?"

"Yes, he is safely in Iraq."

"Well, that is something. What happened in Istanbul?"

"Some bad luck, that's all. Shit happens. We will recover."

Gashi gulped down his cognac. He hauled himself out of his chair, reached for the bottle on Avni's desk and refilled it. This time, to the top. He slopped a few drops on to the front of his shirt as he fell back into his seat. Avni breathed in deeply, but exhaled softly. There was little point upsetting himself over Gashi; the man was a slob, but he needed him.

"You can't go back to Turkey, can you?" Leka asked.

"Not right away, but the cops will lose interest eventually. A few bodies in a warehouse filled with illegal weapons. They have some men to bring charges against, and they have a haul of weapons. This will make them happy. And illegal immigrants drowning at sea? Who cares? The West has no interest. In the meantime, I need to stay out of sight for a few weeks. Keep a low profile."

Leka almost laughed. The man was the size of a small mountain. Keeping him unseen would be impossible. It would be like a hippo hiding behind a blade of grass.

"I suppose you could stay here?"

"I'm not staying, Avni. There have been developments in Bari that need attending to."

Leka raised an eyebrow.

"Really? What developments?"

"Marius came to see me. He wanted protection. His boss had had enough of him, and Marius believed the old man had decided to get rid of him. Easy to understand; it's what I would have done."

"I gather for your protection he had something to offer."

Gashi nodded. "He told me the Apulian crime boss was set to go to war against my men in Bari. Wipe us out."

"I see," Leka said. "So much for agreements. It is becoming difficult to find anyone to trust."

The comment made both men smile.

"Lucky we have each other, Avni," Gashi said.

Leka had taken a mouthful of drink and almost spat the contents across the table. He managed to keep his jaw locked. He took a moment to compose himself before he continued the conversation.

"What do you have in mind for our friends in Bari?"

"They want to go to war. We must attack first."

Avni Leka nodded. As much as he disliked Osman Gashi, he had also come to admire him. Gashi did not get flustered. He was a survivor, and he survived by striking his enemy first, or retreating to fight another day.

"Tell me your plan."

༄

Avni stood on his balcony and watched as the Alfa Romeo drove Osman Gashi from his courtyard. He contemplated the state of events. The smuggling operations were held up for the time being, but Gashi assured him not for long. There was to be a war in Bari, and this might cause him problems. He relied on Gallo for security. Gallo had influence in Rome. Gashi did not. At least Project The Sheriff was going according to plan. In a few more days, The Sheriff would be the world's most infamous freedom fighter. When he released the hostages, the world press would be all over the story. All would know how the Kurdish PKK leader had made fools of the Western authorities, how he had made his escape under their noses and shown his humanity by freeing the hostages. The only casualties would be put down to botched Western rescue attempts. The Sheriff would be idolised by those Leka needed to idolise him the most, and the tribal rebel leaders that controlled his smuggling corridor through to Asia would bow to his will.

CHAPTER THIRTY-FIVE

The Marriott Hotel Sisli was in the city centre on the European side of Istanbul. It was a five-star luxury hotel, and with all the glass, chrome and deep lush carpets, it looked it. Jeff's boots tapped out a steady staccato as he strode across the polished marble floor to the reception desk.

The concierge directed him to The Dish Room Terrace Bar.

"Your friends are always to be found there," the hotel man commented.

Jeff noted the disapproving tone. Soldiers were known to let their hair down after ops. Had there been a few all-night drinking sessions? He found The Dish Room easily enough. From the doorway, he searched the tables in close proximity and did not see a group of men that would fit the SAS mould. A wood-panelled bar stood in the centre. Surrounding it, unoccupied bar stools were pushed in under the ledge of the bar top. The bartender, wiping a glass, gave him a quick once-over, but his eyes didn't send any signals of welcome. Clearly, five-star hotel staff weren't enthused by men in jeans and T-shirts.

Jeff entered. Now he could see throughout the whole room. Circular tables and chairs covered the lounge floor, and at the rear there were more comfortable settees. And behind the white settees, three men lounged in purple-coloured, egg-shaped seats round a square table. One look told Jeff these were the men he was looking for. The jackets and loose-fitting shirts could not hide the bulky upper bodies; biceps the size of a normal man's thigh. Eyes, set back in faces hardened by sun and sand, flickered around the room like an airport radar scanner. Although they looked casual and relaxed and lolling about like they had just eaten Christmas dinner, Jeff knew that each man sat taut, like a piece of bent willow, ready to explode with deadly force should the need arise. Like members of the police, soldiers on active service were never off duty.

Reason had given him intel on the group. They were contract security men working in one of the most dangerous regions on earth. The Middle East was a killing field, and the men he now walked towards were the iron safety wall that stood between killers and the wealthy families they were contracted to protect.

Without invitation, Jeff sat in the spare egg chair. Three sets of eyes gauged the uninvited guest. Curiosity, not hostility. These men feared few, and the sight of Jeff was not going to send them running, no matter if he was big and looked handy.

"Hi, guys," Jeff said. "We need to talk. If one of you is the boss, can I ask who that might be?"

The man opposite Jeff laughed. He shook his head. "That would be me. You can call me Jonno."

"Jeff Bradley, Jonno."

"Let me give you a friendly warning, Jeff. Next time you want to sit at our table, wait for an invitation."

It was Jeff's turn to laugh.

Jonno's eyebrows raised. He sat back in his chair, studied Jeff and then leaned forward. "There is a story I heard from my military days in New Zealand of a Jeff Bradley. He punched out a certain Captain Brian Cunningham on active duty in Afghanistan."

A wry smile from Jeff. "You know what rumours are like in the forces, guys: over-exaggerated and to be listened to with a huge dollop of scepticism. Even if there was truth to the rumour, it's classified and I can't talk about it."

Jonno leaned forward. "And you're the same Bradley who tangled with terrorists in Kosovo and not so long ago in New Zealand."

Again Jeff nodded. "I'm impressed you guys have time to read newspapers."

Jonno scratched under his chin. He sideways glanced to his companions. They both shrugged.

"Seems these two are giving you a nod of approval, so fine, Jeff, you've earned the right to sit at our table. Ex-squadron makes us family. Meet Ginger, and the asshole on the end is Aussie. Born in Australia and trained with the Aussie SAS, but he saw the light and migrated to New Zealand."

"He's bullshitting you, Jeff. I only signed on with him because he needed to beef up his company profile with an Australian flag on his business card."

"Good to meet you, guys." They shook hands. Jonno looked over his shoulder and waved to the waiter. "You'll have a beer, Jeff?"

"Yes, whatever you're having."

Jeff gave the waiter the order.

Jonno said, "Right then. I take it you haven't tracked us because you're short of friends, or you're looking for free beer? So what is it you want?"

"My sources tell me you're out of work."

Three sets of eyes widened. Jonno and his comrades exchanged glances.

"Are we under investigation?" Friendliness had gone from his tone.

"Relax. You are not under investigation by anyone, as far as I'm aware. But I have friends with influence, and did some checking before I came here. You must know international organisations have you on their radar. Your last stint was Abu Dhabi. My connections tell me you got dumped out of your contract. Can I ask you why?"

"What's this about, Jeff? Why the twenty questions?"

The waiter arrived with the beers.

"I want to offer you a job. But first, I want to know who I'm dealing with. What happened in Abu Dhabi?"

Jonno twisted the ring on his left hand as he scrutinised Jeff. Jeff knew the mental debate taking place right now. These guys didn't know him, and their business was confidential. Even if stories of wrongdoing abounded in the public domain, there were always two sides to a story, and in many circumstances the stories were only gossip. But groups like Jonno and his mates could not defend themselves because their work was secretive. He was asking them to let him into their private world where the business of security contracting lived and died on discretion and reputation. For all they knew, he could work for a journalist or, worse, an opposition company.

Jonno stopped fiddling with his ring and a slow nod followed.

"Well, in this case it's no big secret, and the damage to our name is already done. A sheikh offered us a bag of cash to stop his kid running off and joining up with ISIS. The little shit gave us the slip. A maid drove him out of the compound in the boot of her car. She lost her job, but the kid had already given her enough money so she would never have to worry about working again. Made us look like amateur assholes, and daddy was pissed off and sent us packing. Abu Dhabi is a small place and daddy had us blacklisted. So here we are, licking our wounds, enjoying some R&R and waiting for a new job."

Jeff sipped his beer. "What you guys need is good old-fashioned SAS work."

"No way," Ginger moaned. "Getting shot at is not how we make a living these days. Look around, Jeff: five-star accommodation, soft beds and plenty of booze, and not far from here, beautiful women too. Our only worry is making sure we don't get too fat."

"Ginger is right, Jeff," Aussie said. "We left that military crap behind with our berets and boots. We're gentlemen now. Stay in nice hotels and protect wealthy clients in luxury homes. No eating sand or camel dung."

Jeff sat back in his seat and waited until they had said their pieces. Let them grumble and bemoan military life. He understood the men he sat with. He had been one of them. Safety was not a lifestyle they could ever adjust to. Despite their words, he knew that to them adrenalin was like cocaine to a drug addict. The longer away from it the more they craved a snort.

"You said you had a job, Jeff. Is this a paying job, or are you looking for a favour?" Jonno asked.

"A bit of both. I will pay your usual fee, whatever that is, but the catch is the mission is dangerous: lots of risk and a good chance you might get your heads blown off."

Jonno laughed. "You sure know how to woo a guy. Do you use that line on women? Okay, just for curiosity's sake, what type of shit do you want to dump us into?"

Jeff looked over his shoulder. No one was within listening distance.

"You will have been following the news broadcasts of the bus loaded with Australians, New Zealanders and two American women hijacked at Gallipoli."

Three grim faces.

Jonno said, "Yes, real bad shit. We watched that play out on the news. Saw the explosion. What is it you want to do, Jeff, go after the killers? A little payback for killing some ANZACs? We aren't in the revenge business. If we were, we'd never work again."

"No, this is not about revenge." Jeff leaned forward and lowered his voice. "Many died on the bus in Goreme, but none of them were Kiwis or Aussies. The hostages were miles away on another bus, and that bus is now somewhere across the Iraqi border. I'm going there to rescue the hostages, and I need you guys to come with me."

CHAPTER THIRTY-SIX

Barry stretched before climbing to his feet, careful not to disturb Bethany. Their new surroundings were not up to the standard of the warehouse in Istanbul. The bathrooms were filthy. A search through cupboards found some bottles of cleaning fluid. There were three toilets, two showers and two basins. Barry drew up a roster for the showers, and the rule for the toilets was knock on the door and make sure the cubicle was empty. The doors had no locks.

Their captors provided blankets and mattresses and a steady supply of simple food: bread and cuts of meat and cheese, instant coffee, herbal tea and sugar. For anyone who wanted a cold drink there was no milk or fruit juice on offer, only water. The drinking water came in plastic bottles and looked as if it came from an outside tap. Barry asked the guards to fill the water bottles daily. One night would be long enough for microbes to contaminate it. He warned everyone not to drink from the taps in the toilet area. The water might not come from a treated source – it was not worth the risk. No one argued. After the murders of Mildred and Reg they all knew the consequences if they became ill.

When he thought it through, he realised the bottled water probably came from the same source as the water in the bathrooms, but he took comfort from not knowing for sure. At first, the guards had refused the fresh water request, but when Barry explained that if all the passengers became ill with dysentery there would be a bad smell and the guards would be the ones cleaning up, they got the message, and fresh bottles of water came daily.

For a prison it was comfortable enough. As in Istanbul, they had been left to themselves. Earlier that day, the guards had returned the bags stored in the bus luggage compartments. The benevolent manner of their captors continued to puzzle Barry. Why were they being so decent? It made little sense.

They had driven for many hours. The signal on his phone had faded en route, and the battery had died after the last message to Jeff. Bethany carried a spare in her bag, along with another SIM card. When he replaced the battery and inserted Bethany's SIM card with roaming, a signal returned, confirming they were in a new country. That worried him. Where the hell were they?

He had sent a message to Jeff. He left the phone turned on for thirty minutes. The message from Jeff saying that he was organising a rescue was heartening for himself and Bethany. They could not share the news with the others, but he would make sure he did nothing to antagonise The Sheriff.

It was time to retrieve the phone and send a new message. The next text would be to tell Jeff he would turn the phone on every two hours for ten minutes. He needed to save the battery. Ten minutes should be enough for the signal to be tracked. If it needed to be more, Jeff would tell him. He had hidden the phone under a stack of wooden pallets pushed up against the wall. None of the other passengers were aware he had the phone, and he needed to be careful no one found out. The Sheriff's threat to shoot anyone hiding a phone would still be fixed in their minds. Barry wasn't certain what the group's reaction might be if they found he had one. It was best no one knew.

The passengers had little to do. They gathered in groups and the discussion was always the same. What was going to happen to them? Barry theorised the hijackers wanted to hold them until a ransom was paid. The passengers understood the ramifications when it came to kidnapping. Their governments would let them die before paying out money. All agreed they would not leave their fate in the hands of politicians. A few suggested they form a finance committee. Many had homes and sizeable bank accounts. The group appointed Brendon, an accountant from Auckland, the negotiator. When the time came he would bargain for their lives. The decision seemed to placate even the most fearful. It was a plan and, everyone agreed, a good plan.

Barry had used all his money for the trip and to pay for Bethany's engagement ring; any spare cash left had gone into the wedding fund. Not enough to interest a kidnapper. He and Bethany were dead meat. He remembered The Sheriff said that when they reached their destination they would be released. His instincts told him they had arrived at the final destination. And he saw no sign The Sheriff was about to honour his pledge.

Bethany stirred, as he was about to make his way to the pallets.

"Hi, doll." He gave her a peck on the cheek.

"I need a drink of water and to use the toilet," she whispered.

"I was about to use the phone."

"Wait until I get back. We can do it together."

Barry nodded. The other hostages were sitting quietly or dozing. The two American girls had been separated from the group. Where they had been taken, and why, he had no idea. He surmised because they were Yanks they were worth more money. Maybe a ransom had already been paid and the women were on their way home. Good news for everyone if it was like that. It meant the kidnappers were open to deals.

Bethany was making her way back to him. There was something odd about her walk. Head down, she moved quickly, but her legs were unsteady. Water slopped over the rim of her plastic drinking glass. Barry made to rise, but she held her hand up. She fell to her knees beside him. Her eyes were tearful and her face had turned the colour of snow. Barry took the glass from her shaking hand before all the contents ended on the floor.

"Are you okay?"

Bethany shook her head. "No, I'm not." Barry made to speak, but Bethany held up her hand. "Wait a moment; I need a moment." She took deep breaths. Swallowed, then fixed her eyes on Barry. She leaned forward, her lips close to Barry's ear.

"They're going to kill us."

Barry's mouth dropped open. He stared straight ahead. His head unmoving.

"Tell me why you think that?" he whispered.

Bethany's lips trembled against his earlobe.

"I heard two of the Albanian guards talking. They said the order had come from whoever gives the orders – I assume The Sheriff – that all the hostages are to be taken into the mountains. We are to be shot and buried in a secret place where no one will ever find our bodies. The Albanian guards are not happy. They say they are not mass murderers. They worry that if they do this and it is discovered the 'Internationals' will hunt them."

Barry gulped. "Okay, that's something at least. We might be able to exploit that weakness when the time comes. Did they say when this will happen?"

"No. Transport needs to be organised, they said. And they need to be wary of roadblocks. But in the next few days, it sounded like to me."

Barry took Bethany's hand and looked her in the eye. "I promise, with all my heart, nothing will happen to you."

"You can't make such promises, Barry."

"Yes, I can. Nothing will happen to you. Now, I need to text Jeff. He needs to know."

"Jeff might not be able to help. We don't even know where we are. How can you tell him where to come?"

"He'll know."

She turned and pushed her back against the pallets, bringing her knees up to her chest and wrapping her arms around them. Barry waited for her to settle. Her lips tightened and pursed, then she took a deep breath. Bethany nodded she was ready. She lay against him as lovers do. Barry reached behind her and wiggled the phone from the gap. He switched it on and tapped the Text icon, then wrote a message to Jeff. He included Bethany's news that The Sheriff was going to have them killed. Now he needed to wait ten minutes before he switched it off. Bethany nudged him.

"A guard is coming our way," she whispered.

He pushed the phone back under the pallets. Barry stroked Bethany's thigh. Her hand rested on his, and she gave it a squeeze when the guard stopped in front of them. The guard pointed his Kalashnikov at Barry.

"On your feet. Both of you," he commanded. Bethany held Barry's arm. Barry kept his eye on the barrel aimed at his chest.

"Stand up," the guard repeated.

CHAPTER THIRTY-SEVEN

The black SUV drove along the new multi-lane highway in the direction of Baghdad until it reached the outskirts of Erbil, the capital of the Kurdish area of Iraq. The driver made a left turn and drove over a dirt road for fifteen more minutes before taking another left into the darkness. A dozen wild dogs loped across the front of the vehicle and disappeared into the darkness.

"Dogs," the driver said. "Very bad. They have diseases. If they bite you it will make you sick. And they attack in packs. A young girl was savaged to death by these beasts. If you walk in these remote areas at night, you must be careful."

Jeff nodded. He could think of more dangerous animals wandering in the dark in the various regions of Iraq and Kurdistan. Mostly they had two legs.

"At night in the city the police shoot them," the driver added.

Jeff was bounced about in the seat as the driver manoeuvred the vehicle through a copse of trees and stopped in front of a small brick cottage.

"We are here," the driver said.

Jeff, Reason and Jonno followed the driver inside.

The woman they had made the night drive to meet was medium height, and of slim build, but the rolled-up sleeves of her shirt revealed muscled lower arms. Her pretty face had finely chiselled features, and clear, light-brown skin, almost Asian. She had a ready smile and a warm and welcoming disposition, and looked no older than twenty years; her eyes though exuded a wisdom and experience beyond her years. She had graduated university, a genius with computers, Jonno had told Jeff, and had a degree on a wall in her family home to prove it. Jonno said he had seen it. She was Jonno's connection, and Jeff had to take Jonno's word his connection was reliable.

Her black hair was swept back in a single plait that hung loose down her back. A touch of make-up enhanced her beauty. She could have been like many Eastern European women he had met, readying herself for a night out in search of a husband. And, by Jeff's initial assessment, young men would line up to dance with such an elegant and intelligent beauty. But this woman would not be dancing. Unlike other young women, Luka wore a khaki-green military uniform and had a Kalashnikov slung over the back of her chair, and a pistol on the table within ready reach of her hand.

Fellow female soldiers, also uniformed, sat cross-legged on the floor, Kalashnikovs across their laps. Jeff had heard of the Kurdish women soldiers and the stories of their prowess as fighters. He'd read reports in the media describing them as a very effective fighting force. He had also read reports that the PKK women soldiers had shot it out and had beaten back ISIS soldiers on the battlefield on more than one occasion. They looked competent. He was about to find out.

When Luka saw Jonno, her eyes widened and a glow brightened her face. She rose from her seat and rushed to greet him.

"Jonno, my friend. It is so good to see you again."

They embraced and clung to each other more like old lovers than long-lost friends. Jeff made a mental note to question Jonno. He needed to know if there was more to their relationship than just old acquaintances, and he already knew Jonno would tell him to piss off.

In Afghanistan, he had seen these scenarios before in the rebel groups. Romeo and Juliet relationships often occurred, and often the lovers needed to choose sides or had already chosen a side. And if one of them was an informant, the team could be led into a trap. He didn't know Luka, and they were about to place rescuing the hostages in her hands.

Luka returned to the seat behind her desk.

"How can I help you people?" she asked, her eyes on Jonno.

Jonno looked at Jeff. Jeff nodded an okay. Jonno could lead the discussion.

"We need weapons," Jonno said. "What can you get us?"

"Do you have money?" Luka asked.

Jeff nodded to Jonno.

"Give me a list and I will get what I can," she said.

Jeff pulled out the piece of paper with the list they had compiled in Istanbul. He passed it to Luka.

She gave it a quick scan. A nod of her head as she mentally ticked off the items. "It is possible to get these weapons. Even on the streets of Erbil. We have gun shops. Just like in America. What else do you need?"

Jonno said, "We also need a guide and transport to Zakho."

Luka's brow furrowed. She glanced up from the list.

"It is dangerous for us to travel by road. There are many roadblocks, and the town Zakho, my home town, is close to the Turkish border. Turkish forces are near. The West has listed us PKK as terrorists, and now the Turks are taking advantage and invading Kurdish towns. They are happy to kill many innocent people to get a single PKK member. They want us all dead. Also, it is close to Syria, and ISIS and the other rebel groups, and if it wasn't hard enough before, there is the Syrian army and the Russians. Nobody respects borders, and they cross over whenever it suits. In the past we could cross into Syria as we liked, but now it is not such a good idea. When we return, they follow us into Northern Iraq. If we are caught, we suffer as women. They do not treat us like men. They torture us and kill us differently. We must be careful."

"Does this mean you cannot help us?" Jeff asked.

Luka looked up at Jeff. "I did not say that. I said it will be very dangerous for us." She tilted her head. "You must pay more for our services than is normal, because of this danger."

Jeff laughed. Jonno looked to Jeff for affirmation. Jeff nodded. What choice did he have? This rescue was becoming an expensive exercise. Luckily, his grandmother had left him a great deal of money and property when she died. The amount he had spent so far was not a cause for concern; not yet anyway.

"Do you have an exact location?" Luka asked.

Jonno turned to Reason.

"Yes. My contact has narrowed the search area," Reason said.

She opened the map and pointed to the location. Jeff threw her a curious glance, then frowned. It surprised him the target area had been narrowed to a few hundred metres. She had not given him this information. She caught his look and raised her eyebrows, and the corners of her mouth turned up. A hint of humour over her deceit.

Luka rose from her seat and put both hands on the table, leaning forward to study the map. She placed a finger on the plastic-coated surface.

"This location is close to Zakho. I think on the outskirts, but for sure between the town and on the road in the direction of the Syrian border. Zakho is a busy town; it has a university and from time to time it is used as a checkpoint and border crossing into Turkey. It is not so busy nowadays because of the war. The lack of activity means there will be empty sheds and warehouses along this highway. My guess, they are hiding your people in one of those warehouses. Taking them too close to Zakho would invite curiosity. Kurdistan has a buoyant economy, but there is still unemployment. The townspeople have little to do except sit in cafés and drink iced tea and coffee and gossip. If they notice things out of the ordinary, they will tell someone."

Jeff said, "You mentioned ISIS and other rebel groups. Could any of them be involved with the hostages?"

Luka held up her hands. "Who knows? Fighters from these groups are everywhere. And there are so many factions within some of these groups. ISIS has only come to your attention because of the beheadings and brutality against women. This is why we" – she waved her arm towards the others – "joined the PKK. The kidnapping of Kurdish women. We women needed to defend ourselves. The West did not care what happened to us, so we took matters into our own hands. We are PKK, but we're not all terrorists, no matter what the politicians say. But even in the PKK, there are factions that are no more than criminals. On the whole though, Iraqi Kurdistan is okay. The interim government does a good job. The Iraqi forces work with Kurdish troops and there are international military forces in Baghdad if needed, but they do not come to Zakho. In this region, you only need worry about The Sheriff and his men."

"Fair enough," Jeff said.

Luka turned to Reason. "Can we narrow the target area?" she asked. "It is a small spot on the map, but in reality two, maybe three kilometres. Big enough to waste hours trying to find wherever the hostages might be hidden."

"I need to call Istanbul in an hour. I will have an exact location after that call. That's if the hostage friend of Jeff's has turned his phone back on," Reason responded.

"How far to Zakho from here?" Jeff asked.

"It is about 350 kilometres. Five to six hours' driving, depending on the traffic."

"When do we go?"

Luka said, "First, I think a few questions need to be answered. To evacuate forty people has problems. Some will be elderly, possibly suffering from ill health. What if they cannot walk? How do you plan getting them to safety?"

"If the bus they travelled on wasn't still there, we could steal a truck or two, or even another bus," Jeff said. "If needed, could we get you to hire us a bus or a truck? Would that be a possibility?"

Luka said, "This is a Third World country. Everyone is interested in improving their standard of living."

Jeff turned to Reason. "What about an extraction? Choppers from Baghdad."

"That can be arranged."

"If we have to go by bus, would the Turkish border be open at night?" Jeff asked.

"The Zakho border may not be open at all. It is only used every so often."

"Okay, when the time comes we talk with the Yanks. When can we leave?" Jeff asked Luka.

"It will take time to organise a safe passage and identify where it is the hostages are held. In an operation like this, you will want to be in and out as quick as possible."

"Agreed," Jonno said.

Luka was thoughtful. "I think that in four days, maybe five, we can leave."

"Too long," Jeff said. "The last message from the hostages is the kidnappers intend to kill them any day now. The man who sent the text could not say which day for certain. It could be tomorrow. But it means we cannot delay the mission."

Luka puffed her cheeks and blew out the air.

"Very well, we can drive to Zakho tomorrow. Tonight, go back to your hotel and get some sleep. Only bring whatever gear you consider essential. I will arrange for the weapons to be in Zakho when you arrive."

༄

On the drive back to the Erbil International Hotel, Jeff peered out the window, watching the lights of passing traffic. It relaxed him. Cleared his head. He thought through the decision to find a team and go it alone

219

with the rescue. Had he judged the situation correctly? Was this decision best for the hostages? He decided yes it was, and he would live with it.

Right now, questions needed to be asked. He turned in the seat.

"Out with it, Reason – why didn't you give me the coordinates of where the hostages are in Istanbul?"

"Easy answer: I didn't trust you to bring me along."

Jonno, sitting in the back seat with Reason, laughed.

"Fair enough," Jeff said. "You're right, I would have left you in Istanbul, but not for the reasons you might think."

"Really? You mean, it's not because I'm a woman and once you had the information you need, I serve no further useful purpose than maybe a night of sex?"

"No, it's not like that."

"Really. I can't wait to hear. Tell me," Reason said.

"Tell her, Jonno," Jeff said.

"I think what Jeff meant to say is that the four of us make an SAS operational unit. It's how we're trained. We know each other's role. Our survival is reliant on being able to depend on each other. You don't fit, Reason. You're not trained to think like us, and you have no combat experience. Nothing personal."

"Well, guys, I hate to rain on your parade, as we say in good old America, but I'm in the team. Your foursome has become a fivesome; now learn to live with it."

Jonno laughed again. "She sounds like a soldier, Jeff. Can you drink beer, Reason?"

"Not by choice, but if you want a buddy to bond with after this, I'll be there for you."

Jeff shook his head. She was a woman he respected, and as always, he hated putting the women he admired in danger, especially given his past history. More than one friend he'd involved in his escapades had wound up dead. But on this occasion he had no choice but to bring her along. Reason could call in the US troops stationed in Baghdad if needed, and when the hostage rescue started they might need a squad of US Navy SEALs and choppers.

"I'd be interested in what you two think. Is there anything I've missed?" Jeff said to Jonno and Reason.

"I think you're about to land us in a big pile of shit, Jeff," Jonno said. "If we manage to do this, the US forces will be pissed off. The New Zealand SAS contingent in Baghdad will not be happy either. I hope you don't think they're gonna kiss your ass and praise you with a big thank-you-very-much pat on the back. You're making them look like a bunch of assholes. You'll be a leper from here on in. The government may never let you leave New Zealand again."

Jeff said, "That would suit me fine. Anyway, a suicide bomber blew up the gate of Camp Taji, near Baghdad, the other day. Opposition politicians want the New Zealanders off the base and sent home. I don't think now is the time to invite them to a clandestine mission in Kurdistan. But if it turns to shit for me, I'm a wine maker now. If I can't travel abroad, I'll retire to my estate and put my feet up."

"Yeah, sure you will," Jonno threw back. "What about you, Reason? What reaction would you expect from your government when this is over? That is, providing we come out alive."

"It's easy for me. I don't exist on paper except at the highest level. Whatever happens, I'm okay."

Jonno gave her an incredulous look.

Jeff caught it. "She's not kidding, Jonno. Reason wields a lot of muscle; it's why she gets to tag along. She might just pull our asses out of the bloody big hole we're about to jump into." He paused a moment, then turned his attention to Jonno. "Jonno, I need to ask – can Luka be trusted?"

"No worries there, mate."

Jeff was about to question further, then decided it was a discussion best had in private. An image of Barry and Bethany intruded into his thoughts. "In the morning, the mission begins. I hope to hell we aren't too late."

CHAPTER THIRTY-EIGHT

The first roadblock was on the outskirts on the way out of Erbil: a Kurdish military checkpoint. The SUV pulled in behind a slow-moving line of trucks, taxis and other vehicles. A balaclava-clad soldier sat on the back of a pick-up truck, his arm draped over the barrel of a machine gun bolted to swivel brackets on top of the cab. Sniffer dogs poked their heads around tyres and underbodies, while soldiers with long-handled mirrors checked under trailers – for contraband, illegal immigrants, or arms or bombs, was Jeff's best guess. Pedestrians walking into Erbil gave a cursory, uninterested glance at the queue of vehicles and moved on. When it came to the turn of the SUV, a head poked through the window and the driver, also the guide, showed the passports and they were waved on.

The checkpoint guards appeared relaxed, and the search was not as rigorous as checkpoints Jeff had manned in the past. But Luka had said there were many roadblocks on the roads of the autonomous Kurdistan state in Iraq, and because of it little smuggling happened through the day. Groups like ISIS and the PKK moved about at night.

"Kurdistan is mostly peaceful," she had said. "You will not have any trouble from the authorities. My driver will make sure of it."

Jeff was sceptical, but with the first roadblock behind them without hassle, he was a believer. Luka had said neither she nor her soldiers could travel with them, but she had supplied the vehicle and the driver. The decision was made to take the long route over the mountains via Shanidar. Jeff had wanted to steer clear of Mosul, as that close to the Syrian border security would be tighter. The driver drove a pre-planned route, which Jeff assumed Luka had cleared with the police. The checkpoint on the outskirts of Erbil was the first of many along the road to Zakho. Jeff lost count after forty. Mostly, it was police checking passports and, mostly, they were waved on. The police did not ask why a vehicle of foreigners was travelling north. Evidence Luka had done her job, and evidence that she had clout within Kurdistan.

Jeff's observation of Erbil had been that it was a city on the up. There were cranes everywhere, and from the balcony of his hotel, he could see construction was happening all over the city. He had enough of a grasp of economics to understand a buoyant construction industry underpinned a healthy economy. In the villages they had passed through, similar activities were taking place. Kurdistan on the surface was a vibrant country, and the police were actively keeping it safe to ensure the boom continued. Compared to Kurdistan, its neighbours, Southern Iraq and Syria, were lawless lands, where the Western and Syrian Air Force bombers had turned the cities into rubble, and rebel groups and ISIS had reduced the populations to living a nightmarish existence. In these countries, violence occurred on a daily basis, and essential services were years away from being reliable. But as peaceful as most of Kurdistan was, Jeff knew the wars and conflict that surrounded Kurdistan would eventually impact on the developing nation. They always did.

That Zakho was so close to the Syrian and Turkish borders, and the hostages even closer to the border, worried Jeff. At night, remnants of rebel groups fighting in Syria, especially ISIS and the Taliban, wandered the open range like the wild dogs of Erbil. And, like the wild dogs, they scavenged and killed as they liked. Did the hijackers have enough soldiers to fight off ISIS if they decided to make a raid? He had little doubt a group like ISIS would love to get their hands on a bunch of foreign hostages.

∾

In the late afternoon, they drove on to the bridge over the Little Khabur river and into Zakho. The pavements, in need of repair, were busy with pedestrians, but they were mostly men. The few women he saw wore hijabs or scarves. Drab retail outlets built into cement-block buildings occupied every inch of space at street level. Young men stood beside sheets of wood with shelving displaying CDs and DVDs.

They came to an island roundabout. In the centre of the island was a fountain, and beside the fountain a flagpole; at the top of the pole, the national flag of Kurdistan was flapping in the breeze. They drove on to the intersection and down the second street to the hotel Luka had arranged for them.

They were to wait for her to make contact. After showering, Jeff threw on fresh clothes and knocked on Reason's door. She caught her breath when she saw him. A slight flush to her cheeks.

"I thought you might be the waiter. I ordered some nibbles. I'm hungry."

She stood back to let him enter. The smell of soap and mistiness of steam hung in the air. There was a hint of perfume, but she wore no make-up.

"I'm sorry. Have I interrupted you? I can come back."

"No. It's fine. My face needs a touch-up. I can do that while we talk."

He was about to say, 'It doesn't need it, you look great,' but instead he dropped on to a chair by the window.

"Do you have an update on the coordinates?" he asked.

"Yes," she called from the bathroom. "My techie has narrowed it down for us, but he said there was something weird about the signal."

"Weird, how?"

"He said the signal has not been switched off. It has been sending continuously. Your friend Barry had said he would only switch it on for ten minutes every two hours. That isn't happening right now. I think it is significant."

Jeff frowned. He scratched the side of his face.

"It could be he just can't get near the phone. I'm assuming he will have found a hiding place for it. It's unlikely he would carry it on him. Guards might be watching closely. It also might be they have been moved and he could not retrieve it before they left. There are any number of reasons I can think of without thinking the worst."

Reason did not respond. Jeff turned in his chair and looked out the window. She stepped out of the bathroom. "All done."

Jeff was tempted to comment on her glow. But he kept his mouth shut.

"Is this plan of mine to go it alone madness?" he said, looking again through the window. "I've argued it over and over in my head. Am I making the right decisions? Should I hand it over to the military? How can a handful of ex-servicemen and one woman take on so many behind enemy lines? But I keep coming up with the same answer. I trust myself to go in there and make it happen. Find them. Bring them home. No one else." He turned back to Reason. She sat on the bed, watching him.

"What do you want me to say, Jeff – that you're wrong? Okay, I'll say it: yes, you are wrong. You're leading us – me and your three new best friends – into an impossible situation, and apart from the plan of finding the hostages, you really haven't any idea as yet how large the force is you have us going up against, or what to do with the hostages once you find them." Reason looked at him like a school teacher looking over the top of her glasses as she is about to admonish a pupil.

"Oops, I forgot that's why I'm here: to call in the cavalry when needed. You're a smart guy, Jeff. You'll figure it out. And we are all adults. We could have said no. We didn't. Now, let's get focussed."

Jeff nodded. "I'll consider myself reprimanded for being such a whiney asshole. What are these new coordinates?" he asked.

Reason opened the map and spread it on the bed. Jeff climbed off his chair and stood beside her.

"My techie has zeroed it in, to one hundred metres, right here." She stabbed at the spot.

Jeff stared. "It looks to be about ten kilometres along the road in a direct line to the Syrian border. There's nothing on the map. I'd say there might be a small village, a few dwellings, some old storage warehouses. Narrowing the search area to one hundred metres should be exact enough to find the building or shed or whatever construction the hostages are being held in. At a guess, it's unlikely there will be more than five or six buildings to look at. A hundred metres is not a lot of space."

The closeness of Reason and the smell of soaps and perfume stirred up the anticipation he'd experienced on their night together in Goreme. She turned to him. Their eyes held. He leaned towards her and Reason did not pull away. Their mouths were barely inches apart.

A ping on Reason's phone; a text. The phone lay beside the map. She glanced at it, but managed to keep her head still. Jeff gulped.

Reason said, her voice barely a whisper, "It's Luka." His lips tightened. He nodded for her to go ahead and check it. She reached for her phone and opened the message. "Luka is downstairs."

CHAPTER THIRTY-NINE

Jeff rallied Jonno, Aussie and Ginger, and he led the three ex-SAS soldiers and Reason out of the hotel. They followed Luka for fifty metres. Luka stopped outside the entrance to a café. Through the front window, Jeff could see into the crowded café; only men, and mostly young men. Many of the patrons were lounging in comfy chairs, smoking flavoured tobacco through hookah pipes. On the tables sat bottles of water, coffees, tea and bowls of nuts. The groups of men talked over the top of each other; the café was noisy with chatter.

"Wait here," Luka said. She stepped inside and Jeff watched her until she disappeared into the rear.

The pavement was busy, and standing still in one place resulted in them being pushed and jostled. Jeff could see his team begin to become irritated. Aussie opened and closed his fist a number of times. Jeff didn't need locals beaten up and bleeding on the pavement.

"Why don't we step inside and get out of everyone's way?"

He pushed open the door and they filed in. Those near the entrance watched the visitors with more than a hint of interest. Foreign visitors would be a rarity in Zakho, and Jeff had little doubt he and his four companions stood out a mile. A hand over the back of a chair nudged another local, and soon half the customers were looking at the doorway. Jeff searched the café for any sign of Luka.

He turned to Jonno. Jonno stepped up beside him.

"What do you think? Are these guys getting hostile, or just curious?"

Someone yelled out something. The room fell silent. Jeff had no idea what was said, but he glanced over his shoulder at the door; maybe it was time to go back to the pavement. Slowly, the men rose to their feet. All eyes were now on the five foreigners.

To Jeff's astonishment they began to clap.

The clapping increased in intensity, and cheering followed. Luka appeared from the rear and walked up to Jonno and threw her arms around him. Men surged forward. They pushed Jeff and Reason and Ginger and Aussie aside. They all wanted to touch Jonno. One man, who looked a lot like Luka, held Jonno's arm and called him 'my brother'. Jeff looked at Reason, then the others. Ginger shrugged.

"Don't look at me, mate," Aussie said. "I don't have a bloody clue. It's not his personality, that's for sure; Jonno couldn't charm a hooker." Aussie caught Reason's quizzical look. "What I meant to say was . . ."

"I know what you meant to say, Aussie," Reason said. "Probably best left unsaid."

"Yeah, right. Gotcha."

Luka took Jeff by the arm.

"Come, I have a table in the back. Jonno will join us shortly. Many want to shake his hand."

"I can see that," Jeff said. "I had no idea Jonno had been to Zakho before. Why is he so popular?"

"It is not for me to tell you. He swore me to secrecy," Luka said. Her hand swept the crowd. "All of us, in fact."

Jeff turned to Reason. "This has to be a story we need to hear before the mission is over."

"Yes, Captain. At the end of the mission," Reason said, smiling and giving a mock salute.

Jeff ignored her, and allowed himself to be led away by Luka. When they walked through to the rear, Jonno was still surrounded by well-wishers. Whatever he had done to earn such adoration intrigued Jeff, but of more interest was the obvious support network he had in the town. That might prove useful if they ran into any serious trouble rescuing the hostages.

One large table stood in the centre of the room. It had a dozen chairs round it. Two of Luka's female soldiers stood in the corner. Jeff received a friendly acknowledgement. Luka sat in a chair at the head of the table.

"My friends, sit. I will order coffees."

She signalled to a waiter. Jeff and Reason sat down.

Luka said, "I think it best we use the backroom for our meeting. The café as you can see is for men, and even though I am a soldier, I am still a Kurd and must obey the rules of our culture. Secondly, not everyone in the café tonight is a friend. Maybe someone at a nearby table will overhear us. Zakho is no different to any other Northern Iraqi towns. Full of spies – PKK, ISIS, Iraqi intelligence, Turkish intelligence, tribesmen, criminals, maybe even Al Qaeda and Taliban. Anyone expert at selling information for money is in Zakho." She smiled. "There are many factions setting themselves to grab a stake in this new Kurdish nation."

The coffees arrived, and Jonno walked in behind the waiter. He ignored the looks and said nothing. Jeff waited until the waiter was out of earshot. He leaned towards Jonno.

"Are you going to tell us what that was all about?" Jeff asked.

Aussie said, "Yeah, mate, I hadn't realised I was in the company of a genuine Kurdish celebrity."

Jonno offered a sheepish grin and shook his head. He looked at Luka.

"You have the weapons we asked for?" he asked.

Luka nodded. "Close by. I have asked around. The sector where you believe the hostages are being held is Sheriff territory. Word on the street is The Sheriff has been there, but he has left. I am told he left a day ago. He is very strong in the region all the way to Dornaq. He has men everywhere. Dornaq is close to the Syrian and the Turkish border. It is a very good spot for a smuggler like The Sheriff."

"How reliable is the information?" Jeff asked.

"You can rely on it."

Jeff glanced across at Reason. The time tied in with Barry no longer communicating. Could The Sheriff have moved the hostages?

"I am told The Sheriff has a high profile in the PKK," Jeff said. "Your group see him as a potential caliph, and believe that he will build a great nation?"

Luka brushed at her shirtsleeve. She dropped her hands on to the table, her fingers entwined. A teacher set to address her pupils.

"Those close to The Sheriff are frightened of him, but none of us have respect for him. Not for a long time. In the early days, it might have been true. But not anymore. Fighters like us join causes for many different reasons. As Jonno knows so well." Heads turned Jonno's way. He ignored them. "I joined to protect myself and my friends from ISIS. When that danger has passed, I will hang up my uniform and go home. When The Sheriff joined the PKK in his early days, he would have been like any of the other fighters; the cause was just and he would have given his life for it. But something happens when you have lived like a wild animal for such a long time. Your beliefs change. The Sheriff and his men no longer fight for freedom. They have built up many smuggling routes in and out of Kurdistan and through Syria, Iraq, Turkey. They have used this knowledge for drugs, illegal immigrants, weapons and whatever else makes money. The money gives him power. His inner circle of soldiers are ruthless;

too long in combat and too much killing. The Sheriff lost his way. But, as I said, he is powerful and the locals fear him; even his own men are afraid of him."

Jeff drummed his fingers on the table.

He said, "If The Sheriff has left, we need to go tonight. If they intend to murder the hostages, as Barry said they are going to, with The Sheriff gone there is no longer any requirement to keep them alive. If the need for murder is to protect him from the Turks finding out he is still alive, then each day that passes is a risk of discovery. Anyway, right now they won't be expecting a rescue. Not by a motley crew like us. How about you, Luka? Will you and your soldiers help us?"

Luka looked at Jonno.

She shook her head. "I cannot. I dislike The Sheriff and all he stands for, and it is men like The Sheriff who have caused the rest of us to be classified as terrorists, but I cannot take up arms against another Kurd. We will stand by and help with logistics. When the rescue is completed, we will protect the hostages. After all, it will help our cause to ensure the hostages are returned safely."

"Fair enough," Jeff said, but in no way did he mean it.

The look on Reason's face told him she was of the same opinion. But there was no point in arguing or trying to change Luka's mind. This was a woman who lived on the run and faced death daily. She had made her decision. Whatever had happened between Luka and Jonno, when it came to loyalty it was not enough for her to switch allegiance. Begrudgingly, he accepted it. That's how soldiers were, but it meant if it all turned to shit they were on their own in a region surrounded by The Sheriff's supporters.

"Okay," Jeff said. "We go tonight." To his team he said, "Do not leave anything behind. We are not coming back. Any questions?" Jeff waited. No response. "Good. Let's get out of here."

Jeff dropped some US dollars on to the table for the coffees.

෴

Under the cover of darkness, the convoy moved out. They travelled in two SUVs, Luka's vehicle leading the way. The roads were similar to those they'd travelled on from the Kurdistan capital of Erbil: sealed and in a reasonable state of repair. The further they got towards the edge of the city, the less effective the street lighting, and it wasn't long before the road and surrounding area were totally black. Luka had assured them before they left that within the hour the moon would rise.

A half-mile from the target, Luka's vehicle turned off on to a dirt track that ran between two crumbling storage sheds. They had changed into jeans and black pullovers. Jeff had bought a pair of calf-high desert-tan military boots in Istanbul. Jonno, Aussie and Ginger had boots as part of their security uniforms and had brought their kit with them. For a soldier, boots were as important as his rifle. They had decided the only kit they would wear that was military were the boots. If the night turned ugly, and Kurdish authorities or international troops appeared, he didn't want his crew mistaken for mercenaries or ISIS recruits. They climbed out of the vehicles and gathered round the raised rear door of the second SUV. Jonno, Aussie and Ginger picked over the weapons and chose Kalashnikovs.

"Are they in working order?" Aussie asked.

Luka said, "Fired today. They will work. No one uses these buildings anymore. As you can see, they are falling down. We can stay parked here for as long as we like. It is a three-hundred-metre walk to the coordinates. No one is on the street. Not out here, and not in the dark. We will not be seen."

Jeff took Reason aside.

"Please don't take this the wrong way, but I need you to stay behind. We are going to reconnoitre the place, and we will move as an SAS squad, the way we were trained to do. It will be in, locate the target, make a note of any obstacles and out. No more."

"Tell me to fuck off, Jeff, but don't patronise me. I know where you're coming from; I'm not an idiot."

Jeff laughed. "Okay. As long as we're clear. I promise next time you can go in alone and we'll stay back. Just to be fair."

"Get on with it. And don't get shot."

Jeff joined the others.

"We don't have headsets, which means we need to stay close. Ten-metre intervals. The moonlight is bright enough for us to easily navigate the area. We'll keep to the right side of the lanes until we get to the coordinates."

Jonno passed Jeff a tube of grey and a tube of green camouflage cream. Jeff applied it to his face and hands, and passed the tubes back.

"Okay, guys, let's move out."

⁓

Reason stood beside Luka and watched until Jeff and his team disappeared from sight.

"He is your man, Jeff Bradley?" Luka asked.

"No. Why do you ask?"

"When you look at him, it is like a woman does when she is proud of her man. When she has claimed him for herself."

Reason laughed.

"You might laugh," Luka said. "But it is in your eyes, and the eyes do not lie."

"Is this how it is with you and Jonno?"

"For me, yes. For Jonno, no, but I love him in a different way."

"What happened between you two? Tonight in the café, the warmth for Jonno from all the men — what is that all about?"

Luka pointed to the boot of the SUV. "Take a seat."

"I will tell you because someone should know, but I ask you, until Jonno says it is okay, you must keep it to yourself. This is woman to woman because what Jonno did to help can only truly be understood by another woman. I need to talk about it, but I cannot here in Zakho. Such things as this we are forced to live with in silence."

Reason shifted in her seat to fully give her attention to Luka. The rebel leader looked at the ground. Kicked her boot into the dirt.

"For me, what happened three years ago has become a blur. I try not to remember, and mostly I don't, but some nights in the dark, when I sleep, it comes back so clear I wake screaming. But the scream is silent. My mouth has opened, but there is no noise."

Luka paused. Reason waited.

"One morning, my sister and my mother and I went to the markets. I was on a break from university. The morning was crisp but sunny. A nice day and we were happy. Then the men in black appeared. The rifles in their hands spat death. The men already at the markets and any men who came near when they heard the shooting were shot. Me, my mother, my sister and twenty other women were loaded on to trucks and taken across the border into Syria. We had become a number among the many hundreds of women kidnapped by ISIL or ISIS, as this scum has become known. We were lost to our families."

Luka stood and took a few paces forward. Stared into the sky.

"I don't think I need to explain to you what lay ahead for me, my mother, sister and the other women."

Reason shook her head. "No, I have read the news stories."

"Many Kurdish women have suffered at the hands of these pigs of men. We all heard the stories of the Yazidi women. Raped, and turned into nothing more than prostitutes. Passed around like bowls of food, and tossed into the trash or murdered when finished with. In those first hours, I held on to my mother and sister and we wept."

Luka turned back to Reason.

"And praise to Allah, he sent a saviour. My brother had been working in Baghdad as a translator for the New Zealand soldiers. This is where he met Jonno. They became friends, and he invited Jonno to our village for a visit. We were excited. A foreigner not only coming to dinner, but to stay. This is why we were in the market that day. Buying food to make a great feast for our honoured guest.

"Late that afternoon, my brother and Jonno arrived in Zakho. The news of our kidnapping at first left my brother in shock. My father said he became as white as flour and fell to his knees. But for my brother there was more bad news to follow. Two of his best friends were among the men killed in the markets. Poor Jonno, he was in the house of our family and he could see the distress, but my father did not speak English and my brother would not speak."

Luka returned to sit next to Reason.

"After an hour, my brother came out of his trance and, still not speaking, he went outside and to the back of the house. Jonno followed him. We had weapons hidden in a garden shed. My brother took out a Kalashnikov and ammunition. As he made to walk back to the house, Jonno stepped in front of him and demanded to know what was happening. My brother told him we had been taken and he was going to rescue his family. He would arrange for Jonno to be taken back to Baghdad. He apologised for his rudeness, but it was his duty and he did not know how long it would take; best for Jonno to return to his camp.

"Then, praise to Allah, Jonno said he would not let my brother go alone. That he would go with him. But they would not leave until nightfall. He wanted this time to plan. He wanted weapons, and he wanted to know the crossing points. My brother called to the house everyone he knew would be useful. Those who knew the Syrian border crossing were of course the PKK soldiers, and they were ready to help.

Jonno told them he had the experience, and would lead and selected a team of ten experienced PKK fighters and my brother. At dusk, Jonno, my brother and the PKK fighters made for the border."

Reason could imagine Jonno becoming involved. She had met men like Jonno and Jeff in the Special Forces units from America and Britain. They believed they were invincible. She reconsidered, and decided that was not a fair comment. Special Forces men, when they decided a job needed to be done, got on and did it.

"What happened to you and the others during this time?" Reason asked.

"Not a lot. We had no idea what our final destination might be, but we crossed into Syria. My guess was they would take us down through Syria, cross back into Iraq and end up in Mosul. Most of the kidnapped women were taken to Mosul to be given as wives to the ISIS soldiers. Anyway, the sun was going down and I guess the ISIS shits must be frightened of the dark. We stopped at one of their border bases and we were locked in a room. We assumed this would be until morning, and we would be moved on. After a few hours, the guards returned. Maybe they had been drinking. I don't know. They needed comforting. Four young women were selected. Myself and my sister and two others. My mother screamed at them. One of the guards punched her in the face. We were pushed from the room."

Luka stopped. Her head fell to her chest. Her right hand rubbed the bridge of her nose. She stayed that way for a minute. Reason did not reach out to comfort her. Luka was shedding her demons talking with her, and Reason knew enough to leave her to go through it alone. Sitting with her, giving her space and listening was enough.

"Jonno and my brother crossed into Syria around midnight. The PKK soldiers knew where to cross safely. Then Jonno took over. They saw lights in the distance and they parked the trucks. They walked to the small village. Jonno selected two of the PKK men. Seasoned fighters. He told my brother and the others to wait. And he and the two PKK men entered the town. I have no details of what happened, but when they returned they had extracted our location from an ISIS soldier.

"In the room where we were held we heard the gunfire. We huddled together, frightened of course. The door was smashed down, and I will never forget the sight ever: Jonno stood in the light as big as a god. I had never met him, and screamed. Then my brother rushed past Jonno and held us. My brother said Jonno was like a superman. Charging into building after building, firing his Kalashnikov and bodies dropping everywhere. The PKK soldiers avenged fallen comrades. None of the ISIS soldiers lived. By morning, all the women taken from Zakho the day before returned home.

"Jonno did not stay the night. Too much sorrow pervaded the house. My sister and I were so ashamed. We hid ourselves in our rooms. Jonno said he needed to return to his base and told my brother that what happened in Syria was never to be spoken of and swore us all to secrecy. He said what he had done was against army regulations. It would be very bad for him if it was ever found out. Tonight is the first time he has been back to Zakho. The men who welcomed him were the husbands and brothers of the women he saved."

Luka smiled.

"And there you have it. I will always love Jonno, and for our town he will always be a hero."

"That is some story, Luka. You have my word. Jonno's secret is safe with me."

∽

The hostage building identified itself. Beams of light flooded out through the windows. The surrounding buildings were in total darkness.

It was also the only building that looked solid enough not to collapse at any moment. It had a roof. The other visible buildings looked as if they had suffered the worst effects of a bombing raid. Jeff knew the Turkish Air Force had flown bombing missions in the area.

He gave the signal for the team to move forward. Jonno and Aussie were on his left flank, Ginger on the right. The warehouse had a wall round it. When they reached it, he held up his hand to stop. A few metres to his right, Jeff found a spot where the concrete blocks had crumbled away. He could see into the compound. While there was light coming from within the building, there were no lights on the outer wall. However, the moonbeams emitted enough light to clearly see any obstacles that lay ahead. It also meant that they could be spotted easily by a sentry when crossing the dead ground.

"There are two buildings in the compound. With me, Jonno. We'll check the closest building first. Ginger, you and Aussie stay here and cover us. Any shooting, and we're going to come back running. Don't open fire until you identify your target."

"Is that right, mate?" Aussie said. "Who would've thought that's what you do. Fuck me – if only I'd joined the army and got some bloody training."

"Okay, okay. Sorry, fair point," Jeff said.

Ginger said, "Don't worry about it, Jeff. He is an Aussie; he needed reminding."

Jeff climbed through the gap. Jonno followed. A quick scan showed the ground clear to the warehouse wall. Jeff ran at pace. The ground was loose dirt. No sound. They crept up to a window at chest height. Jeff peered through the bottom right corner.

He pulled back. "The hostages are in there."

Jonno tapped him on the shoulder as an acknowledgement he had heard and understood.

"The road entrance into the compound is on the other side of the building," Jeff whispered. "Any guards will likely be near the gate."

Jonno gave Jeff another tap on the shoulder and moved ahead of him, leading the way along the outer wall. He poked his head round the corner, and turned back to Jeff.

"Two guards by the gate."

"Okay, you cross over to the other building and check it out. I'll cover you."

Jonno ran across the twenty metres to the second building. Jeff watched the guards, but the soft ground again meant no sound from Jonno's boots. After a few minutes, Jonno was back at Jeff's side.

"We've a major bloody problem," he said. "Let's get the hell out of here so I can tell you about it."

CHAPTER FORTY

They've got us outnumbered," Jonno said. "Maybe there are too many of them." He looked at Jeff. "This rescue might just be starting to take on the appearance of a suicide mission."

"Not yet, Jonno. Let's talk it through before we jump to conclusions."

They had re-assembled back at the vans. Jeff had not given any information to Aussie and Ginger at the wall. They were in enemy territory, and he wanted them fully focussed on the patrol formation and to remain alert. He also didn't want to repeat himself.

Now, he paced while Jonno leaned against the side of the vehicle, arms crossed, and Ginger and Aussie sat on their haunches. Reason and Luka sat in the boot and waited for Jeff and his team to settle. Aussie opened a bottle of water. Ginger plucked it from his hand and gulped half.

"The hostages are in there, all right," Jeff said.

"How many guards?" Aussie asked, snatching his water back from Ginger.

Jonno said, "Six inside the building and a couple of sentries outside. There is a detached building thirty metres to the left. I didn't get a good look, but from what I did see, it's set up like a barracks. I saw bunks and into another room at the end of the sleeping quarters; men were sitting round a table, nibbling titbits and drinking cognac or raki, or whatever it is they drink in Iraq. I couldn't see enough of it, but it looked like a typical army camp mess to me. At the other end, I could hear running water. Had to be an ablution block, is my guess. The living quarters looked ordered. I think in their day these guys might have been army."

"Could be some of Saddam's old troops," Luka said. "If that were so, I would question why they are with The Sheriff. Many went to join up with ISIS, but none would have gone near the PKK."

Jeff said, "I think, Luka, if we have learned anything over the last few days, it is that The Sheriff has little interest in fighting to build a Kurdistan state. He is working with Avni Leka, and that is scary stuff. Anyway, let's continue with the briefing. Jonno."

Jonno said, "But our worry is there are at least twenty of them inside the barracks building. We can easily take care of the six with the hostages and the two outside guards, but that small garrison in the barracks is a problem. Once the shooting starts, we'll be outgunned. And we have to consider more reinforcements will come from the town. In fact, I think we have to bank on it."

"Okay, it's simple really," Jeff said. "We need to take that garrison out of play before we go get the hostages. Luka, you have a stack of RPG rocket launchers in one of the vehicles. How many?"

"There are six."

"What do you think, Jonno – will six be enough?"

"Overkill, but I'm happy making sure none of them crawl out of the rubble."

Jeff turned to Reason. "When the time comes, we are going to need the SEALs and a Chinook helicopter to pick up the hostages. And tell them to send an Apache, or any heavily armed chopper available. We won't know how many we're up against until the shooting starts, and if more of The Sheriff's men come from the village, there's no better deterrent than an Apache. We need to get them on the way. I'm guessing they will come from Baghdad. I didn't see any sign of choppers at Erbil Airport."

"I'm on it."

"Right," Jeff said. "Time to kick butt. We move out in twenty minutes."

CHAPTER FORTY-ONE

This is it, Reason. Keep your Glock at arm's length and aim your barrel at the chest and pull the trigger. Identify your target, then shoot to kill. You aren't the police. We aren't here to arrest anyone. Got it?" Jeff asked.

"I have fired a weapon before, Jeff. This one in fact," Reason said. She held her Glock shoulder high and waggled it. "You might have noticed how handy I was against Marius in Istanbul."

Jeff blew air through his lips like he was playing a trumpet solo.

"In the military we repeat ourselves a lot. Think of it as the same as a checklist routine a pilot and co-pilot go through before taking a passenger jet into the air. Yes, you are a fighter and you can handle yourself; I know that, but night fighting is different. When the bullets start flying, you won't know where they're coming from. You won't see your enemy, and when you do see movement, it will be shadows. Your first reaction will be hesitation. Are they bad guys or not? Your gut will churn, and you will wish to hell you were someplace else." Jeff reached out a hand and touched her arm. "Just remember to keep your head down."

"That's twice you've patronised me. Don't let there be a third time," Reason said, tight-lipped.

"Okay, guys, let's get out of here before I make a complete ass of myself."

Each member of the team had an RPG-7 launcher slung over their shoulders; Aussie and Ginger carried an extra rocket. Kalashnikovs at the ready, they made their way through the gap in the wall. Jeff glanced over his shoulder. Reason leaned across the opening, her Glock 17 in her hand and at arm's length, ready to give covering fire. He allowed himself a smile, then switched into mission mode.

Jeff led his team in single file and spread out in patrol formation across the open ground. When he reached the corner of the hostage building, he held a hand up and the men behind dropped to one knee, taking up a firing position. Jeff peered round the corner. Fifty metres ahead were the barracks. The internal lights illuminated the area outside. He could see all the way to the road. There was no movement. He leaned out further and checked for the guards out the front. They were nowhere to be seen; all clear. He waved the others to him. They gathered round.

They had discussed in the briefing that the way to gain the deadliest effect from the rockets was to fire them through the windows at the inner walls. The barracks building was built from concrete block and brick, and internally it looked like it had been rendered with some type of plaster. The back blast from the explosion after the rockets hit the solid walls would cause enough damage and maximise the kill zone. RPG-7s were mostly anti-tank. A rocket fired directly into the outer wall might make a big boom and nice hole and sound scary, but it would not be as deadly efficient as Jeff needed it to be.

He spoke in a whisper.

"Okay, guys, you know what to do. Let's get it done."

They moved into position. Excited chatter could be heard from within the barracks; for Jeff, it was a good sign. Relaxed soldiers, slurring from too much cognac, and probably exaggerating anecdotes about past adventures meant they were not in battle mode. Jeff and his team had the element of surprise; a huge advantage when dealing with a much larger force. He was thankful for the distance between the barracks and the hostage building. It minimised any danger of hostage casualties from the exploding rockets.

Jeff gave a thumbs-up for go to Jonno, who passed the signal to Aussie and Ginger. They readied the launchers. From his vantage point Jeff could see through to the mess. He targeted the space between a line of cupboards and the bench and fired. The ground shook as the rocket exploded inside the building. More rockets smashed against the back walls. He saw Aussie and Ginger reload. Flashes of light and debris spat back through the shattered windows. Rock and dirt flung into the air sprayed down around them. The roof lifted, then collapsed. Smoke billowed skyward. Flames plumed. Then the sounds of the explosions died away. An eerie silence followed. Seconds passed. Seemed like minutes. And then came the guttural screams from men in agony lying and staggering inside the smoking wreckage. Strange words in a language Jeff did not recognise.

Jeff dropped his launcher and ran towards the front of the hostage building. Aussie trailed. Jonno and Ginger raced towards the barracks. As Jeff rounded the front of the building, the two soldiers guarding the entrance were scrambling to their feet. Jeff, the Kalashnikov against his hip, tightened his finger on the trigger and sprayed one of the rising men with two automatic bursts. The bullets thumped into the man's chest, flinging him backwards. Jeff swung his head as he heard shots fired beside him.

Aussie aimed at the second guard. The man's head exploded.

Aussie spun round and dropped to his knee, bringing the Kalashnikov's sights to his right eye. He took aim at the front of the hostage building. Two men charged through the doorway. Flashes of light spat from the barrels of their rifles. Aussie and Jeff had already flattened to the ground. Aussie shot the first man, and he fell back, knocking his companion off balance. Jeff leaped to his feet and ran on to the slate-covered verandah. He smashed the butt of his Kalashnikov into the side of the second man's head. The Sheriff's soldier collapsed to the floor.

Jeff turned towards the barracks building. In the light from the flames, he could see survivors from the RPG strike staggering from the destruction into the path of Jonno's Kalashnikov. Jeff heard smaller explosions. Ginger was lobbing grenades into the building. The raid had been ferocious, the devastation complete. No one had survived.

Jeff turned his attention back to the hostage building. By his calculation, there were still four of The Sheriff's men unaccounted for. He tried the door. Locked. He took a few steps back and shoulder-charged.

"Shit," Jeff cursed.

The door hadn't budged. He rubbed his shoulder.

Aussie gave a slow head shake and stepped forward. He reached out and pushed Jeff to the side. Raising himself on to his toes, he aimed his Kalashnikov downward at the lock. A short burst and then there was only a hole where the lock had been. He looked at Jeff. Jeff nodded he was ready. Aussie raised his leg and booted the door open.

Jeff dived through the gap, hitting the floor, his weapon sweeping back and forth.

"Clear," Jeff called.

Aussie leaped over him and ran along the corridor, Jeff covering. A head poked out through a side door. Jeff's Kalashnikov spat lead, and he heard a grunt and a satisfying thud as a body crashed on to the wood floor.

"Three to go," Jeff yelled.

He was back on his feet. Jonno and Ginger were now behind him.

"Jonno, stay out until we clear. If anyone shoots into this tunnel, we'll all cop it."

They heard gunfire inside the room holding the hostages.

"We need to go, Aussie; sounds like they might be shooting the hostages," Jeff yelled.

Aussie smashed through the door into the warehouse as Jeff caught up with him. They both dived through, and Jeff rolled to the left and Aussie to the right. Weapons sweeping the room. In his peripheral vision, he caught sight of frightened faces. The hostages huddled together to his left. Jeff ignored them. He remained focussed on danger. He could see no more guards.

Aussie yelled to the hostages, "Keep down. Stay flat to the floor."

Bodies dropped. No one needed a second warning.

"Where are the guards?" Aussie demanded from no one in particular. Shaking arms pointed towards an open rear door.

Aussie signalled to Jeff he was going for the door. Jeff held up a hand: wait. He looked back. Jonno and Ginger were now in the corridor. Weapons trained back towards the entrance.

"Jonno," Jeff called out, just loud enough to be heard. "Aussie and I are going to clear the rear. Take care of the hostages."

A thumbs-up.

From outside, machine gun fire shattered the eerie silence. Then single shots, followed by a further staccato of machine gun fire.

"Reason," Jeff yelled.

He scrambled to his feet and dashed to the door, leaping through it.

"Fucking hell, Bradley. Wait for me, you stupid asshole."

Jeff ran for the wall. He saw the shape of a body on the ground. He ran faster and dropped to his knees beside it. Relief spread through him. It was one of the guards.

Aussie leaped through the gap. Jeff followed, and on the other side dropped to one knee, aiming his weapon into the darkness. Both men scanned the ground in front of them. No movement.

"Reason, are you out there?" Jeff called.

"Behind the tree," Reason called back.

Jeff identified Reason's cover. It was thirty metres away.

"I've got you. Don't move. We're coming to you." Jeff turned to Aussie. "Ready?"

"I'm always ready, mate."

Jeff darted to the tree and hit the ground. Aussie ran ten metres past them. Jeff reached out for Reason. He found her hand. She grasped his back.

"Are you okay?" he asked.

"I'm okay."

"Stay where you are. See anything, Aussie?"

"Nothing," Aussie said. "I think they've done a runner. They probably thought the whole fucking Iraqi army had arrived."

"Okay," Jeff said. "It looks all clear."

He climbed to his feet and, still holding Reason's hand, he pulled her on to her feet. Aussie walked back to them. Jeff reluctantly let Reason's hand go.

"Thank you, guys," Reason said.

"*No problemo,*" Aussie responded.

Jeff said, "Let's get back to the hostages. We still have a job to do."

At the door, Jeff turned to Aussie.

"Stay out here, Aussie. We might still get visitors."

When Jeff re-entered the hostage building, he made straight for Jonno. He was in the hallway with Ginger.

"It's all clear outside, Jonno. Ginger, get out front and find a spot. Secure the area."

Ginger moved off along the corridor and disappeared from sight. He returned after a minute pushing a groggy guard in front of him.

"It must be the guy I bumped on the head," Jeff said. "Come on, my friend."

Jeff took hold of the prisoner's shirt collar and pulled him into the main room with the hostages. He pushed him against the wall. "Keep an eye on him for a moment, Jonno. Reason, with me."

Jeff and Reason made their way across to the hostages. Some of the women wept into comforting shoulders; others held on to arms. Pale faces watched as he approached. Mouths opened and closed. It would take them a few moments to adjust, realise what had happened and pass through the fear barrier. A woman Jeff guessed to be in her sixties sat cradling the head of a man of the same age on her lap. He swallowed when he saw the blood spreading across the man's chest.

"They shot at us as they ran through the door," one of the hostages explained.

Jeff knelt beside the couple.

"I'm sorry," he said.

The woman looked at him and nodded. "It's okay, young man. Graeme Beattie was once a fine soldier. I'm sure he would have approved. He's at peace now."

Jeff wanted to walk across to the wall and kick it. Instead, he climbed to his feet, sucked in some air and composed himself. He saw Reason watching him from a few feet away, her eyes alert and her demeanour controlled. The more time he spent with Reason Johanson, the more he liked her.

Jeff addressed the hostages. "Anyone ex-military?"

"I'm ex-air force," a man in his sixties answered.

"That will do." Jeff gripped the wrist of his outstretched arm and helped him to his feet. He took a handgun from his belt. "Follow me." Jeff waved for The Sheriff's man to sit on the floor. "Back against the wall," he further instructed. "Good." Jeff passed the weapon to the ex-air force man. "Stand back ten paces and keep this on him. If he moves, shoot. Just pull the trigger."

"No worries. I won't need much of an excuse."

"Good man."

"Okay, Jonno, time to go check the corridor. We need to clear those rooms."

The danger seemingly over, the hostages slowly got themselves on to their feet. Two women went to comfort the woman holding her dead husband. Jeff gave the group a quick scan.

His heart sank. There was no sign of Barry or Bethany.

CHAPTER FORTY-TWO

W hy are Barry Briggs and his fiancée, Bethany, not with you lot?"
Jeff asked.

"They were taken away earlier today," the air force man said over his shoulder, his aim on The Sheriff's man unwavering. "We don't know where. Ask this guy," he said. "He was one of the phoney cops who kidnapped us at the beginning of all this. He was in charge."

"Really?" Jeff eyed the prisoner and walked across to him.

Jonno entered. "There are a number of rooms off the hallway, doors bolted shut from the outside. They must be hiding something. It means there is no risk to us from an attack from within. I'm thinking we leave the doors shut, Jeff. They could be booby-trapped and we don't have the time or the equipment to clear them."

Jeff stepped up to the phoney cop. He put his thumb and forefinger under the cop's chin and lifted his head. "Do you speak English?"

A nod of the head.

"Are the rooms booby-trapped?"

A shake of the head.

"Are the two you took away today in one of those rooms?"

A shake of the head. "No, they are not."

Reason observed the interaction over Jeff's shoulder. She stepped up beside Jeff. "Are the two American women in one of those rooms?" His eyes widened. He nodded. "Which room?" she asked.

"The one at the end of the corridor."

"For your sake, they'd better be alive."

She turned on her heel. Jeff and Jonno followed.

"What about the bus?" Jeff asked Jonno. "Any sign of one outside?"

"Never saw one, Jeff, but with the choppers on their way we won't need one, will we?"

"They aren't here yet."

Reason stopped outside the last door. She pulled out her Glock and emptied half the magazine into the hinges. She turned to Jeff. He moved forward, lifted his leg and kicked it open.

The two American women sat on the bed, holding each other. Reason rushed to them, and the women threw their arms around their rescuer and burst into tears. Jeff made the decision to leave Reason with the women. There was nothing he could do.

"Let's try the other doors, Jonno."

Jeff walked up to the first. He aimed his Kalashnikov at the wood around the bolt as Aussie had done on the front door, pointing the barrel down so the bullets would hit the floor on the other side. He pulled the trigger. The door splintered. The bolt held the door, but only just. He pushed against it and it flung open. Jonno stepped in. A man lay on the bed. Of Middle Eastern origin. His eyes bulged at the sight of Jonno. His hands came to his mouth and he retreated into a foetal position.

"Well, bugger me," Jonno said.

Jeff gave him a sideways glance. "You know this guy?"

"That's the bloody kid from Abu Dhabi. The one who did a runner and cost us our jobs."

Jonno bent forward and helped him sit up.

"Leave him until we clear the other rooms," Jeff said.

Jonno pointed a finger at the kid's forehead. "Don't move," he growled. The kid nodded.

Two more rooms revealed two more prisoners. Both young Arab men. The two women and young men were brought through to join the hostages.

Jeff turned to Reason. "We need those choppers. The Sheriff's reinforcements could arrive at any time."

She turned away as she pulled out her phone.

Before she could dial, the mobile rang. With it to her ear, she waved to Jeff.

"Luka says there are locals running in different directions like headless chickens, but no sign of any of The Sheriff's men. Not yet anyway. But she says someone will be making contact with The Sheriff and asking for instructions. We need to move."

Reason put her call through to the US base in Baghdad.

Jonno joined Jeff.

"How is the kid?" Jeff asked.

"He's good. Seems when ISIS found out who he was, they decided he would be more useful to the cause as a hostage and have daddy pay a big pile of money to get him back. The other two are also from wealthy families. I think they've lost interest in the cause and want to go home."

"It does bring into question, just what the hell is The Sheriff up to? And why keep them here? Why not keep them in Syria, where ISIS is stronger?"

Jonno said, "If I was a betting man, my money would be on a breakaway group looking to make money on the side."

"You might well be right."

Reason folded her phone. "The choppers are still twenty minutes away."

The hostages were gathering around them.

Jeff said, "In twenty minutes, helicopters will arrive to take you to safety. Please gather together your belongings and be ready."

Jeff walked across to The Sheriff's man.

"You and I need to talk," Jeff said. "I want to know where the two people you took away from the group today have gone. I don't have time to debate the issue with you. Tell me; if you don't, we're going to take a walk outside and only one of us will return."

The Sheriff's man shrugged. "There is no need to make threats. You only need to ask. It is of no interest to me if you have them back. I have done the job I was paid to do. I am an independent contractor, as you say in the West. How much will you pay for this information?"

Jeff almost laughed.

"I tell you what I'll do: if you show me where they are and they are safe and unharmed, I won't put a bullet in your head. How does that sound?"

"I can trust you to let me go?"

"I only want my friends back, but I want them back alive."

"Okay. I accept your kind offer."

"Where are they?"

"The Sheriff has taken them to one of his strongholds close to Dornaq."

"How far?"

"Not far from here."

Jeff nodded. "Why did he take them there?"

"I only follow orders. Osman Gashi is my boss. He ordered it. Even The Sheriff was confused, but he took them anyway."

Jeff knew the answer, and he felt sick to the core. He threw his head back and looked up at nothing. Osman Gashi and Avni Leka had ordered The Sheriff to hold Barry and Bethany. His two friends were to be bait. He clung to the hope that The Sheriff would keep them alive until he walked into the trap that no doubt was being set for him. Time was important. The Sheriff would know by now of the attack on his compound.

What was Leka's endgame? What the hell was going on? He didn't believe for one moment that Leka had gone to all the trouble of freeing

The Sheriff, hijacking the hostages and blowing up a busload of alternative passengers just so he could set an elaborate trap for a dumb-ass New Zealander named Jeff Bradley. Something else was going on, and given Leka's past history of not caring how many innocents died, it scared the hell out of him. If the mad criminal had tried to blow up a nuclear submarine in New Zealand, who knew what he might be thinking of this time round?

Jeff said to The Sheriff's man, "All right, get up. You and I are going to The Sheriff. Jonno – you, Reason, Aussie and Ginger stay with the hostages and get them on the choppers."

"Wait until the choppers have been and gone, Jeff, and we'll come with you," Jonno said. "Better we stick together."

Jeff shook his head. "There is no time. When The Sheriff learns of this attack, he might panic and kill my friends. I might already be too late. Your job is done."

Jeff cast his eye over the hostages. Some were elderly and looked in need of medical care. The SEAL team would have a medic.

"What about the choppers?" Jonno asked Reason.

She checked her watch. "Fifteen minutes."

Jonno nodded. "I'll get this torch out to Ginger; he can guide them in." Jonno returned after a few minutes. "There's plenty of room out front for a Chinook."

He'd barely spoken the words when automatic weapons crackled in the direction of the rear wall.

"Get down!" Jeff yelled.

Bullets slammed into the wood, sending splinters flittering about like fireflies. The hostages began screaming and threw themselves to the floor, eyes widening in fear as the shooting intensified.

Jeff raced across the room and switched off the lights.

CHAPTER FORTY-THREE

J onno, Reason, to me."

Shadows crawled towards him.

"What do you think?" Jeff asked.

"Same as you," Jonno said. "The Sheriff's men have rallied. There could be a few hundred of the bastards out there, for all we know. This is not good."

"We need to think of something quick time. They will outflank us."

"Let's hope to hell they don't have rockets," Jonno said. "If they fire the bloody things into this building . . ." He lowered his voice so the hostages wouldn't hear, even though over the sound of the firefight it would be impossible. "Well, I don't have to spell it out."

A body brushed against Jeff. The perfume told him it was Reason.

"The choppers aren't far away," she said. "I have their command on my cell phone. Any instructions?"

"Not yet," Jeff said. "When they get close tell them to stay back until we give an all clear. In the daytime we could throw a few smoke grenades, but at night they'll never see them. If Ginger starts waving the torch about, The Sheriff's men will turn him into a pile of mincemeat. I need a landmark.

"Jonno, you go out the back and support Aussie. I can hear return fire, so he's still making them keep to their side of the wall. Reason and I will go out front with Aussie. Once I've found a beacon of some type, Reason can guide in the choppers."

"They have the GPS coordinates," Reason said. "They know where to come."

"Yes, but in the dark they can't identify us from the enemy. We need to tell them where to shoot."

"Okay, my lack of military training is showing."

Jeff crawled across to the air force man guarding the phoney cop, who was lying flat on the floor like everyone else. Jeff tapped the air force man on the shoulder.

"Make sure he doesn't go anywhere."

"Roger that," the air force man responded.

Jeff climbed to his feet and ran along the hallway, Reason close behind.

As they ran through the doorway and leaped off the terrace, Jeff grasped Reason's jacket at the top of the shoulder and flung her to the ground. He hit the dirt beside her and flung an arm over her.

"Sorry about that; instinct."

"Would you have done that if I was Jonno?"

"If Jonno looked like you, of course."

"Always the chauvinist. Women can look out for themselves, you know. But thanks, Jeff."

"Ginger, where the hell are you?" Jeff yelled.

"Right here, mate, behind the rock." He waved an arm. "The bastards are all round us. I dropped a couple, and since then they haven't shown their ugly faces. Luckily, there are no heroes on The Sheriff's team. But I'm running out of ammo. One more mag, and whatever's left in this one."

The shooting intensified. Reason lifted herself up, but Jeff pushed her head back to the ground.

"That's twice, Jeff."

"You can thank me later. But keep your bloody head down."

He swept the barrel of his rifle across the open ground. No heads. Then the sounds of the shots changed. The automatic fire switched to sporadic. "Hey, Aussie, I don't think we're being shot at anymore."

A pause. "I think you might be right, mate. Then if they're not trying to kill us, who the hell are they shooting at?" The firing stopped. "A ceasefire, maybe."

"Jonno." A female voice called from behind the outer wall at the rear of the building.

"Over here," Jeff heard Jonno cry.

"It's Luka," Jeff said as he scrambled to his feet.

He held out a hand for Reason. She ignored it and rolled back, then flipped forward on to her feet like an Olympic gymnast.

Jonno led Luka and ten of her soldiers round the corner of the building.

Jeff walked towards them. "You're a welcome sight, Luka," he said. "Why the change of heart? I thought you said you wouldn't fight other PKK members."

"I have given it some thought. The PKK does not kidnap people from foreign countries and we do not work with ISIS. Whatever it is The Sheriff is up to, it has nothing to do with Kurdistan. I decided to bring in my soldiers to help. I also know the local commander and I said we are here to reinforce his units, so they let us through. They have stopped firing until me and my soldiers are in place. They don't really want to get into a fight, so for them it is a game to make sure when the hostage rescue gets back to The Sheriff, he will think they made a good fist of putting up a fight but were outnumbered."

Jeff asked, "So they aren't going to try and overrun us?"

Luka shook her head. "I explained to the leader what The Sheriff is up to. He didn't care. They're afraid of him. Disobeying an order could get him shot. But no, as I said, do not worry; they are not going to charge us. They might fear The Sheriff, but none of the locals is that interested in getting killed for him. But they will keep us pinned down and make it difficult. They have not got enough troops yet to surround the area, so they are concentrating on blocking off the road back to Zakho."

"Reason, where are we at with the SEALs?"

"Five minutes."

Jeff said to Luka, "So right now, you're saying the road to Dornaq is open."

"Yes, they figure you won't be looking to go in the direction which is The Sheriff's territory. But men are coming. Soon the circle will close."

Jeff said, "Well done, Luka."

"What do you want from us?"

"Spread yourselves around the perimeter; use the wall as cover. Keep The Sheriff's men out of here until the choppers arrive. Only a few minutes away."

Luka said, "You've got it. No one will get through."

Jonno put his hand on her shoulder and gave it a squeeze. Jeff noted the affectionate display. What the hell, it was their business.

"I'm taking that black Mercedes car over there and our crooked cop. He knows where The Sheriff is holding Barry and Bethany, and he can take me to him. Jonno, you and your team stay here with the hostages, get them on the choppers and go out with them."

Jeff went back inside. He flicked on his torch and waved its light over the huddled group.

"It's okay, everyone. Please prepare yourself to leave on the helicopter. You will be taken to Baghdad or Erbil. Not certain where, but you will be safe."

Jeff turned his attention to the phoney cop.

"We heard The Sheriff had given orders to execute the hostages. Is this true?"

The cop nodded. "But neither I nor my Albanian companions were happy about it. We aren't mass murderers, no matter what you might think. But the men in the other building. I don't know who they were, but they would have done it."

"It doesn't matter now. You and I are going for a ride."

Jeff dragged the cop to his feet. He took the pistol off the air force man. He pointed it at the cop and waved towards the corridor. The cop walked ahead.

Outside, it was still quiet. He said to Reason and Jonno, "Okay, I'm off."

"I'm coming with you," Reason said.

"Like hell you are."

CHAPTER FORTY-FOUR

Reason followed Jeff to the car. She stepped in front of him, forcing him to stop.

"You can't drive and watch this guy at the same time. I told you I have a special interest in The Sheriff, and after tonight I've added the rape of two American women to the list."

Jeff's mouth slackened. "I'm sorry, I didn't know. Thoughtless of me not to ask." He closed his eyes for a fraction of a second. "Are they okay? Stupid question. Of course they aren't."

"I want him, Jeff."

Jeff's lips thinned. He took hold of the cop's shirt front and pulled him close. Their noses almost touching. Jeff put the pistol against the cop's temple. "Did you rape those girls?"

Reason's hand touched Jeff's arm. "No," she said. "He wasn't one of them. It was the men in the barracks. The consul's daughter said the Albanians tried to stop it."

Jeff relaxed his hold and dropped his gun hand to his side.

"I'm coming with you, Jeff," Reason repeated.

Jeff nodded. "Okay, I don't have time to argue." He looked through the window at the dashboard. There was enough light from the moon to make out the dials. "It's still got keys in the ignition. The cop can sit in the back and give us directions. You want to come, you can drive. Let's go."

"Is it safe having him in the back?" Reason questioned.

"What can he do? He is unarmed. He can't take us both on at the same time. And if he tries to jump from a speeding car he'll be injured and we will stop and I will shoot him."

Jeff smiled at the cop.

The cop shrugged then said, "He is right. If I try to escape I would have no chance."

They heard sounds, distant. "The choppers are here," Jeff said. "Now Luka has joined the party, we're not needed anymore. Ginger can use the torch to guide them in. The gunship will take care of any of The Sheriff's men who want to fight on. Let's get out of here."

When Reason switched on the ignition, Jeff checked the petrol gauge. The tank was full.

∾

Jonno heard the choppers and looked upwards, searching for the telltale lights. Spasmodic shooting started up again, but it was over their heads. This told Jonno The Sheriff's men were flat to ground and firing at who knew what, but they were not going to put their heads above the wall. Reason had switched the contact with the SEALs' base to Jonno's phone and he was in direct contact. The choppers were ready to come in.

"Luka, where are you?"

Luka appeared by his side.

An Iroquois hovered above. Ginger looked into the sky and waved the torch above his head. Jonno was talking directly to the SEAL commander. The helicopter banked and swooped into a wide arc before disappearing from sight. Jonno heard the roar of the engines and the *whoop*, *whoop* of the Chinook's twin propeller blades. He looked for it. The sound grew louder then; like an apparition, it appeared over the rooftop of a warehouse fifty metres away and made for his waving torch. The downdraft flung dust and debris in all directions, forcing Jonno and Ginger to shield. The Iroquois circled like a hawk looking for a rabbit. An airman attached to a harness manoeuvred his machine gun, looking for a target. Jonno raised his arm and gave the airman a thumbs-up. The Sheriff's men had run.

The Chinook touched the ground, and the back ramp hit the dirt at the same time. Blackened figures ran down the ramp. Seven of the SEALs sprinted into position. They encircled the big helicopter. Eyes looking for movement, fingers tight on triggers.

A SEAL walked up to Jonno.

"You in charge?" the voice commanded.

"Call me Jonno."

"We're here to collect civilians, is this correct?"

"They're inside the building. Did you bring a medic?"

The SEAL commander spun round. "Johnson, with me." He turned back to Jonno, "Right, show me."

∽

Jonno, Ginger, Aussie and Luka stood back at a safe distance as the last of the hostages were loaded on to the Chinook. Graeme Beattie was lifted aboard in a body bag. The big double blades had not stopped rotating. In a minute it would be gone.

The SEAL leader dashed across to Jonno.

"Are you sure you guys want to stay behind?"

"Certain," Jonno said.

"What should I say about all this?"

Jonno said, "American SEALs operating under cover found the foreign hostages thought to have been killed in Turkey, and rescued them from somewhere along the Syrian border. The exact location is classified. They are believed to have been kidnapped by The Sheriff working with remnants of an ISIS terrorist cell. All the terrorists were killed during the rescue. Something like that would work."

"You don't want any credit?"

"No. Leave us out of it."

The SEAL commander held out his hand and Jonno shook it. "Good work. If you ever need us again, call."

Jonno gave a half-hearted salute, and the SEAL commander ran up the ramp into the rear of the Chinook. The monster flying machine was in the air before the rear door closed. When it was high enough, it turned and drifted away, the Iroquois in pursuit.

"Why didn't you go with them, Jonno?" Luka asked.

Jonno smiled. "I have to make sure you get home safely," he teased. "But mostly those three young Arab men need to go home." Jonno tilted his head towards the three.

"Yes. Let's get back to the vehicles," Luka said. She waved to her troops.

Jonno looked down the road towards Dornaq.

"Good luck, Jeff," he whispered.

CHAPTER FORTY-FIVE

Reason slowed at the outskirts of The Sheriff's village. The first strands of light from the rising sun silhouetted the minaret of a mosque. Jeff imagined that thirty minutes earlier the imam had climbed the internal staircase and sounded the call to prayer. Or more likely, as in other modern Islamic towns, the imam might have used a loudspeaker. The phoney cop had sat in silence throughout the drive, head resting against the window, eyes half closed. Now he sat up, fully awake. His eyes flitted about, searching the streets, the shadows; a touch of concern. Jeff grinned. The cop was nervous. Good. The Sheriff would know by now the hostages had been rescued. He wouldn't be expecting the men behind the raid to come looking for him. No one but his inner sanctum would know where he was. But he would certainly have sentries posted. Normal security precautions for sure.

Jeff turned in his seat. "Okay, cop, where to?"

"I think two streets past the mosque. I am trying to remember exactly."

"You aren't seriously going to screw with us now, are you?"

"No, of course not," the cop blurted out whilst eyeing the door.

Jeff caught the look. "Don't try it," he warned. "You'll never get twenty metres."

"I've only been here a couple of times. All the streets look the same." He pointed. "There, turn there."

Reason followed the directions and parked thirty metres short of the next corner. Jeff drew his pistol and climbed out of the car. He opened the rear door. "Okay, out." The cop stepped on to the pavement. They stopped at the corner.

"Halfway down," the cop said. "The red door."

Jeff used his binoculars. Three small trucks were parked in a line in front of the house as close to the outer wall as possible. It was standard security practice for gangsters like The Sheriff, living in Third World countries. Drive-by shootings and rockets fired into homes by rivals were commonplace. The trucks made it difficult, and anyone wanting to try would need to find a gap to fire through, which would mean stopping the car. The armed guards could empty a magazine into their vehicle before they got a shot away.

The two armed guards outside The Sheriff's house had Kalashnikovs slung over their shoulders. And they looked handy enough.

One of the men stubbed out a cigarette and lit another.

Jeff passed the binoculars to Reason.

"What's the plan?" she said, passing them back.

"Do you know these men?" Jeff asked the cop.

"Yes, I do."

"Well then, the three of us will take a casual stroll. You can lead. Give them a friendly wave, and when we get close, ask to see The Sheriff. My friend and I will take out the guards. Are you up to it, Reason?"

"I have a black belt in karate." She opened her jacket and tapped the handle of her knife with her index finger. "But I think I will use this. Less noise."

"Good thinking. I wish I had one."

Reason reached behind her back and produced a second knife. Jeff pushed the blade up his sleeve, keeping hold of the handle. With the back of his hand facing towards the guards, they would never see the weapon.

"Okay, cop, lead the way," Jeff said.

As Jeff, Reason and the cop approached, the guards unslung their rifles. The cop waved to them. His manner friendly. They relaxed when they recognised him. Another few metres and Jeff had selected the spot on the body of his man, up under the ribcage and into the heart. His fingers caressed the knife handle, and as arranged, the cop walked across in front of him, shielding him from the guard's scrutiny. Jeff pulled the knife from his sleeve, and as the cop stepped aside, he leaped. His left hand grasped the front of the guard's jacket and he sunk the blade to the hilt. He pulled his hand away and let go of the guard's shirt. The dead man fell across the body of Reason's guard, her knife in his throat. Jeff gave Reason a quick check. No sign of emotion.

"Okay?" he asked.

"Just get on with it."

Jeff turned to the cop. "How many in the house?"

He shrugged. "Your two friends and The Sheriff is all I know. But if there are guards on the outside, there will be guards on the inside. This is his house. They will be relaxed. The Sheriff would never expect anyone to come here. His house is not known to many."

Jeff tried the door. It opened. He pulled his pistol. Checked the mag. Reason did the same. "Stay behind us," he said to the cop. "Any noises, and you will not live to see the outcome."

The cop held up his hands. "Don't worry. I have nothing to gain by betraying you."

"Why not put a bullet in him and be done?" Reason said. "If you're too squeamish, I'll do it."

"And if Barry and Bethany are not inside?"

Reason looked the cop square in the eye. "Well, when the time comes, the offer is there."

Jeff gave Reason another quick scrutiny.

"I'm a man of my word; if the cop is on the level, he can walk. Let's go."

They entered a small courtyard. Three paces wide. The door into The Sheriff's house was slightly ajar. Jeff pushed at it and it swung open. No squeak. An oiled hinge. There was a light at the end of a darkened corridor. He could hear voices. Mixed in with the banter in Arabic was an English voice. As Jeff moved closer he recognised one of the speakers. Something was not right. He stepped into the room. A kitchen. A long table covered with plates of food, coffees and cognac. Seated at the table were Barry and Bethany, both tied to their chairs. Two of The Sheriff's men were standing behind them. Two other men holding a suitcase in each hand were just exiting through the back door.

Jeff moved in.

Bethany saw him first. An incredulous stare, then a nervous look towards the kidnappers. Jeff put a finger to his lips. She nodded.

He held his pistol out in front of him and aimed it at the two men behind Barry and Bethany. As he had done with Bethany, he put his finger to his lips. Shocked, the two men lowered their weapons to the floor and pushed them across to Jeff. He kicked the weapons into the corridor, and gestured for the two men to lie on the floor and put their hands on their heads. The men obeyed.

The knives they had used to kill the guards had been left in the bodies.

With Reason covering, he stepped forward, grabbed a knife from the table and cut Barry and Bethany free. The two men who had left the room a moment earlier returned nonchalantly through the back door. When they saw what was happening in the room, one of the men's mouth dropped open, his eyes wide with fear. The second man, though, did not appear alarmed. He stood, legs wide, and flashed a row of yellow teeth at Jeff. "Mr Bradley. We have never met. I am known as

The Sheriff. Welcome to my home. I have been expecting you. Please, you and your friend sit."

Without waiting for a response, The Sheriff sat, as did his man. He glanced at the two men lying on the floor and spat something in Arabic at them.

To Jeff it sounded a lot like, 'I'll deal with you two later.'

Bemused, Jeff pulled out a chair for Reason. He stayed standing. The Sheriff's blasé attitude intrigued him.

The Sheriff said "Thank you" to the cop. "You have completed your task. I will tell Osman Gashi how helpful you have been. You may go."

Jeff turned his pistol on the cop. "I don't think so. Sit on the floor."

The cop looked to The Sheriff. The Sheriff nodded to him, and the cop slid his back down the wall until he was sitting too.

The Sheriff said, "Mr Bradley, did you believe you could come into my territory, rescue the hostages and walk away? This is naïve of you. As we speak, my men are surrounding this house. There is no way out for either of you. And if you have any thoughts you might want to play hero and are prepared to fight to the death, think of your friends. I do not want to hurt them. My contract is only for you. I give you my word: give up, and they and your woman can leave safely."

Jeff suppressed a laugh.

"The problem with warlords such as yourself, Sheriff, is that your area of operation and expertise is limited. I've been in many Third World countries where assholes like you are a dime a dozen. Like you, they surround themselves with a few thugs and truly believe this makes them invincible. But today we live in a new world. You did not account for this," Jeff said, and held up his mobile phone.

"This is to impress me, Mr Bradley. I have one of those too." The Sheriff held up his own phone.

"Yes, but your phone doesn't have a location beacon monitored by the Americans. I don't have to tell you how excited they were when I told them I had found you. They really aren't your best friends. A drone is on its way. The type that fires missiles." Jeff checked his watch. "You have three minutes."

"You're lying."

"Did you think I would trust this crooked cop? I know his boss. I used him to find my friends and now I have found them. Three minutes, Sheriff. Believe me. A drone is on its way. This place is about to be blown to bits and you with it."

The Sheriff looked about. His eyes narrowed on Jeff. Jeff knew what he was thinking: 'Is he lying? And do I take the risk?' It was time to act.

Jeff sprang. He pushed the table forward, smashing it into the seated Sheriff. Then he gripped the edge and flipped it on its side. He brought his pistol to bear on the man next to The Sheriff. The man's gun was rising. Reason beat Jeff to it and shot him in the chest. Jeff swung his attention to the two on the floor. They scrambled about looking for an escape. Jeff fired two shots into the floor beside them. They froze. Now the danger was over, Jeff switched his attention back to The Sheriff. The warlord was now up and running for the door.

Jeff took careful aim.

"No!"

Jeff heard Reason's scream. It distracted him enough to turn his head. A blue denim leg flashed upwards and the weapon flew from his hand.

"What the hell!"

He turned on Reason. Dumbfounded. "Are you kidding? What the hell was that about, Reason?" When he turned back, The Sheriff had disappeared. He switched his attention to Barry and Bethany. "You two, quickly. We need to get out of here." Jeff retrieved his handgun and, ignoring the cop and The Sheriff's two men, pushed Barry and Bethany towards the hallway. "Come on, guys, move it. We need to be gone before the drone arrives. Oh, one second." He opened a hall cupboard and placed his phone in it. "If I carry this with me they'll end up firing the missile at us running away."

"What do we do about these three?" Reason asked.

"Leave them. I'm not going to shoot them in cold blood, and they aren't going to follow us. Leave them for the drone if they're silly enough to hang about."

Outside, Barry said, "Bloody hell, Jeff, that was cutting it fine. It's good to see you, mate."

"Great to see you too, Barry."

Bethany kissed him on the cheek.

They ran back through the gate. Jeff kept them moving until he was confident they had some distance. He led them to the car. A light truck with a cab painted bright blue and a khaki-green canvas canopy covering the flat deck sped past them leaving a dust cloud in its wake. His gut told him The Sheriff was making his escape. Then he heard it. A faint buzz at first, then louder. A lawnmower in the sky. He looked up, his hand shielding his eyes from the now-rising sun. He knew what it was, and he knew it wasn't a microlight.

Jeff yelled, "Come on, everyone, get behind that wall."

They sat with their backs against the cement blocks. Jeff continued to look skywards, searching. He caught Reason's eye.

He said, "I'm grateful you arranged the drone. Snazzy gadget, the tracker you inserted in my phone. But I thought you wanted The Sheriff dead? Why did you save his ass back there?"

"The drone was insurance to get us out. It worked. And Barry and Bethany are free. A job well done, I think," Reason said.

"That doesn't answer my question. Why did you save The Sheriff?" Jeff asked, still searching for the flying machine.

Looking into the sun, it was impossible to see. Then he spied a shadow speeding across the walls of the surrounding buildings like a black wraith from the crypt of the damned. The MQ-1 Predator came into view. The US Air Force drone turned towards its target and released its payload: two AGM-114 Hellfire missiles. Moments passed. Jeff set himself for the explosion. The ground shook. Once the pressure wave passed over him, he looked over the top of the wall and watched the fireball erupt into the air. In less time than it would take him to run ten metres, The Sheriff's house became rubble. Anyone still inside would be dead.

When the debris had stopped falling, Jeff stood up. He pulled Bethany to her feet.

"So, all this was to use Bethany and me to trap you, Jeff?" Barry asked, leaning on the wall.

Jeff turned to Barry, but kept one eye on Reason. She stood apart.

"Not really, Barry. I think you and Bethany were a lucky extra. Avni Leka is behind all this; he is funding them in a big way, and it seems he still has the hots for me on the side. Osman Gashi recognised you two and informed Leka. He guessed that if he had you and Bethany, I'd come after you. He was right. But no, this is not about you two."

Barry hugged Bethany.

Jeff focussed on Reason. In a single stride he was next to her.

"Okay, tell me. Why did you help The Sheriff?"

CHAPTER FORTY-SIX

Barry leaned back against the Mercedes, Bethany in his arms. The gentle roll of her shoulders told Jeff she was sobbing, relieved that finally it all seemed to be over. Local people were emerging from houses, drawn to the burning wreckage that was once The Sheriff's hideout.

Reason walked for a few metres. Until she was out of earshot of Barry and Bethany. Jeff followed.

She stood legs apart, arms folded. "I want The Sheriff alive. He has information I need."

"Go on," Jeff said. "This better be good."

"I told you I had been a stuntwoman. I worked on a number of movies. The last movie I worked on was set in Egypt, in the south, near Abu Simbel. The director wanted to use the temples and spectacular landscapes as backdrop settings. Great for the movie, but Abu Simbel was in the middle of nowhere. A three-hour drive from our hotel each day. But the film-maker wanted to use temples built by an ancient pharaoh, Rameses II, so that was that. His word was law.

"My husband was my stunt assistant. Because of my work for most of our marriage we travelled. The children had a nanny and my mother to look after them when my husband and I were away. This film shoot in Egypt was to be in the school holidays. I thought, why not take the children? The hotel had a pool. My mother agreed to come along to help. So when we trudged off for our daily shoot, she stayed at the hotel with the children.

"Each day we convoyed out to the different locations. On one occasion, we were to stay overnight. We took the kids and they loved it. We were in the wilderness. They saw wild animals and they had a ride on a camel. It wasn't all that rough, as we had caravans and generators and all the comforts of home provided by the film studio."

Reason paused. Jeff waited. He would not interrupt. He knew Reason well enough now to know that she wasn't someone interested in frivolous chatter. There would be a point, and he would let her get to it in her own time.

"My big stunt was to jump a dirt bike over a river. It was more than thirty-five metres across. It took a couple of days to build the launch ramps and clear a path for the run-up. Fortunately, it was not the rainy season, otherwise it would have been impossible.

"On the second day of the camp, the time had come to make the jump. Another crew waited on the opposite bank. When it was over, the landing ramp would be dismantled, and that, the bike and me would be floated back on a barge. Cameras had been strategically positioned to capture the best shots. Every angle the cameraman could envisage had a lens aimed at it. My husband, mother and children had ringside seats to watch the main event. The children were jumping out of their skin with excitement, and my mother was having trouble keeping them in their seats.

"When I was ready, I said the prayer I always said before that type of stunt, and buried the accelerator. I hit the ramp at the right speed and soared through the air. As always, butterflies danced about in my stomach, but I knew the take-off had been perfect. But no matter how certain I was all had gone to plan, there is a nervous moment until touchdown. When the bike's wheels touched down on to the landing ramp I breathed a sigh of relief. Knowing my family was watching, I decided to show off for the kids, dropping my boot into the dirt and sliding the bike to a stop in dramatic fashion. I jumped off, laughing, and waved to my family; they waved back. The children blew kisses."

Reason stopped talking. Her eyes welled and a curtain dropped on their sparkle. She clasped her hands behind her head. Her lips tightened.

"The rebel soldiers came from all sides, firing as they ran. At first I thought it was part of the movie. And then I saw my husband staggering backwards as the soldier walking towards him emptied every shell from his magazine into my husband's chest. He fell next to the children, who were already dead. My mother screamed as she was pulled to her knees, and we locked eyes as her throat was cut. Then I was grabbed from behind by one of the film crew, and we ran until we found somewhere to hide. The rebel soldiers could not get to us. The boat was on our side of the river. We hid for hours, then walked for more hours, and finally came across a village. Someone went for the authorities."

"My God, Reason, I am so sorry," Jeff said.

He touched her arm. She pulled it away. She did not want comforting when speaking of her dead family. Jeff had come across that reaction before. Reason walked with the guilt of the living. Why had she not died?

"And this has to do with The Sheriff, how?" Jeff asked.

"I'll get to that," she said dismissively. "The men who attacked the camp were Islamic rebels from the Sudan. The Egyptian military managed to catch them before they crossed the border, and most were killed. A few were captured, but the leader and his second in command managed to escape. For me, my life was over. I was no longer interested in the film industry, and quit my stuntwoman career. I went back to my home in the States, and pretty much became a recluse.

"Time passed, then one day I received a message from the head of the company I now work for, Devon Securities."

Jeff nodded.

"The man who was to become my boss," Reason continued, "told me that the two men I wanted to find had been recruited into ISIS and were somewhere in Syria or Northern Iraq. After some training, I was ready to go look for them."

Jeff nodded.

"Part of my brief is to hunt terrorists who kill American citizens, and make sure these men never kill again."

"I see," Jeff said. Had he learned a little more about his friend, Caldwell? Had a tragedy befallen him? Did Devon Securities only recruit people who had suffered great loss and had nothing left to lose? Those prepared to risk all to exact vengeance?

"And how does this bring us to The Sheriff?"

Reason looked in the direction the truck had taken. "The Sheriff is an ISIS recruiter, and I discovered that it was him who brought these men here. They are either here in Northern Iraq or in Syria. I want the men who killed my family, Jeff, and The Sheriff can lead me to them."

∽

Reason drove. There was only one road to Mosul and Baghdad. All she had to do was drive fast enough to catch The Sheriff's truck. Jeff clung to the handhold above the passenger side door. Reason flung the Mercedes round each bend. Barry and Bethany bounced about on the rear seat until they managed to secure their seat belts.

"Bloody hell, Jeff, I'm not certain this is any safer than life as a hostage," Barry yelled.

"Barry, the suitcases at The Sheriff's house – do you have any idea what was in them?"

"No, mate, but he did handle them like his life depended on them. You only saw a few of them. There were lots more that went on to the back of three or four other trucks. They had gone before you arrived. The last was the truck The Sheriff escaped in."

Before they'd left the village, Reason rang Luka. She wanted to leave Barry and Bethany behind. Luka had agreed to collect them, but Bethany refused. Now she was safe, she wanted her and Barry to stay near Jeff. She didn't trust anyone else to keep them secure. When Reason tried to convince her otherwise, Bethany held up a hand and firmed her jaw. No amount of reassurance was going to change her mind.

Jeff had told them to get in the back of the car. He didn't agree with Reason. Now he had his friends safe he wasn't about to let them out of his sight. At any rate, there was no time to argue. They needed to get after The Sheriff before he made it to the safety of an ISIS enclave, or wherever else he might be headed. Reason increased speed, and Jeff fought the urge to tell her to slow. He would prefer to drive himself, but he had to admit her driving skills were exceptional, better than his. And she must have been going twice as fast as the truck.

After ten more minutes, they rounded a bend and saw the bright blue cab. The truck was less than five hundred metres ahead.

"What now?" Jeff yelled into Reason's ear.

"You're the bloody Special Forces soldier – think of something, but we need him alive."

"Okay, best scenario: we shoot out the tyres. Get us close."

Reason nodded and accelerated. The car jumped.

"Barry, pass me the rifle."

Jeff took hold of the Kalashnikov and held it in his right hand, the butt clamped to his side by his elbow.

"Keep to the left. When they shoot, don't stop. They won't hit us. It's impossible to hit anything accurately firing from a truck at a moving target, especially if you aim at the target, and I'm guessing these guys will. But just in case I'm wrong, throw in a few weaving manoeuvres when we get close."

Reason gave Jeff a thumbs-up.

They had now closed to less than two hundred metres. Figures on the back of the truck were pointing in their direction. Still no weapons aimed. Good. They would be confused. Unsure about the speeding vehicle; in these countries, everyone drove like an idiot and this might just be another bad driver. But they wouldn't stay confused for long. Reason had closed to fifty metres. The Sheriff's men had raised their weapons and were readying to shoot. One of them hit the top of the truck cab and yelled a warning to the driver. The truck increased speed.

"They know we're on to them," Reason yelled. "They've increased speed."

Reason sped up, and Jeff was having difficulty aiming his weapon. He tightened his grip and pushed the top half of his body through the window. Hands grabbed at his shirt. Barry held him.

Reason veered to the left. Jeff pushed the safety down to the middle position. He needed the rifle on automatic; he didn't need to aim, just spray the wheels. He dipped the barrel. As Reason closed on the rear wheel, he squeezed the trigger. The weapon bucked in his hand, but he had anticipated that and had aimed low. He held his finger on the trigger and swung the barrel back and forth until the magazine emptied.

The tyre exploded. Shredded rubber ground into the surface of the road as the truck dipped on to the wheel rim. Sparks spat into the air. The out-of-control truck slid sideways and, unable to stop, disappeared over the bank.

Reason slammed her foot on the brake and the Mercedes's anti-lock-braking sensors worked to maximum capacity, bringing the car to a gentle stop.

Jeff scrambled back inside the car.

"Magazine, Barry."

A hand appeared holding the metal ammunition container. Jeff changed magazines.

"You lot stay here," he ordered – not to anyone in particular, but he had meant everyone.

He flung the door open and leaped out in one movement. He cocked the Kalashnikov as he ran. The truck had crashed cab first on to the surface below, and then rolled on to its side. Two men holding weapons stood beside the vehicle. Dazed, but when they heard an avalanche of small stones as Jeff slid down the embankment they reacted instinctively, bringing their weapons to a firing position. Jeff let off two bursts. Their chests exploded and they fell to the ground. The driver climbed out through the window, holding his arms out in front of him in a gesture of surrender. Jeff waved for him to move clear of the vehicle. When he was clear, Jeff gestured for him to lie on the ground. He fell face first and did not look up.

Jeff half turned at the sound of footsteps. Reason stood beside him, her Glock in her hand.

"The Sheriff is in the cab," Jeff said.

The cab roof hid him from sight. They could not see inside from their position. "I don't know if he's conscious or not."

She touched him on the arm. A gentle squeeze. "Thank you, Jeff. The Sheriff is my business now."

CHAPTER FORTY-SEVEN

The truck lay on its side, the passenger door buried in the dirt. Reason inched along until she reached the cab. She leaned forward, far enough to allow her to see in the reflection of the cracked wing mirror that The Sheriff was slumped against the passenger door. Unmoving. She stepped into the open, aimed at the driver's end of the windscreen and fired off two shots. The screen shattered. She reached round and pushed the Glock between her back and belt. Hands free, she stepped forward, grabbed two fistfuls of the front of The Sheriff's jacket and dragged him through the shattered windscreen frame and on to the dirt.

She patted him down and, satisfied he had no hidden weapons, stood and looked down on him. With the toe of her boot she pushed against his ribs. The Sheriff stirred. He groaned and rolled on to his back. Eyelids flickered and slowly opened. Confusion transformed into alarm as he saw the sky, then Reason. He scrambled into a sitting position. Reason did not budge.

"You are very persistent. You and your man have rescued your friends. Why are you not driving them to safety? You must know that sooner or later my soldiers will find me?"

Reason bent over. "Still very cocky, aren't you? Well, okay, I can put up with that at the moment. As long as you answer my questions. I'm looking for two men. Sudanese. Yusef Ahmed and Mohamed Jawari."

"And I should know these men, how?"

"You have been recruiting soldiers for ISIS and whatever other shit organisations you can make money from, but you personally recruited these two men. I want to know where they are."

The Sheriff shrugged. "Many have been through my hands. I never know their names or where they come from. No one cares. How would I remember two individuals among so many? It is nonsensical that you think I would."

"These two men were African. Black Africans. How many Black Africans have you come across? I'm sure their skin colour alone would make them stand out."

"No. I cannot help you."

The Sheriff's eyes flicked to the right and Reason caught it. He was lying.

She straightened.

"You leave me no choice. If you cannot help me, I will hand you over to the authorities."

Again The Sheriff shrugged. His nonchalance irked Reason.

"What will the Americans do?" he asked. "Put me in jail? I don't think so. I am not wanted in Iraq. My men are fighting against ISIS. I have American funding. They are my friends. That is why I have kept the hostages alive and my men have been protecting them until it was safe to hand them over to the authorities. I had no control over the kidnapping. This was not me; this was the man you have had contact with, Osman Gashi. It was he who put the hostages in jeopardy. Not me."

Reason smirked.

"You misunderstand me, Sheriff. I would not take you to the Americans. I'm going to hand you back to the Turkish police. You know them, don't you? You killed some of their men a short time ago," Reason said.

The Sheriff's eyes narrowed. He wiped spittle from the side of his mouth. Reason smiled as his eyes flicked about like those of a wild animal caught in a trap seeking an escape. Right now, his demeanour had switched to dangerous. She pulled her pistol from behind her back and held it by her side ready to swing it on the target if needed. If The Sheriff so much as twitched, she would empty her magazine into him. Then his shoulders sagged. Defeated. Reason had won the first round.

"I'll ask you again. Do you know where the two men I'm looking for are?"

"Their exact location, no."

Reason lifted her gun. The Sheriff raised a hand.

"Look, I have no desire to die, so I am not going to lie to you. I have no allegiance to any of these people, and I am not going to get myself killed for them. My men, they are usually shooting at these groups. I got paid for delivering, and that was it. I smuggled them across the border into Syria, and after that they were out of my hands. They could be anywhere now, but they are not here, in Iraq."

Jeff moved up to stand beside Reason.

"What do you think, Jeff?"

"I'm sorry, Reason, but I think he is telling you the truth. He has no conscience or loyalty to anyone other than himself. He would not risk being killed to save another, especially anyone signing up to join ISIS. They truly are natural enemies."

He placed a hand on her shoulder. She did not remove it; instead, she placed her free hand on it.

"This is the end of the line, Reason," Jeff said. "You can't track them now. It might be they have been killed, or they might be with another ISIS unit somewhere else in Africa or even Asia. Who the hell knows where you might find them?"

Reason looked off into the distance. Her eyes welled. Jeff put his arm around her and she fell into him. She had carried a burden for so long. Vengeance had been her driving force and had kept her family alive in spirit. Now that journey had ended and her vengeance needed to be buried as she had buried her family. She needed to grieve. Jeff knew of the mix of emotions tormenting her; he carried his own ghosts. Faces inside his head he could never erase.

"Time to go home, Reason," Jeff said. "To the States, and rebuild your life."

She nodded.

Barry and Bethany had made their way down the bank to join them.

Jeff picked up a Kalashnikov rifle dropped by one of The Sheriff's men. He removed the magazine and checked it contained bullets. He cocked the rifle. No round flew out. Empty. The magazine reloaded, he cocked the weapon again. Satisfied a round had slid into the chamber, he thrust the Kalashnikov into Barry's hand. "Keep this trained on The Sheriff. The safety is off and it is set on semi-automatic. You only have to pull the trigger to fire a bullet. Just keep pulling the trigger if you want to fire more rounds. Do you think you can do that if he moves?"

Barry, a hardness in his eyes, said, "I've seen him murder innocent people in cold blood. I won't give it a second thought."

Jeff patted his shoulder. "Good man."

The Sheriff nervously licked his lips as Barry set his eyes on him.

Jeff walked to the rear of the upturned truck and unloosed the elastic cord securing the canvas hood. There were a dozen suitcases. He pulled one out. He lay it on the ground and flipped the lock. The lid opened.

Dumbfounded, Jeff stared at the contents.

"Holy crap."

CHAPTER FORTY-EIGHT

W hat is it, Jeff? What's in the suitcase?" Reason asked, as she walked across to join him.

Jeff said, "Take a look. Money. US dollars. The case is full of them." He reached into the truck, pulled out another case and flicked the lid. "More money. Bundles of one-hundred-dollar notes."

He turned to The Sheriff.

"What did you do, Sheriff, rob a bank?"

The Sheriff sat stony-faced.

"I wonder how much there is," Jeff said.

Barry butted in. "A shitload mate. If you count all the cases. One, two, maybe three million dollars. There's enough here to fund a small army, or buy a bloody beautiful home on the Sydney waterfront."

"And you say there were more cases in other trucks?"

Barry nodded.

Jeff scratched his chin. He walked across to The Sheriff and looked at him. "Why have you got so much money?"

The Sheriff licked his lips.

Jeff shook his head. "You don't have a lot of options. Tell me what I want to know, and you can walk." Jeff gestured with his thumb towards the suitcases. "Not with the money – I'm taking that – but with your life. You can start again, but I think the deal is fair."

"How do I know I can trust you?"

"You don't, but I am a man of my word."

Reason, Barry and Bethany gawked at Jeff. Disbelieving.

"He wanted to kill us, Jeff," Barry said. "Kill everyone else, and who knows how many he has killed over the years? The guy is a mass murderer. Should he be allowed to walk away? He murdered Mildred and Reg."

"I have to agree with Barry, Jeff," Reason concurred.

Jeff stayed focussed on The Sheriff as he spoke to the others. "This man has a short life expectancy. Sooner or later, he will get a bullet between the eyes. But not today. I need to know what's going on here. That's more important." Jeff stepped a pace closer. "Are you going to tell me what I need to know? Information for your life?"

The Sheriff shrugged. "Okay, I will tell you. What does it matter? I have more money, and can get more when I need."

Jeff waited. The Sheriff swallowed.

"Substituting the bus with the hostages was a ruse, as you already know, to get me across the border and out of Turkey. But what you do not know is that smuggling the money was the main purpose. As your friend said, there are many cases. Added together, twenty million US dollars to be exact."

"Holy shit," Barry said.

"The money was given to me by Osman Gashi. One of his men came to the jail and made a deal. They would break me out of jail and get me safely across the border into Northern Iraq, and once there I had two jobs. The first job was to build a fortress in the mountains and raise a small army to defend it. Osman said that one day his boss might need a secure refuge. It was a priority."

Jeff stood. "Avni Leka. This is all about bloody Leka and him building a hideout." He looked at The Sheriff. "Could this be done?"

"Of course. In Qandil mountains he would never be found."

Jeff nodded. "And the second job?"

"At the same time I am building the fortress I was to open a gateway through to Asia. Make deals with the tribal leaders in Iran, Afghanistan and Pakistan."

"To smuggle arms and people?"

"Yes, and whatever else might make money."

"The people on the bus you blew up? Who were they?"

The Sheriff smiled. "In this case, do not worry yourself – they were ISIS recruits. It was easy to get them to play act. For them, they were helping the cause."

"Except they didn't know they were to be blown up at the end of it."

"No, they didn't know that and, as I said, that wasn't the plan. But when you join such an organisation, it is accepted life will be short. For them, it was very short."

"And one last question: why did you decide to kill the hostages?"

"This was easy, really. I did not blow up the bus. I do not know who did. My best guess is it was the Turks; they had the most to lose if I crossed the border. But really it could have been any number of groups. Maybe someone wanted to take over my smuggling business. Who knows? But once in the eyes of the world I was dead, then Osman Gashi thought it best I stay dead. If the hostages were found, the authorities would know I had not been killed. They might come looking for me and find his boss and the fortress."

Jeff shook his head.

"In the end," The Sheriff went on, "I thought it was not such a bad decision. It is not easy to sleep at night when men with guns are hunting after you. No one is going to look for a dead man."

Reason touched Jeff on the arm, then led him away until they were out of earshot. "What are we going to do with him?" she whispered.

"What can I do? I gave my word."

Reason glared.

"I gave my word, Reason," Jeff said again. "I was not speaking on your behalf. If you want to put a bullet in the prick's head, do it. I won't stop you."

Crack! Crack! Crack!

The air behind Jeff and Reason exploded with gunfire. They flung themselves sideways. As they fell to the ground, they grabbed their pistols and searched for a target. Jeff relaxed first. He dropped his gun and leaned on his elbow.

Barry stood over The Sheriff's body, the Kalashnikov still aimed. Jeff picked himself off the ground. He slowly walked across to his friend. Bethany clung to Barry's arm. She turned at Jeff's approach. Barry stood still.

Between clenched teeth he said, "He murdered Reg and Mildred, Jeff. I couldn't just let him walk away."

Jeff looked down at the lifeless body of The Sheriff. Blood oozed from the holes in his chest. Jeff placed a hand on Barry's shoulder.

"Come on, Barry. Let's get the hell out of here." Barry loosened his grip on the rifle and let it fall on to The Sheriff's legs. Jeff gave Bethany a nod, and she led Barry back towards the road.

Jeff watched them walk away, then turned to Reason.

"Contact Luka. Tell her we have a gift."

Reason gave Jeff a quizzical look.

"Many of the women in her troop lost their families and their homes," Jeff said. "Maybe Leka's money will help them build new lives. Life as a rebel can't last forever."

Reason nodded an agreement.

"And tell her we need an escort to Erbil."

❧

The phoney cop watched from a safe distance. When The Sheriff had escaped, and after the American woman and the New Zealander,

Bradley, had taken the two hostages, he ran out through the back door. He had been to the house a number of times. He knew a car was parked outside. One of The Sheriff's getaway vehicles. It had weapons on the back seat, a full tank of petrol and a mobile phone on the front seat. If nothing else, The Sheriff was always prepared. The phoney cop knew where Bradley had parked their car. He waited until they drove away, then followed.

He phoned Osman Gashi.

Gashi ordered him to follow but keep his distance. If The Sheriff did not escape Bradley, then he was to kill the PKK rebel leader. And, if The Sheriff did escape, he was to lead Bradley to him and make sure Bradley saw The Sheriff killed. Whatever happened, Gashi wanted The Sheriff dead, and he wanted Bradley to bear witness. It had surprised the phoney cop that Osman Gashi wanted Bradley left alive, but he was not about to argue with the boss. When Gashi gave an order, Gashi expected it to be obeyed. He said killing Bradley was not as important as having him confirm The Sheriff had been killed. With the hostages rescued, the Turks and other security forces would set about hunting The Sheriff. The pursuit would be relentless. And that would make it difficult to re-establish the business. The Sheriff needed to be dead. They would have someone else take his place and carry on with the project. With this in mind, Gashi ordered him to stay on, make contact with the rest of The Sheriff's men, and secure the money in the suitcases.

To his relief, The Sheriff had not escaped. One of the hostages had saved him the task of killing the PKK soldier. He could report the good news to Gashi.

The phoney cop climbed into his vehicle and drove back to Dornaq. He had much work to do.

CHAPTER FORTY-NINE

The media converged on the town of Lecce, in the Apulian region of Italy. The occasion had a voyeuristic aspect that had the news producers salivating. They had already screened titbits from YouTube videos uploaded by the locals. One amateur cameraman was lucky enough to be in the right place and caught the mafia chieftain Pietro Gallo climbing out of a car. Excitement was building. The gathering of Gallo and his family at his granddaughter's wedding in the Basilica di Santa Croce was becoming big news. The Basilica had begun construction in 1549 and was completed in 1606. It seemed fitting that such an historic building should now be the focal point of the coming together of members of one of the world's oldest known criminal organisations. Real live gangsters on television.

Hundreds of the most influential members of the Gallo family had packed into the church. A hush descended over the congregation as the priest brought the bride and groom together to exchange vows. Gallo, leaning against the rail of the pew, looked on with a mixture of pride and boredom. He'd been to too many weddings in his lifetime. When he was younger, at the later festivities he would screw a bridesmaid; nowadays, when the sun went down, all he wanted to do was go to bed.

The shaking floor shook him from his reverie. His hands tightened on the rail as he heard a sound like a thousand galloping horses rumbling beneath his feet. Then thunderclaps burst his eardrums. His eyes widened and his mouth stretched his wizened skin as it opened to release a scream that would never be heard. The interior of the church erupted like an exploding volcano, flinging Gallo through the air.

Outside, fragments of stone and wood rained down on the shocked crowd. Black smoke and flame spewed through the roof and the smoke billowed above the imploding cathedral. Spectators, far enough away to be safe from the explosion and falling debris, captured the demise of the Gallo family on mobile phone and tablet cameras.

In the following days, the main news item on all the world's media was a message from the ISIS leadership. The bombing of the Basilica in Lecce was a warning to NATO to stay out of Syria, Iraq and the Middle East, or more Westerners would die.

᠎᠎ᡄᲧ

Avni Leka poured two cognacs. This time, the tray sat on a small table between two leather sofas. Leka picked up both glasses and passed one to Osman Gashi.

"*Gazeur.*"

They clinked glasses.

"How has it worked out for you in Bari, Osman?"

"As I expected it would. The Gallo family is no longer a force. Gallo himself was killed in the blast. Any important survivors have been taken care of, and my men have moved into all the towns."

"Good."

Leka looked up at his map of the world.

"Has anyone stepped up to take The Sheriff's place?"

Gashi nodded. "He was one of The Sheriff's lieutenants. The soldiers respect him. He is as ruthless as The Sheriff was, and he knows the route through to Asia. It will be up and running in a few months."

"He has all the money he needs to build his army?"

"More than enough. We only lost two million dollars. I was able to secure the rest of it."

"How about the operation in Turkey?"

"All is in its place."

Leka sipped his cognac. When he looked at the map on his wall, he saw he now controlled the territory from India and Pakistan through to Turkey, the Balkans and into Italy and the rest of Europe. A smuggling pipeline. He would light fires of discontent through all the developing countries. And flood Europe with illegal immigrants.

He carried his glass to his desk. Gashi poured himself another drink.

"I still think we should have killed Bradley when we had the chance," Gashi said. "My man had him in his sights."

"I agree, Osman," Leka said. "And one day I might live to regret it, but it was more important he bear witness to the death of The Sheriff and that the world believed it. Business comes first. What about the fortress in the mountains in Kurdistan? Will the new man still build it?"

"Yes. This will be started as soon as he has built up his power base."

Leka clicked on his computer.

A photo of a vineyard appeared on the screen. Bradley's vineyard in New Zealand. In the photo, Bradley was standing alongside his adopted family, the Shalas. The day would come when he would make the Shalas and all Bradley's acquaintances regret the day they ever laid eyes on the New Zealander. For Bradley, he had something special planned. A storm was coming his way, and for him and his countrymen there would be no escape.

Captain Balboni sat in his office at the Carabinieri headquarters and read through the latest intelligence reports. The Albanian Mafia were taking control of the territories left vacant by the killing of the Gallo crime family. There was a nastier group of criminals in town. More drugs were on the streets in Rome and other major cities, and supply had been tracked back to Bari. Illegal immigrants were flooding the coastline, and the Italian navy was finding it impossible to stem the tide.

The name *Osman Gashi* appeared on a number of his reports as the man in charge. None of his spies had seen the man. The other name linked to the new criminal gang was *Avni Leka*. This was a name known to him. He had heard it before and searched through his files. He found the document he was looking for and placed it on the table.

With his pen, Balboni circled the name *Jeff Bradley*.

~

Fati drove Jeff and Reason to the airport.

Jeff was not disappointed when Barry and Bethany put off their wedding plans. For now, they needed time to get over the trauma of their kidnapping. Barry had killed a man. He appeared to be coping, but Jeff knew he would never get over it. The Sheriff's face would return in his dreams. Over and over. Bethany and Barry assured Jeff he would be the first to know when they had set the new date. And Jeff had promised to be there.

There was time to kill as they waited for their boarding calls. Jeff and Reason kept the conversation to minor details of the mission and what they might have done differently. Both knew they were parting to begin new lives, and it was unlikely they would meet again anytime soon. They were purposefully avoiding a discussion that might lead them to make false promises of a future together.

Reason's flight to the States came first, and when it was time for her to go through, Jeff walked her to the departure gate. They stood close. Less than the tilt of a head between them.

"I guess this is goodbye," she said.

"What will you do now?" Jeff asked.

"I have a house and a job to get back to. There are friends in my local church who knew my family. I need to sit with them and remember the joy of my family. Be told stories about them. I need that closure, and I think only my close friends can give it to me."

She kissed him on the cheek. Then stepped back.

Jeff reached out and stroked her arm.

"Have a happy life, Reason."

Her lips broke out a smile as intimate as a kiss, and then she turned away. He watched her show her boarding pass to security, and carried on watching until she disappeared from sight, and then a little longer.

He checked his watch. Two hours before his flight. He went in search of a restaurant that served bacon and eggs.

ACKNOWLEDGMENTS

I apologise to anyone I have forgotten. A special thank you to Trevor McGarry, Nick Abbott, Adrian Blackburn. To my military advisors Chris Kumeroa and Capt. K. E. McKee-Wright MBE Rtd. My guiding light, assessor Cate Hogan, and as always, a big thank you to Emilie Marneur, Mike Jones and the rest of the Thomas & Mercer team.

ABOUT THE AUTHOR

Thomas Ryan has been a soldier in a theatre of war, traded in Eastern Europe, trampled the jungles of Asia and struggled through the trials of love and loss: ideal life experiences for a would-be author. Schooled by professionals who have helped him hone his literary style, Ryan is quickly establishing himself as a skilled writer of riveting thrillers and short stories. He considers himself foremost a storyteller, a creator who has plunged his psyche into the world of imagination and fantasy. Taking readers on a thrilling journey is what motivates Ryan as a writer.